SOFRITO

SOFRITO

By **Phillippe Diederich**

 CINCO PUNTOS PRESS EL PASO, TEXAS

Printed in the U.S.

First Edition
10 9 8 7 6 5 4 3 2 1

Library of Congress Cataloging-in-Publication Data

Diederich, Phillippe, 1964-
  Sofrito / by Phillippe Diederich. —First edition.
     pages ; cm
  ISBN 978-1-941026-14-4 (softcover : acid-free paper)
  ISBN 978-1-941026-15-1 (e-Book)
  1. Cuban Americans—Fiction. 2. Cuba—Fiction. I. Title.

PS3604.I338S67 2015
813'.6—dc23
                          2014031844

                             ✳

Book and cover designed by BluePanda Design Studio
Cover and title photo by Phillippe Diederich
Author photo by Selina Roman

FOR MY PARENTS

"Sofrito is the mother sauce of our food.
All Cuban cooking must begin with
a good sofrito. It is the heart of the recipe.
Everything else grows from there."

—Nitza Villapol
during an interview after the publication of
her book *Cocina Al Minuto*, 1956

Frank Delgado was sitting alone in the back of Maduros, contemplating the presence of his father's ghost. The old man was all over the fancy white dining room—its white floor, its white walls, its white tables. Frank imagined his father's imposing figure sitting at the bar, sipping on a rum and Coke, watching him—passing judgment on him.

Frank was despondent and a little confused. It had been four months since his fiancé walked out on him. After Julie left, his heart didn't break. He hadn't suffered remorse or even sadness. He didn't feel a goddamn thing. It was just the same uncomfortable angst he'd been carrying around like a cross for most of his life.

He pushed away the papers in front of him—stacks of unpaid bills, collection notices, and a ledger that showed how deep in the red the restaurant had fallen. He leaned back on his chair, front legs off the ground, back against the wall, and stared at New York City out of the restaurant's tall windows that faced 1st Avenue. He loosened his tie and sighed. For the first time in his life, he was putting on weight. It wasn't what he had expected, not at thirty-three. He had never been athletic, but he was tall and had always been on the skinny side. Now he was getting soft. His dark, moody eyes were losing their glint and taking on a permanent gloom. He ran his hand over his hair and took a deep breath when a long scream pierced the dining room.

The few customers in the restaurant stared at him. If it had been only that, he could've lied and said it was nothing, that the chef was simply a cantankerous old Cuban with a short temper. But then came the crash of breaking glass and Justo bellowing at the top of his lungs, cursing the mother of the goat who gave him birth.

Later, Frank would joke that Justo had spilled his blood as part of a Santería ritual that promised to bring life back to the restaurant. But the accident—because that's exactly what it was—was only another blunder in a series of mistakes that had taken them to the brink of ruin.

The kitchen was thick with smoke. The stench of burnt sofrito— olive oil, onion, garlic, peppers and cilantro—had charred into a bitter ash that stung the eyes and throat. The waiters and the cooks yelled and threw food and banged on pots and pans like a conga back in Cuba. Justo danced in circles, his hands pressed against the center of his chest, kicking and cursing every saint in the book. There was blood on the counter and all over his white chef's coat. A sharp butcher knife and a large blood-spattered leg of roast pork lay on the floor.

Frank's older brother Pepe wobbled his heavy frame past the prep area and took long swipes at the grill with his suit jacket. With every slap, the flames swelled.

Frank reached past him and turned the knobs on the grill. The fire died.

"He cut his hand!" Pepe cried. He was frantic, moving in quick jerks, the fat hanging from his jowls jiggling like thick slices of membrillo. "It's bad. Really bad."

Frank stared at him, at the panic in his tired eyes, tiny beads of sweat forming over his brow all the way to the top of his balding head. Maybe that was it. They had reached the end. He shook his head, the copper-like taste of defeat lingering on his tongue like the poison the restaurant had become.

They fell quiet. He imagined their father—Filomeno—waving a thick finger at them, angry at their failure. Filomeno had refused to be a part of anything of theirs except this restaurant. It had been the only time he'd ever stretched his arms out and hugged them like a real family. Even Justo. And Filomeno was the one who named it after the sweet fried plantains he loved so much: Maduros.

The mayhem slowly settled. The kitchen staff took over. The dishwasher began mopping up the mess. The waiters shuffled back to the dining room. Frank and Pepe joined Justo behind the prep counter. He'd wrapped his hand in a towel and was sitting on a plastic milk crate, his lanky frame hunched over, his dark skin glistening with sweat, a half-smoked Winston between his thick lips.

Frank shoved his hands in his pant pockets and avoided their eyes. "So what now?"

Five years ago it had been perfect. When Maduros first opened, they were *the* restaurant on the Upper East Side. There were celebrities, write-ups and feature articles about the Cuban brothers who struck gold with their magic blend of Cuban fusion and European chic. But that was a lifetime ago.

"I'll take him to Lenox-Hill," Pepe said. "He'll probably need stitches—"

"I'm talking about the restaurant."

"This is not the time."

"Coño, it's never the time." Frank cursed and gestured with a wave of his arm at the catastrophe of the kitchen. "Damn it. We're bleeding money, Pepe. Every day I'm the one who has to face our suppliers and creditors and invent excuses and beg for more time. We're sinking. And we're sinking fast."

"You know..." Justo stood and adjusted the towel. "...we could always pay my friend Ramón Juárez a little visit over in East Harlem. He can make a...tú sabes, un trabajito. An offer to Yemayá never hurt anyone. We can drop some flowers and fruits into the East River and..."

"What's the matter with you?" Frank cried, but it came out soft, like everthing he did. Like when he said goodbye to Julie for the last time. His tone was always laced with acquiescence. Maduros had been hanging by a thread of debt and favors for months. They had pumped everything they had into it. They had nothing left.

But what made him angry was that he was willing to accept it.

The following afternoon Frank stood at the espresso machine. It hissed a cloud of steam that reeked of bitter coffee, filling him with memories of his childhood in Houston. He could still hear his father singing in the shower, stretching his baritone to sound like Beny Moré singing *Preferí perderte* or *Corazón rebelde* while his mother Rosa, in pink and blue plastic curlers, paced around the kitchen, the clap-clap of her plastic sandals slapping against the bottom of her feet as she made tostadas and café con leche.

Justo came out from the kitchen and joined him and Pepe at the bar. "I brought some new recipes."

Frank served him a café. "How's the finger?"

Justo held up his hand. It was wrapped in a clean white bandage. "Only four stitches." His small deepset eyes had a shine, a happiness that never faded. It was as if the trouble with the restaurant didn't exist.

Pepe took the folder from Justo and leafed through the recipes. "I was thinking we could run a promo," he said. "Like a two-for-one. Like the Indian restaurants on East 6th Street."

"Coño, Pepe. Get real."

"And what's this?" Pepe held up a sheet of paper. "A love letter?"

Justo smiled and took it from him. "It's from my brother."

The fight was quickly seeping out of Frank. Or maybe he'd never had it. He wanted to say it, tell them they had to declare bankruptcy. There was no other option. Accept the loss and move on. Do something else with their lives. But at that moment his mother walked into the restaurant.

Frank met her at the front and gave her a kiss on the cheek. "How was church, Mami?"

Rosa wore a long black dress like she did every day since her husband had passed five years ago. "Fine," she said, and maneuvered her heavy frame between the tables, her soft gray hair covered with a black lace mantilla. "Jesus sends his regards. He says you should come visit him more often."

They took a table at the back. Frank went to the bar and mixed a batch of mango mojitos. He thought of the last five years of his life adding up to nothing. Not long ago he'd had so much ambition, hope. And now here he was—alone on the fast track to broke. He wanted to get away from the trouble of the restaurant and the ghost that seemd to squeeze his will. But he and Pepe had made a promise to their father. They had to take care of Rosa. No matter how he looked at it—restaurant or no restaurant—he was trapped. All he could do was tap the counter with the back of the thin mixing spoon and add an extra jigger of Bacardí to his drink.

When he came back to the table, Rosa was inspecting Justo's bandage.

"Of course it hurt." Justo used his good finger to draw the length of the cut along the knuckle of his index finger. "Look, from here to here."

"Well, what in the name of the virgin were you cutting, chico?"

"A leg of pork. The knife caught the bone and I lost my grip."

Rosa covered her mouth. "I do not see why you need such big knives. All my life I have been cooking, and I never had a need for such fancy cutlery."

"Come on." Frank raised his glass. "Let's have a toast."

"Yes, certainly. To Maduros!" Rosa took a short sip of her mojito. She let out a long sigh, and her eyes wandered around the dining room. "And tell me, how is business?"

"You know..." Pepe glanced at his brother.

"No. I don't know," Rosa said.

"A bit slow," Frank said. "But that's normal for this time of year."

"And what time of year is that?" Rosa turned her palms up. "Where is everybody?"

"It's Sunday afternoon, Mami."

"Por favor, Cubans eat all day on Sunday."

When no one said anything, Rosa touched her glass and turned to Justo. "And what is new with you? How is Amarylis?"

"Fine. We went to see a fertility doctor."

"Ay no, be careful, chico. They will take all your money and do nothing for you."

"Mami—" Frank said.

"But it's true. Leonor's daughter Chiquita paid a doctor in Queens ten thousand dollars and she is still not pregnant. Pobrecita."

"Yes, but—"

"I do not believe in any of that," she said flatly.

"And neither did I," Justo said. "But Amarylis is not getting any younger."

"But there are other ways, chico."

"No." Pepe laughed and winked at his brother. "There's only one way to make a baby."

"And I also got a letter from my brother," Justo added. "He says they're all doing fine."

"No, mi amor." Rosa waved violently. "Not in Cuba. Nobody can be fine living under the rule of that butcher."

Frank rolled his eyes. He knew her speech by heart. But Justo interrupted her before she got started. "And there's good news. My sister is expecting."

"She got married?"

"Yes, and expecting twins."

"Twins? ¿De verdad?"

"That's what Eusebio said. He also said he got a job at El Ajillo, a restaurant of—"

"¡El Ajillo!" Rosa cried. "No me digas. They reopened El Ajillo?"

"Yes, he's a waiter there. He says he makes very good tips. And in dollars."

"I am sure he does." Rosa sighed. "You know that used to be Filomeno's uncle Nestor's restaurant. It was very popular back in my day. They made the most delicious chicken in the world. Ay, tan sabroso. It was famous. Te juro, I have never had anything like it."

"Really?" Frank leaned back on his chair. "You never mentioned it before."

"There is a lot I have not mentioned. Your father did not like it when we spoke of Cuba. It was too painful for his weak heart."

"Didn't I tell you?" Pepe smacked Frank on the arm. "The restaurant business is in our blood."

"Nestor Quesada. He was quite eccentric, that one. He never told anyone where the recipe came from. There were all kinds of rumors about it. Your father suspected he stole it from an old gypsy."

"Did you know him well?" Frank asked.

"Claro." Rosa waved. "He used to be a machinist at my grandfather's ingenio in Oriente. He was not a cook. We were all surprised when he opened the restaurant."

"And when they saw it succeed, no?" Justo asked.

"Imagínate," Rosa said. "People thought all kinds of things. Some believed the recipe was cursed."

"Why, what happened?"

"Ay, the misfortunes that befell that poor man. His four year-old son passed away from a terrible bout of pneumonia. His wife was so grief-stricken, she committed suicide three weeks later. She tied a rock to her waist and jumped into the Almendares River. Can you imagine? Nestor became a recluse. He was quite wealthy, but he rarely left the restaurant. They said he slept in the kitchen because he was afraid someone would steal his recipe."

"So it was cursed?" Justo asked.

"I don't know about that. But just before Filomeno and I left Cuba, we heard they found the body of the head cook floating in the Bahía de La Habana."

"The curse," Justo said.

"No chico, those are just superstitions." Rosa looked away. "Sometimes I think that chicken is what I miss the most from Cuba. I would give anything in the world to try it again."

"What was it like?" Justo asked. "Maybe I can come up with something like it."

"Ay, no." Rosa laughed. She waved her index finger and her expression turned serious. "Only Nestor knew the recipe. God only knows what Fidel had to do to get the recipe from him."

"Maybe he paid him a nice—"

"Qué va." Rosa dismissed the idea. "Fidel only knows how to steal. If the State reopened the restaurant...Ay no, poor Nestor."

"But what did it taste like?" Frank asked.

"It was very different. Let me see. It—" she touched her eye with the tip of her napkin. "Dios mío, it is difficult to describe. It was delicious, of course, but it was more than that. It tasted earthy...a little bitter. And sweet...like when there is a storm and the sea is raging against the Malecón. Óyeme," she said suddenly and waved her finger. "That chicken tasted just like Cuba."

Justo laughed. "Who could cook something like that? I mean, what does Cuba really taste like?"

"Ay, don't worry." Rosa took his arm. "How about a little plate of moros and some of your maduros endulzados, eh?" She smiled and focused past him at the empty restaurant.

After lunch, Rosa went home. Frank, Pepe and Justo gathered in the kitchen to review the new recipes. Justo spread out the papers and began making notes. Frank sat on the prep counter and glanced at the bizarre artifacts on the shelf behind Justo. When they first opened the restaurant, Justo had brought a Santero to bless the business. Justo insisted they place an Elegguá effigy of sandstone and seashells by the front door. He promised them Ayé-Shaluga would watch over them and bring them good fortune. The three of them argued. In the end they settled for a small altar in the back of the kitchen. It was only supposed to be a pink conch seashell and a red, black and white bead collar, but with time the altar grew as Justo added picture cards of catholic saints, candles, a small wooden ax for Changó, a decorative plate with otán stones, and an arcane collection of aluminum and ceramic urns holding various offerings to the Orishas.

Frank looked at the collection around the altar. Maybe they should have placed it at the front of the restaurant. He really didn't know about these things. Justo could have been right all along. He glanced at him, leaning over the counter, sorting through the recipes, and recalled that September evening eighteen years ago when Justo entered their lives. Frank came home from school and there was Justo, sitting on the couch between his parents. The first thing Frank noticed was Justo's dark skin. Then he noticed his father's excitement.

"He came in a raft," Filomeno said proudly. "It took him a year to build it and three days to cross. Increíble, no?"

Justo was introduced as his ahijado, Filomeno's godson. And therefore, it was Filomeno's duty to offer him a place to live. Later that night, Frank lay awake in bed listening to his father and Justo whisper about Cuba until three in the morning.

Now, so many years later, he still harbored a certain jealousy for the passion Justo had stirred up in his father.

"How about this duck with truffle trumpet?" Pepe said. "Sounds powerful, no?"

"Duck?" Frank couldn't believe it. "Are you serious? Mancini and that other meat distributor from Brooklyn refuse to extend our credit. We can't afford to change the menu."

"Well, what about this mango grouper?" Pepe said and handed Justo another recipe. Then he looked at Frank. "If we can still afford fish."

Frank hopped off the counter and began to pace, his eyes combing the ground, searching for an exit. As much as he wanted to keep the restaurant, he couldn't see how to turn things around. They were in too deep.

"Here's one for a stuffed chicken breast," Pepe said.

Justo took the recipe and looked it over. "Can you imagine if it's anything like that chicken in Cuba?"

"Mami really liked it, no?"

Justo leaned against the counter. "You think it could be that good?"

"Sounds like it was a big deal back then," Pepe said.

"Sounds like it's a big deal right now," Frank added. "Maybe if we knew what it tastes like—"

"Sí claro." Justo laughed. "Let's call them. Maybe they deliver."

"Chicken that tastes like Cuba," Pepe whispered. And for a moment they were all silent, reading the recipes. Then Pepe slammed his hand against the counter. "I got it!"

He looked around the kitchen. The linecook was slicing Chilean sea bass filets for ceviche, and the dishwasher was stacking plates. He motioned for Frank and Justo to follow him into the walk-in freezer.

Pepe rubbed the palms of his hands together. Then he pulled Frank and Justo into a huddle. "Here's what we'll do. We'll get in touch with your brother and offer him some money to get the recipe for us."

Justo shook his head. "Too dangerous. He could go to prison for stealing. The government checks everything—mail, phone calls."

"Fine," Pepe said. "Then Frank can go."

For a long while all they could hear was the low hum of the freezer's fan as little white clouds of condensation floated from their lips, their eyes skipping back and forth from one to the other.

"Very funny." Frank backed away. This is what they always did— Justo and Pepe ganging up on him. He was the youngest. He always got the short end of the deal. He waved a finger at his brother. "Very funny."

"No, no, it's a great idea," Justo said and lit a cigarette.

"And if that chicken's as good as Mami says, it can turn Maduros around just like that." Pepe snapped his fingers.

"You're insane." Frank shook his head and looked at Justo. "We'd be stealing from the government. You just said your brother could go to prison."

"Yeah, but he's Cuban," Justo said. "You're not."

"Didn't you notice how Mami's eyes glazed over when she talked about it?"

"That's Mami." Frank stepped back and waved. "Her eyes glaze over every time she talks about Cuba."

"Yeah, but Justo's brother said something along the same lines in his letter."

"Coño, you're right." Justo pointed at Pepe with his bandage. "It's like they're both in love."

"And who knows, maybe the Quesadas still work there. A relative or someone," Pepe added.

"If they're still there, they're in business with Castro." Frank turned away and ran his hands over his hair. "It's a terrible idea. I could go to prison."

"No, Frank, Think of this: every Cuban who left in 1959 is probably dreaming of El Ajillo and—"

"The taste of Cuba," Justo said.

"Then maybe we should just find out about the Quesadas before we do anything rash," Frank said. "And what about the curse?"

"It's just a superstition," Pepe said.

"And the secret police? Mami says—"

"No, no," Justo interrupted. "Your mother, she likes to exaggerate."

"Then why did you leave?" Frank asked.

Justo waved his cigarette from side to side. "It's different for the tourists."

"And besides." Frank turned and flaked the frost off a shelf with his fingernail. "Mami would freak if she knew I went to Cuba."

"We'll tell her you went to Ft. Lauderdale or something."

"Why can't you go?"

"Because I was born there," Pepe said. "Justo and I would have to get Cuban passports."

"And that would take forever," Justo added. "You can go just like that. We'll buy one of those tour packages. You can fly in through Mexico or Canada. One week. Así como si nada."

"But what if your brother doesn't want to help us?"

"No, óyeme, my brother will help us. I'm sure he'll find a way to get it for us. Coño, I think this is a great idea." Justo patted Frank on the back and took a long drag from his cigarette.

"Besides, we can get some press coverage," Pepe said. "We'll tell them the story about how the government stole our recipe and how we went to Cuba and took it back. The press'll love it. It's like that whole Bacardí, Havana Club thing. We can really play this up for publicity."

"Listen to your brother," Justo said. "It might not be the best idea, but it's the only one we have."

"No." Frank turned away to face the back of the freezer. "This is ridiculous."

"Frank," Pepe circled around him. "Ever since Julie left you've been moping around like a stray dog—"

"No I haven't."

"Well, that's the point, no?" Pepe said. "You never seem to care about anything."

"I care about the restaurant."

"Well?"

"We have this chance," Justo said.

"Besides," Pepe went on. "You know how you always talk about doing something important and making a difference?"

"No." Frank turned away and avoided his eyes. "I'm not doing it."

"Think of the restaurant. Think of Papi." Pepe pleaded, his hands gesturing, clutching desperately at the frozen air between them. "You have to do it."

"No," Frank said flatly. "I could go to jail, or worse. Besides, for all we know this business of the chicken is just a bunch of mierda."

Frank left the restaurant early that night and went home to an empty apartment. When Julie moved out, she'd left him the small dining room table, the futon and an abstract painting they'd bought at a flea market in SoHo. In the darkness, her absence was palpable. But it wasn't because he missed her. Her company had only been a welcome distraction from the problems of the restaurant. Being alone meant he had to face himself—his regrets. There had been a time when he believed in himself, that one day his life would come together and he would earn the admiration of his family. It wasn't about achieving his father's American Dream: a small suburban house with a fenced yard. He had expected more: adventure, love, maybe even wealth.

He moved slowly around the apartment, his shoulders slouched forward, his fingers tracing the places where no memories existed: the wall, the radiator, the window that was screwed shut, the side lamp without a shade. Lately, the smallest tasks had become too much for him. There was a pile of dirty laundry on the floor and a stack of unopened mail on the kitchen counter. The whole place had the sour smell of an old wooden trunk.

He pulled off his shoes, took two Advils and lay on the futon with his arms extended. He stared at the ceiling wanting for the whole thing to go away—Maduros' imminent bankruptcy, the constant restlessness in his heart, and his father's ghost chipping away at what little confidence he had. He blamed Filomeno for the way his life had turned out—stuck at the restaurant, unable to find love, unable to commit. He closed his eyes, squeezed them tight, clenched his jaw. He thought of something his father had told him during one of those rare moments when rum had softened the old man's heart.

"Things happen for a reason." Filomeno had waved a finger in Frank's face in his usual dramatic fashion, his breath bitter with alcohol and nostalgia. "But do not be fooled by fate, Frank. It is your responsibility to take advantage of opportunity whenever it presents itself."

Maybe it was true about the recipe. Maybe it could save Maduros. He understood one thing: if they didn't have the restaurant, he had nothing. All this about dreams and ambitions was a lie. He was more like his father than he cared to admit. But his father had taken one risk in his life. He had fled Cuba. He'd sought freedom—for Rosa and Pepe. He had given up everything in Cuba, even his own family, to give them all a better future. And he had given Pepe, Justo and him his savings to start the restaurant.

Now Frank had an opportunity to save it.

"I don't know about measurements.
I don't even know how to read. I just look at whatever
I'm going to prepare and add what I need.
It is something I just know, something I feel inside.
And when I'm finished it always tastes the way I want it."

—Justina Dominguez

cook for the payroll manager at the Chaparra Sugar Mill, Oriente Province, 1909

W hen Frank stepped out of Havana's José Martí International Airport, he was engulfed by a wave of human longing, of desperate Cubans trying to catch a glimpse of a relative they had not seen in ten or twenty or thirty or forty years. They called out names, waved, cursed, pushed, grabbed and jostled for a better position. Everyone thrust forward trying to be the first to see Frank, to claim him as one of their own and scream his name and hang onto him and cover him with love and tears. But he was not there for any of them.

His spine tightened. This was la tierra de Papi y Mami: the forbidden island, the place his parents had escaped forty years before. This was a Cuba mired deep in the myth of exile. It was the genesis of his mother's horror stories. She had whispered them to Frank and Pepe like bedtime stories, telling in excruciating detail the atrocities the government had committed on his unknown relatives. She told them about Fidel's coldhearted cruelty, about how in the days after the Revolution he had rounded up thousands of innocent people in the streets of Havana and executed them without trial and in cold blood, about how he stole land and property to compensate the illiterate peasants that had helped bring him to power, about how he turned one of the richest countries in the world into one of the poorest, about how his beard stank of death, and how the tobacco they used to make his cigars was soaked in the blood of his enemies because he believed it endowed him with power and longevity.

Frank forced his way through the crowd and found a seat in the back of the air-conditioned tour bus. He leaned his head against the window and searched the crowd for the infamous secret police his mother had always warned him about. But all he could see was an innocent mass hoping to reconnect with long lost family.

On the route to the hotel—Avenida Independencia and then Boyeros—depressing gray concrete buildings and apartment complexes followed one another like a long forgotten proletarian utopia. Everyone dressed as if they had acquired their clothes from a thrift store in New Jersey. They waited at traffic lights on the street and outside bodegas. They looked old, tired, their faces creased with the complexities of socialist life, their postures folded by the weight of differential acceptance. The entire panorama was short on charm and long on depression.

But as they came around the Plaza de la Revolución and entered the Vedado neighborhood, Frank's paranoia dissipated at the sight of the majestic older homes with long verandahs and lush gardens. All of it beautiful. All of it slowly turning to dust.

The lobby of the Hotel Sevilla was a vintage postcard: tall ceilings, huge open windows, dark wood shutters, and walls dressed with colorful Moorish tiles. The percussion of a conga drum and the picking of a guitar flowed from the patio and blended with the loud conversations of brightly dressed tourists and their Cuban friends

The desk clerk flipped through the pages of Frank's passport and smiled. "Americano. Miami?"

"No." Frank's eyes strayed nervously about the lobby. "New York."

"Ah, New York City. The New York Yankees, eh? You know El Duque?" He slammed the palm of his hand hard against the counter. "Ese hombre es un fenómeno. Is he not the best pitcher in the world? He was with the Industriales before he defected. Now he goes and wins the World Series for the Yankees. I guarantee you he will do it again. And again."

A man at the end of the long counter turned away, unfolded a brochure and appeared to read. Behind him, a trio of young Cuban women in tight-fitting dresses and high heels loitered at the entrance of the hotel.

"Please tell me," the clerk said, "do you go see them play at Yankee Stadium?"

Frank shook his head. "I don't really follow the game."

"Ah, señor. If I lived in your country I would attend every game. You know, I have two uncles and a brother in Miami. Fanáticos de los Marlins. They went during Mariel in 1980."

Frank locked eyes with the clerk for the first time. "It must be difficult, them being so far."

The clerk waved. "No, qué va. It's not far." He stamped the hotel vouchers and handed Frank a guest card and a coupon for his complimentary cocktail at the patio bar.

Frank asked the bartender to make his mojito a double. As he drank, the muscles around his neck slackened. The Havana Club rum, the lime, the fresh yerba buena, and the sugar took him away to a place that was primitive and tropical. Exotic. The musicians fell into a soft romantic song about flowers and love. European perfumes and sweat and the smoke of a distant cigar blended into something reminiscent of his mother's nostalgia for the Cuba of her youth.

Then a fleeting memory from his own childhood filled his head— playing catch with his father in the backyard, Rosa singing in the kitchen, the family gathered together in the living room. Filomeno laughing.

But it was too quick. The clerk's words came back to haunt him: it's not so far. Not so far. For Filomeno, Cuba had been a world away. No country could have been farther from Houston than Cuba, as a place or a memory. It had been Filomeno's decision not to settle in Miami after escaping Cuba in 1959. He refused to contact his extended family. He badgered Rosa and trampled all over her nostalgia with his own ideas of what it was to be American: watching sitcoms, mowing the lawn and spending Sunday afternoons grilling hot dogs and hamburgers in the backyard. It was as if he were trying to live inside a television commercial, eating eggs over easy with too much Tabasco sauce and his hot dogs with mayonnaise. He smoked filtered Viceroys and loved chocolate ice cream.

Frank hated the charade, not because he was Cuban, but because he was American. To him Filomeno was a caricature of the other suburban fathers in the neighborhood—working at a refinery in Pasadena, hanging out at Ice Houses on Friday afternoons after work. He'd liked Gilley's long before they made *Urban Cowboy*. He took his shoes off when he got home from work and ate dinner while watching *Wheel Of Fortune*, calling the words and phrases out loud to Susan Carney just like any other father. He argued with his wife, bought a Lotto ticket every Friday, snored, kept a bottle of Tums by his bedside and hated Swiss cheese.

But Rosa refused to give in to him. She loved Cuba and she hung on to it through her kitchen. She spent hours cooking arroz con pollo, boliche, picadillo, and ajiaco from scratch. She infused the house with the permanent aroma of sofrito.

For all his effort, Filomeno's American style remained rough around the edges like the Spanish accent he couldn't completely shake off. And there was always the silence.

What had hung over their little ranch house—the three bedrooms, two baths and a one-car garage with a live oak tree in the backyard—was more than the sadness that accompanies a life in exile. There was resentment. Anger. Filomeno's hate for Cuba ran so violently in his veins, it was as if he wanted to erase the past completely. As far as Filomeno was concerned, he and Rosa would forget Cuba and become Americans if it killed him. And perhaps it had.

*"I prefer my rice cooked with a few habanero peppers.
Not just for a little spice,
but for the familiar flavor of my mother's kitchen."*

—Cuban heavyweight boxer, Téofilo Stevenson
after winning his third Olympic gold medal. Moscow, 1980

F rank moved quickly around his hotel room, looking for peepholes, microphones, bugs, cameras, anything suspicious. He mimicked the spy movies he had seen, running his hands over the plain wood furniture, the lamps, the curtains. He checked behind the mirror and under the bed.

Nothing.

He dug out the card where Justo had written his brother's contact information and asked the operator to put the call through. After a few tones and clicks, she came back on the line or—as Frank suspected—had never left the line and informed him there was no answer.

He set down the receiver and stared at a faded photograph of the Morro Castle hanging on the wall. His mind spun like a pinwheel, thoughts and fears racing to catch up to the present. He unpacked his bag. He placed half his cash in the room's safe deposit box and spread the rest between the pages of his soft cover copy of Dostoyevsky's *Crime and Punishment*, which he had brought specifically for that purpose.

It was Monday evening. His flight out was on Sunday morning. That gave him five full days to get the recipe. He had no time to waste. He tried Justo's brother's number again, but there was still no answer.

The noise from the courtyard and the lobby filtered up to his room.

It sounded like a party. He went downstairs and took inventory of the security guards in the lobby. They were big men in beige guayabera shirts. One was posted by the elevator, another at the stairs. Two stood by the hotel's entrance and another near the patio bar where the trio was playing Guantanamera for what must have been the fifth time.

It was dark out. At the entrance to the hotel, the doorman was flirting with the same three women Frank had seen earlier. They appeared to be old friends, but as Frank approached, the doorman quickly separated himself and greeted him with a formal nod.

Frank's gaze lingered on the pretty girl with the blue dress. In less than a second he took in the outline of her shoulders, her deep reddish skin and the arch of her back as it curved down her legs all the way to her magenta colored toenails.

She noticed him looking and smiled, but one of her friends had already moved past her and was reaching for Frank's arm. The doorman pulled her back.

"Do you know the restaurant, El Ajillo?" Frank asked the doorman.

"Cómo no, would you like a taxi, caballero?"

"Oye," the pretty girl in the blue dress said loud enough for him to hear. "Listen to him. He almost sounds Cuban."

"Ya, Marisol." The doorman waved her away. Then he stepped outside and signaled a man who was sitting on the hood of a turi-taxi parked across the street.

Marisol's friend approached him again. "What's your name, amigo?"

"Frank."

"Español?"

He shook his head. The girl glanced past him at the doorman who was making his way back into the hotel. "You want company tonight?"

He had never been good with women. He was shy. In all his relationships, it had been the women who approached him. When he entered into a relationship, he hung onto it with mild apathy until it became obvious to both parties that love had never been part of the equation.

The doorman came back and shooed the girl away. "Yoselin, por favor."

Frank stole a quick glance at Marisol, then walked out to the car.

"Oye." Marisol caught up with him as he reached the taxi. "You don't like my friend?"

"It's not that—"

"You don't think she's pretty?"

Yoselin and the other girl were staring at them, waiting.

"Everyone thinks she's pretty." Marisol crossed her arms. "Italians in particular."

There was something easy about her, like they'd been friends a long time ago. Frank leaned against the side of the taxi and crossed his arms over his chest. "I'm not Italian."

"¿Entonces?"

"Americano."

"No me digas. Yoselin has cousins in Miami."

Frank smiled. He knew about jineteras, Cuba's famous prostitutes. His first instinct was to walk away, but then he noticed every foreign man around the Sevilla had a pretty Cuban woman hanging on his arm. If he dined alone it might raise suspicion. And there was something else. He found her cockiness attractive. Challenging. Besides, she wasn't trying to pick him up. She was trying to hook him up with her friend.

But then she took his arm and said, "Why don't you take me to El Ajillo with you? No one likes to eat alone."

In the street, people were going about their business, walking in and out of the hotel or simply waiting. In Cuba, that was what they did. Wait. What was happening between Marisol and him was just one moment in many. Yoselin and the other girl had gone back inside the Sevilla.

She was quite beautiful. And it was just dinner. He met her eyes. There was something tender in them. His stomach quivered. He stepped aside and allowed her into the taxi.

"El Ajillo?" the driver asked.

"Yes. I've heard it's pretty good, no?"

"Señor," the driver said with authority, "es el mejor. The best in the world. I can promise you, never in your life have you tasted such food."

Frank leaned back on the seat as the taxi left Prado behind and traveled down the Malecón, Havana's seaside boulevard. Marisol sat with her face pressed against the window. She seemed sad, absorbed in her own problems, a dark world of lost nights. But he knew nothing of her life.

"So." He swallowed his fear. "Have you ever been there?"

"Qué va, chico, and how would I pay for it?"

Maybe it had been a mistake. He had misread her eyes. He had to be careful. She could be anybody.

"But tell me," she said, "how is it in Miami?"

"I live in New York."

"I would love to go to Miami. They say it's just like another Habana."

"Yeah." Frank laughed. "You could say that."

She adjusted the thin dress strap that had slipped down her arm and turned back to the road. Frank watched her for a moment. Suddenly she seemed shy, distant. Perhaps it was all a game. Or business. Not all jineteras were professional prostitutes. Something about Marisol seemed tough and innocent at once. He wanted to pull her close, hear her story. But instead he turned away and watched the buildings race past on his left. Dim lights spilled out of open windows, all amber and green. Along the Malecón there were no billboards, no neon, no signs, no crowds, no drive-thrus. Havana was everything New York City was not: the traffic was light, the streets were dark, peaceful. People strolled without hurry. He rolled down the window and breathed in the salty ocean air spiced with refinery fumes and a thousand perfumes of flowers and women and cooking stoves and the life that was Havana. When he exhaled, he released all of New York City, all of Maduros and Pepe and Justo and Filomeno. The tropical night swallowed it whole without so much as a gasp.

"Caballero," the driver said, "I have the air conditioning for your comfort."

Frank caught his eyes through the rearview mirror. He could be an informant. A spy. He'd often heard taxi drivers were the eyes and ears of the Castro government.

El Ajillo was a rustic open-air restaurant in the style of a bohío. It had a thatched roof and long wooden tables set under the canopy of a pair of thick almond trees strung with Christmas-style lights. The place was packed.

A conjunto played Chan Chan over the buzz of dinner conversations. Waiters moved between the tables delivering large family-style platters of chicken along with rice and beans, plantains and yucca served from huge clay casseroles. The aroma of the food floated over the restaurant like something sacred. It was a smell without definition, like a fresh rain—a storm—but so much more: exotic and ethereal, yet vaguely familiar.

The maitre'd informed them it would be at least an hour before they could be seated. They nudged their way through the crowd and found a place to stand at the end of the bar.

Marisol sipped her Tropicola and looked casually around the restaurant as if she were trying to recognize someone. "So what do you do in New York?"

It sounded like she was turning on her program. "My brother and I have a restaurant."

"¿De verdad? What kind, McDonald?"

"No. A real restaurant. Cuban food." But that was a lie. Justo's culinary inventions—appetizers of garlic octopus, chorizo and grilled shrimp in sugarcane skewers, entrees of roast quail with a ginger and sherry reduction, lamb steamed in banana leaf with a tart and spicy guava sauce—had nothing to do with Cuba.

"I'd like to go to the McDonald one day and eat a Whopper."

Frank laughed and took a long sip of his mojito. He loved the simplicity of her wish. But it also made him sad—simple, innocent dreams like those of a child. It was something he saw in himself at times.

Marisol peeked into her glass. "So, in your country, are you very rich?"

His eyes traced the smooth line of her arm. "I wish."

"I wish," Marisol said seriously, "that one day I'll meet someone who will take me away from this place."

He stirred his drink with the small plastic straw. "Is that what Cuban girls dream of?"

She didn't look up. She just sipped her drink and made a small gesture with her hand. "That's the only dream a Cuban girl can have."

"Does it happen a lot?"

"What?" She threw her head to the side and stared into his eyes. "That they find a foreigner who marries them and takes them away like in a fucking fairy tale? Yes, it happens." Then she lowered her head and whispered, "To the lucky ones."

Frank thought she was playing him like a game, but there was something delicate in her manner, like her emotions were made of glass. "Has it happened to someone you know?"

She stared at the ice floating in her Tropicola, the reflections sparkling like tiny stars. "To some friends. And to my sister." Then, she tossed her head to the side and called the bartender, "Oye, dame un ron con Coca Cola."

"Where did she go?"

"Who?"

"Your sister."

"Too far."

She was dropping this on him like a line. Perhaps that was all it was. Maybe sympathy was her weapon. He reminded himself to be careful. After all, she was a prostitute. Reality was upside down here. This was a place where doctors drove taxis, waiters were rich and a girl's best chance for a future was to offer herself to a foreigner. Or she could be a government agent. Anything was possible.

"She went to Spain."

"What part?"

"What part of Spain? Chico, how would I know?" She threw her arms in the air and her lip trembled. "Spain, that's all I know. She hasn't written or called since she left almost a year ago. She promised she would arrange for me to come, even if it was just for a visit. But I've heard nothing. Nada. ¡Coño!"

"I'm sorry." She had pulled him in. He wanted to hold her in his arms and have her tell him more, but all he said was, "Do you want to talk about something else? What do you do? I mean when, tú sabes…"

"When I'm not jineteando?" she said with a hint of humor. "I'm waiting to get into the tourism school. I want to get a job in a hotel or a restaurant, somewhere where I can make some real fula. I was studying literature at the University but, chico, you don't know how useless that career is now. I could just as well study Marxist theory." She shook her head. "Can you imagine the fools that spent six years studying that mierda? What will they do now? Nada, chico, they're lost!"

"You don't have to be so angry."

She was trembling.

"At least not with me."

"¿Sabes qué? I don't have to be here. I don't have to be with you. I don't have to have sex with you."

"Who said anything about sex? You were the one who asked me to take you to dinner, and now you're arguing with me like I was the cause of all your problems."

Their eyes met and the corners of her lips turned upwards in the slightest hint of a smile.

"I'm sorry," she said softly. "I'm new at this. And sometimes I'm not in the mood, tú sabes? I get so sick of foreigners. I get sick of their stories and how they love Cuba. They think everything is perfect here because their vacation is perfect. I hate the looks I get from Cuban men when I'm with a foreigner. Like how the bartender looks at you when I order my drink. Like he needs approval from you."

"Entonces, why do you do it?"

She made a motion with her hand, the tip of her fingers grouped together, back and forth into her mouth. "I have to eat, no?"

"But—"

"Oye, It's not like I sleep with everyone. We go out, if I don't like you, I don't sleep with you. I'm not like Yoselin. She sleeps with so many guys, one day she's going to be rich." She laughed and turned away. "Money's not everything. Sometimes it's just about going out and doing something. We all need to escape this nightmare."

"Sorry, I wasn't—"

"Ay, Frank." Her eyes moved quickly about the bar. Then she leaned close to him and whispered, "It's very unfortunate what Fidel has done to Cuba."

They were shown to a table under the low branches of an almond tree. Frank ordered a plate of the famous chicken. He kept reminding himself of where he was. His mother's voice whispered to him, "Beware." He searched the dining room for a waiter who might resemble Justo, but the place was too busy. He spotted a pair of security men, one by the entrance and one by the kitchen.

A waiter arrived with a large platter of chicken. Frank inspected the unimpressive brown morsels and breathed in the scent. He thought of his youth—cinnamon or cloves and a pleasant memory that wasn't quite clear. It was just there, slightly beyond his grasp, like a cloud caught in a violent wind.

Marisol reached across the table and touched his hand. "Are you okay?"

He broke from his trance and stared at her dark, tender eyes. A warm, pleasant feeling circled his gut.

The chicken smelled earthy, inviting. He examined its texture, his fingers moving about the mild roughness of the skin. It wasn't breaded, but it had a thin coat of powder, like brown sugar or coarse spices the color of copper. He closed his eyes and sank his teeth into the meat. The flavor was completely unexpected. It was the ideal balance of sweet and sour without being either. It was tropical and painful and tender.

He took another bite, oblivious of the waiters crisscrossing the dining room filling plates with rice and beans, of the conjunto at the other end of the dining room. He dropped the bone on his plate and glanced at Marisol.

"It's so good," he said. "It's better than sex."

Marisol eyed him with curiosity.

He paused to analyze the chicken, but it was useless. It was everything, and it was nothing—a complex blend that confused him. It took him away to another time. He was on a beach in Puerto Rico running with Pepe under the broken shade of palm trees, hunting for fallen coconuts. A breeze brought the smell of garlic and fish and charcoal from cooking fires. The ocean made soft swishing sounds with the tide. His father held his mother's hand as they walked together along the water.

Then time skipped forward to when he was seventeen, excited and afraid. The smell of sandalwood incense mixed with the aftertaste of the joint they'd smoked and a soft hint of musk that came from a place he had never been. Lizzy Fernandez. It was the first time he touched her breast, soft and forbidden. Lizzy. He explored her skin and her muscles, her bones and her hair and the back of her neck, her thighs.

And then there was his father, lying on the bed at MD Anderson, tethered to a machine by thin green tubes and wires. The only sound in the room was the slow suction of the mechanical lung and the sharp rhythmic beep of the heart monitor. He was gaunt, his skin pale like rice paper.

"Frank." His voice was weak, but deep. "Is that you?"

Frank nodded and took his hand. Filomeno said nothing more. They remained like that for a long while until Frank felt a light tug at his hand followed by the soft remorseful sigh of his father's last breath.

"Pork is the food of the masses in Latin America.
The pig is a robust animal that is easy to keep.
It eats almost anything. Once it is butchered, it can feed
a family for a month, or even longer. And it is also very delicious
when it is well roasted and served with a good mojo sauce."

—Fidel Castro

talking to a group of newsmen after a popular rally. Holguín, 1964

F rank woke up feeling dizzy from all the mojitos and the late night, his body languid from lovemaking. The taste of the chicken from El Ajillo had vanished, leaving behind a peculiar sensation similar to the air in Havana after a tropical storm.

Marisol was sleeping at his side, her breathing calm and rhythmic, her face relaxed. When they had come back to the hotel from El Ajillo, she had pressed her body against his. Her nails had accented the path of her hands as they moved under his clothes to the places he wanted her to touch. They remained fondling him, running shivers across his body as she moved forward and he stepped back onto the bed. He lay naked, watching as she ceremoniously removed her accessories: the high heeled sandals, the plastic earrings, the thin bracelet. He picked up the condom she had placed on the side table and examined it with curiosity.

"Communist?"

She laughed. "No, qué va."

"It's red."

"Yes, red," she said, "and with the flavor of cherries."

She climbed on top of him, her legs at his sides, and slowly pulled her dress over her head. She placed her hands on his chest and slid down. He could feel the warmth from between her legs burning against his skin. Then she leaned forward so her face was close to his and her breasts pressed against his chest.

"Y ahora," she whispered. "I'm going to show you why that chicken is nothing like sex."

He sat on the side of the bed and tried to call Justo's brother. But once again, all he got was a series of clicks and tones.

He looked at the address on the card: Calle Concordia 45 between San Francisco and Espada in Centro Habana. It was a stark reminder of why he was in Cuba. The muscles in the back of his neck tensed. He ran his hands through his hair and recalled a day in late 1967 when the evening newscast confirmed that Che Guevara had been killed in the mountains of Bolivia. Frank was only two years old. Pepe told him the story over and over. "Remember?" he would say. "Papi stormed out of the house, and Mami went into hysterics?"

"Remember?" Pepe went on and on, reminding him how Rosa had shouted all manner of insults at Fidel, at Che, at the communists, at the devil, her voice echoing across the empty living room and down the hallway. She wielded an accusatory finger at the radio, cursed Cuba, and leapt with joy. Then she grabbed Pepe, held him tight against her bosom and danced. When she noticed Frank staring at them with a blank expression, she knelt by him and caressed his head, whispering, "They are murderers, Frank. Every one of them. Butchers. They thirst for blood. But God is finally making things right. God," she added proudly, "is on *our* side."

His eyes fell on Marisol's naked body. He didn't know what to do: wake her, pay her, drop her off at her house. He'd never been in this position. It wasn't just that they'd had sex. He had enjoyed her company. She softened the sharp edge of his fear. In a strange way, he felt safe with her.

He leaned over and kissed her hip, her shoulder, her lips.

"Frank."

"Good morning."

She rubbed her eyes. "Chico, what's wrong with you, getting up so early like this?" She ran her hand over her hair and propped herself up on one arm, her cheek resting on her shoulder. "Did you have a nice time last night?"

Frank blushed.

She smiled. "I thought so."

"Marisol." He leaned closer and laid a hand on her shoulder. "What did you think of when you ate the chicken?"

"Coño, and go on about the chicken."

"I'm serious."

"When I was eating?"

"I had these strange memories. I was a little kid. And then there was something about my father. I can't remember them exactly, but it made me happy."

Marisol buried her face in the pillow. "You'll think I'm silly."

"Please." He caressed her hair. "I want to know. It means a lot to me."

She turned. The light from the opening in the curtains cut like a line across the side of her face. "I was thinking of butterflies," she said. "Many beautiful butterfiles of all colors flying in the air. They could fly anywhere they wanted and were so pretty, Frank. It made me feel very—I don't know—relaxed."

"Butterflies, really?"

She looked away. "Silly, no?"

"No. Of course not." He leaned over and kissed her on the forehead.

"When I was little," she said, and bit her lower lip, "my mother had a flower garden behind the house. My sister Mayelin—the one who went to Spain—my little brother and my cousin and I used to lay face up on the ground in the garden. We'd stay very still. If we were patient, the butterflies would land on us. We used to make a contest of it to see who could have the most butterflies land on them. We imagined that the more butterflies landed on you, the more people loved you."

He caressed her cheek. "I bet you won every time."

She forced a laugh, and her eyes stared at the empty space between them. "Then everything changed. My mother had to take a job and my father built a room over the garden for my grandparents. My aunt who had left for La Habana came back to Cienfuegos to live with us. The garden became a tiny patio where we raised chickens and pigs and grew vegetables. Flowers and butterflies were, sabes, unessential."

Frank glanced away at the ripples in the sheet along her legs, afraid of the intimacy her words offered him.

"That's how it is here," she said. "Anything that is beautiful is destroyed for the sake of what is practical. With Fidel, it's always sacrifice, sacrifice, and more sacrifice. We've become a country without beauty. We have only what is essential. And sometimes not even that."

"It's a shame," he said quietly, but it felt cheap and insincere. He wanted to say more, do more, but he didn't know how.

Marisol dropped back on the bed and stared at the ceiling. "In Cuba, the government tells us what is beautiful and what is essential."

Frank turned away and clenched his jaw.

She closed her eyes. "The thing is, I don't think I've seen colors in my dreams since I was seven years old."

He had no words. He gently brushed a strand of hair from her face and curled it behind her ear the way she'd done at the restaurant.

She smiled. "Thank you."

"For what?"

"For all this. For taking me away for a night and reminding me that there is beauty in the world. It gives me hope."

He leaned forward and kissed her on the lips, his hand moving softly over her breast.

"Ay, Frank." She turned away and covered herself with the bedsheet. "Qué coqueto. And so early in the morning."

They took a table at the patio bar and ordered coffee. In the light of the tropical morning, the cracks began to show. The fountain in the patio was out of order. The bartender appeared tired and detached. The hotel security guard carried his permanent frown from one side of the lobby to the other. The noise of trucks, car horns, children crying, men and women arguing filtered through the cracks in the building. In the morning, Havana was not so different from New York.

Frank drank his coffee in a few quick sips. He was invigorated. It was as if he'd finally been cleansed of something that had been polluting him for years. He took a quick inventory of the lobby and excused himself. When he stood, Marisol grabbed his hand. "Are you coming back?"

"Claro, I'm just going to make a phone call."

"Frank..."

"Oh." He pulled out his wallet and counted a few bills.

Her eyes, like he had known them, faded away and came back with the venom of the previous night. "That's not what I meant."

"¿Entonces?"

"I just didn't want you to leave me alone. The security will kick me out if they don't see me sitting with a guest."

Two security guards were talking by the elevators. He glanced at the telephones on the other side of the lobby. "I'll be right there. If anyone says anything, tell them to come talk to me."

He stood by the telephones and looked around. Marisol was talking with a waiter. An official looking man with a thin mustache walked toward him. He turned away hoping to avoid eye contact.

He waited.

When he looked up again, their eyes met for an instant.

Frank turned to face the wall and waited until the man had passed and there was a good distance between them. Then he picked up the receiver and gave the operator Justo's brother's number. It was more of the same. Nothing.

He rejoined Marisol at the patio. She was working on her second cup of coffee. "Do you know where Centro Habana is?"

Marisol laughed and waved her arm. "All this is Centro Habana, from here, that way until you get to Vedado."

"I need to find a place." He waved to the waiter and ordered another coffee.

"If you like I can come with you. I can be your guide." Marisol ran the tip of her index finger around the inside wall of the empty coffee cup, then placed it in her mouth. When she looked up, Frank was staring at her.

"Coño." She shrugged. "So I love coffee."

*"When I make tostones, I press the plantain so it's flat.
Then I fry it in oil, but I allow a small bit in the center
to remain uncooked so they won't get too dry.
It also gives them a more pleasant texture."*

—María Ramírez de la Garza
cook at La Tropical restaurant on Calle Ocho, *The Miami Herald*, 1995.

T he city of Havana was covered in a thin haze. Everything was gray. The buildings, the street, the cars, the sidewalk, even the people carried an overcast texture that was drab and without color. But slowly, hues introduced themselves in a yellow dress, a flower print shirt, a red '57 Chevy convertible decorated with pink and white balloons parked in front of El Palacio de los Matrimonios.

Frank took Marisol's hand. They walked down Prado's center esplanades to the Malecón where a melancholy ocean shifted in a dark, metallic monochrome. Fishermen casting their lines sat on inner tubes that bobbed up and down with the tide of silver waves. East of the city, a long streak of dark smoke rose from the refinery and stretched like a shoelace across the sky.

The avenue was flanked by a long row of faded pastel buildings, their tattered facades held in place by skeletons of two-by-fours and scaffoldings that looked as old and delicate as the buildings. And behind them, more buildings rose, each a tone grayer than the next, their own forgotten histories buried deep within apartments that were separated into rooms, which were divided into smaller rooms by makeshift walls of wood and cloth sheets.

They crossed the avenue and made their way into the grid of

streets and buildings that rose three, five, sometimes eight stories high, their facades covered in smog and soot from bad gasoline and dust from the crumbling of the city. The rooftops were littered with television antennas and small homemade satellite dishes put together from recycled oilcans and wire mesh. The balconies were dressed in drying laundry and potted plants that desperately reached out for the Caribbean sun. Women leaned over windows, smoking Popular cigarettes. A man rode past with a basket of fruit on the back of his bicycle followed by an echo of calls, "¿Tienes mango?"

Shirtless men leaned against walls, door stoops, and over balconies, admiring the women who strutted past, their buttocks swinging to the rhythm of a Pérez Prado mambo.

"Oye, mi amor," they called, "ven acá que tengo algo pa' ti. ¡Candela!"

On the side of the street, a '53 Buick rested on blocks. A couple of shirtless men prodded under its hood. A few doors down, a group of women were gathered at the entrance of a building trading gossip. Across the street, a pair of old men sat sideways on a doorstep sharing a drink from a plastic bottle that had been filled and refilled with chispa.

Frank absorbed the details. In every conversation he longed to hear his father, his voice rising above another, arguing. He wondered if these same streets had been the genesis of Filomeno's volatile temper. His father had been a man of few words, but when anyone mentioned Cuba, he came alive.

Like that afternoon when they'd visited one of Rosa's friends in Pearland. Frank, Pepe, and their friend Jorge were watching television. In the background they could hear the voices of the grown-ups rising in argument. They heard, "Cuba," and someone yelled, "Fidel," and then, "Cuba," again. The next thing Filomeno was shouting, "Cuba, where the hell is it now?"

They watched him storm out of the house like an angry teenager. And Jorge, who was younger than Frank, said, "Oye, what's wrong with your papá?"

It was as if Filomeno did not want to be reminded that somewhere southeast of Houston, just past Miami, there was a place he once called home. He seemed angry at Cuba just because it existed.

Rosa could be relentless. She wielded that country like a knife. It always led to the kind of violence that prompted Frank and Pepe to escape the house or shut themselves in their bedroom. But deep down, with his head buried in a pillow, Frank found the arguments a relief from the silence and indifference that otherwise permeated their lives. Now, as he walked the streets of Centro Habana, he could not imagine his father here. He could not see him on the street corner or leaning over a balcony or waving at a relative or fixing his old Chevy or smoking a cigar or being Cuban—not like this. Filomeno had lived as far away from Cuba as the moon.

At the crossing of Calle Lealtad and Concordia, the street was closed off to traffic by rusted yellow barricades where Pioneros— elementary students—in their burgundy and white uniforms skipped rope and sang rhymes.

The sun began to find its way out of the clouds. The haziness subsided and the day became progressively warmer. The blue of the Caribbean sky was finally showing in the distance towards the ocean.

At the intersection with Calle Espada, Marisol stopped. "Which one is it?"

"Number forty-five. It's a gray building." But there were no numbers. And all four buildings on the corner were gray.

Marisol looked up and down the street. "Who are we looking for?"

"Eusebio. And Esperanza."

Marisol stepped forward. "Eusebio! Esperanza!" The people on the street went about their business without raising an eyebrow. She called again, "Eusebiooo! Esperanzaaa!"

"No está." A little boy poked his head out from the balcony of a building across the street.

"Eusebio?" Frank called.

"Eusebio doesn't live here anymore."

"What about Esperanza?"

"She went out. To the choppin."

Frank glanced at Marisol. "And you, niño?" he asked. "Who are you?"

"I'm Pedrito. The son of Capitán, the one who is married to Esperanza."

"Do you know where Eusebio lives?"

"Yes."

Frank waited, but when Pedrito said nothing, he asked, "Where does he live now?"

"In Vedado."

Frank shook his head. "Do you know where in Vedado?"

"No. I'm only a little boy."

"¡Compañera!" A pair of skinny teenagers in baggy shorts and T-shirts with opulent Nike logos approached them from the other side of the street.

The one with the bleached, spiked hair moved his shoulders as he spoke, his hands gesturing below his waist. His eyes skipped from Marisol to Frank and back. "You're looking for Eusebio? We used to be neighbors."

"Do you know where he lives?" she asked.

"Claro, en Vedado. We can take you there. We were just now talking about Eusebio and—"

"How far is it?" she interrupted.

"Coño, not far. We can take Orlando's Moskvitch, but we'll need a little money to help with the gasoline."

"Ah." Marisol shifted her weight and her eyes narrowed. "Y dime, what were you going to do if we hadn't shown up?"

"Well." He pulled a cigarette from behind his ear, glanced at it and gestured with it as he spoke. "I was just telling Orlando here how we hadn't caught sight of Eusebio in so many weeks and that it would be nice to pay him a little visit. ¿Sabes? And Orlando was saying how we needed to figure out something to procure some gasoline. And then we hear your pretty voice calling for him."

"Divina providencia." Orlando, the one with the dark skin and a trim afro, leaned forward and lit his friend's cigarette.

"How much?" Marisol asked.

"I don't know." The other glanced at Orlando. "¿Cinco, seis dólares?"

"Okay," Frank interrupted, "vamos, let's go."

"Coño." The one with the bleached hair offered Frank his hand. "¿Español?"

"No, Americano. Let's go. Where's the car?"

"¡Coño!" He glanced at Orlando whose eyes had also lit up at the word Americano. Then he raised his hand and bought it down for Frank to take again. "Miami?"

"New York."

"¡Coño! New Yor', I'm Michi and this is Orlando. Whatever you require during your stay in La Habana we can get it for you: rum, cigars, girls—"

"Let's go."

"Coño, el Yuma's in a hurry." Michi put the cigarette between his lips and led them around the corner where a square blue automobile covered in gray patches of primer was parked. But when Orlando turned the key nothing happened.

Michi jumped out and got to work under the hood. "¡Dale!"

Orlando tried again and the car exploded with a loud backfire. Michi hopped back in, and they were off, leaving behind a thick cloud of black smoke.

"Inferior gasoline," Michi complained. "Entonces, Frank, you think Clinton will lift the bloqueo before he leaves office?"

"The embargo? How would I know?"

"Never mind, it's of no consequence. We can get what we want now." Michi counted the items with his skinny fingers. "Nike, Levi's, CNN, Marlboros, Heineken."

"Don't tell me—you have family in Miami."

"No." Michi patted Orlando on the back. "We work. We're a team. You see, Cuba is not like the United States. Here, you can't work a job and expect to make a decent living."

"Here you have to invent your own living." Orlando glanced at Marisol through the rearview mirror. "Isn't that so?"

"Óyeme, don't bring me into this. What you two do is your business."

"Coño," Michi said. "He means you're Cuban, hay que resolver, no?"

Michi studied the road to gauge their location and gave Orlando directions. They drove in silence for a few blocks. Then Michi leaned forward and tapped Orlando on the shoulder. "It's here." He pointed at a small blue and white house with a narrow front porch.

"Are you sure?" Frank said.

"Coño." Michi frowned. "Of course."

Michi knocked on the door. A brindle pit bull barked at them from the roof of the house. "Huracán," he called and glanced at Frank. "That is one mean dog."

"But only to other dogs," Orlando added.

A pretty blonde wearing tight red shorts and a Cubanacan T-shirt opened the door.

"Hola, Guajira," Michi said. "Is Eusebio home?"

Guajira rubbed her eyes. "'Pérame." Then she closed the door.

Michi turned to Frank and smiled. "And you didn't believe me."

When the door opened again, a man who was a darker, heavier version of Justo studied the group.

"Eusebio." Michi offered his hand, but when Eusebio didn't take it, he made a self-conscious gesture and dropped it at his side. "We brought you some friends."

Eusebio's drowsy eyes inspected the group and landed back on Michi. "¿Y? Who are they?"

"Frank and Marisol. They were calling for you at your sister's house on Concordia."

Frank offered his hand. "I'm Frank Delgado, a friend of Justo's in New York."

Eusebio's eyes grew, and his lips parted in a large white smile. "I don't believe it!" He embraced Frank. "What a pleasure. I had no idea. What a terrific surprise, but tell me something, Frank." Eusebio glanced over at Michi and Orlando. "How did you hook up with these two comemierdas?"

"Óyeme, Eusebio," Michi complained, "por favor. We were doing them a favor."

"Here." Frank dug into his pocket, counted out five dollars and offered them to Michi.

Eusebio frowned. "¿Qué fue?"

"Coño, Eusebio. We need it for gas. The Moskvitch is almost out."

"Michi, he's my brother, por el amor de Dios."

"I didn't know." Michi glanced at Frank, then at Eusebio. "But, coño, there seems to be a minor discrepancy in the color, no?"

"I tell you he's my brother. What else do you want, a fucking birth certificate?"

"It's okay." Frank pushed the money into Michi's hand.

"And this mulatica," Eusebio stared past Frank at Marisol. "Is she with you?"

"She's with your brother," Michi smiled. "Candela, no?"

Eusebio buttoned his shirt. "Come in then. We'll have some coffee. You drink café, no?"

Eusebio led the way into the house with his arm around Frank's shoulder. They walked through the living room. A bulky Panasonic television dominated the room like a special prize. On the wall was a poster of Fidel Castro in the midst of a fiery speech.

"Guajira, coffee for six, mujer." Eusebio turned to Frank. "We better go out to the patio, it's too hot to sit inside."

They found places around a plastic table under the shade of a large ceiba tree. A gentle breeze stirred the smell of jasmine.

"Coño, Frank, it's such a pleasure to meet you," Eusebio said. "Tell me, how is my brother? And Pepe, right?"

"Everybody's fine. Working all the time. You know Justo's married."

"I know, I know. With a Dominican, no?" Eusebio leaned forward and frowned.

"Yes. She's a wonderful woman."

"Good for him." Then he glanced at Michi, rubbed his nose and turned to Marisol. "And you, my love, how do you fit into all this?"

Marisol shrugged and crossed her legs. "Nothing. We met last night. I'm just helping him get around."

Eusebio laughed and clapped his hands. "You're a tourist guide, qué bien. I like that."

Frank found his tone intrusive. He placed his hand on Marisol's leg and changed the subject. "So, this is your new house?"

"Yes. I am finally coming into some modest money. You know, with Esperanza getting married and the twins on the way, I got together with Capitán and we, I, acquired this place so they could have the apartment on Concordia to themselves."

Guajira appeared from the kitchen carrying a tray with tiny blue coffee cups.

"And this beauty here is Yemanki." Eusebio pulled her by the hip and sat her on his lap. "But we call her Guajira because she's from Cabeza, in Pinar Del Río. And besides, Yemanki, what an ugly name, no? Poor woman, another victim of Cuba's generation Y."

A green parrot in a large wire cage squawked. Eusebio turned to Michi. "And you two?"

"Nothing, Eusebio, we just wanted to see you. Since you moved to Vedado we don't see as much of you as we used to. You should stop by the old neighborhood once in a while."

"I stop by all the time when I visit Esperanza and Capitán—and that little devil Pedrito."

"Well." Michi turned uncomfortably. "I suppose we figured we could kill two birds with—"

"You wanted the money," Eusebio interrupted.

"Coño, Eusebio." Michi waved. "But we wanted to visit you too. How was I to know he was—"

"Bueno." Orlando drained his coffee and stood. "I think it's time, no?"

"Coño, Eusebio." Michi pressed his hands against his chest, "I didn't mean any disrespect."

"Next time just say it like it is."

After Michi and Orlando left, Eusebio leaned back on his chair and sighed. "Those two never stop. I know it's not easy, pero, coño, one must have a little dignity." Then he smiled at Marisol, "Coño, But what a beautiful mulata you have here, Frank. For real."

Frank smiled. Marisol looked away.

Eusebio turned on his chair and drank what coffee remained in his cup. "So, how long are you here for?"

"Just a week. I leave on Sunday."

"Where are you staying?"

"The Sevilla."

"Coño, the Sevilla. It's a great place. But next time you must stay here in our house," Eusebio declared. "La Habana has a housing shortage, but we're lucky we have plenty of room for guests."

"Gracias, that's very hospitable, Eusebio."

"Coño, you're family." He spread his arms. "I would not expect any less from you if I was to visit New York. Us Cubans, we prefer the warmth of a home and family to the coldness of a hotel, no matter how luxurious." Eusebio leaned forward and frowned, "But Dominican?

Coño, are there no good Cuban women in New York? I mean, Dominican?"

"If you met Amarylis you'd understand."

They shared a brief silence. Then Eusebio clapped his hands. "Coño, you're right, Frank. And besides, the Dominican Republic is like a sister country, no? Máximo Gómez helped us fight for independence. He's buried right over there in the cementerio Colón." Then he paused and glanced at his empty cup. "And you, are you married?"

"No." Frank laughed. "I was close, but we broke up right at Christmas."

"Was she Cuban?"

"No, American."

Eusebio waved his index finger. "That's good, Frank. But you know, a Cuban man needs a Cuban woman. With American women it's just not the same, eh?"

Frank smiled and glanced at Marisol. It was what his mother always said. But he had never met a Cuban woman until now.

He leaned forward and rested his arms on the table. "Eusebio, I need to speak with you. In private."

Eusebio's lazy grin faded, and his brow dropped over his round dark eyes. He dug into his shorts pocket and handed Guajira a handful of dollar bills. "Guajira, go down to the choppin and get some beer." Then he turned to Frank. "Or do you prefer rum?"

"Beer's fine. Thanks. Con este calor."

"You're right. It will be good with this heat." He turned back to Guajira. "Get some beer, de la Cristal, and whatever you need for lunch." And to Frank, "You're staying for lunch right?"

"Sure, thanks."

"Okay, get whatever you need for lunch," he said. "If you want ham, Montecristi stopped by yesterday and said Lázaro's brother butchered a pig. You can stop by his house and see what he has."

"Sí, mi amor."

"Marisol," Eusebio added, "why don't you go with Guajira so Frank and I can have a little man to man, no?"

Frank followed Eusebio to the parrot's cage. On the roof, the dog barked after Guajira and Marisol walking down the street.

"Listen, Eusebio," Frank stepped away from the cage. "Justo, Pepe and I...we have a restaurant in New York."

"Of course. Maduros, no?"

"That's right." He sighed and stared at the ground. "We're in trouble. We're being pressured by the bank. We might have to close the restaurant."

"That's a shame."

"Eusebio, the reason I'm here is to ask for your help."

"Coño, my help? But I am only a poor waiter. I don't have any money." He tore a leaf off a bamboo plant and held it between the bars of the cage.

Frank watched the bird. He thought of the restaurant, of Justo's blood flowing down his arm, of his mother looking around the empty dining room, too embarrassed to say anything, of the mountain of unpaid bills on his desk, his constant arguing with suppliers and vendors, begging them for time and credit. Maduros was all they had. It kept them together.

"It's not money," he said, and his eyes took a dance around the yard, skipping from the cage to a green lizard crawling on a wall to the empty little blue cups on the table.

"Coño, Frank, what is it then?"

Frank focused on Eusebio's eyes, but he couldn't hold the stare. "The recipe for the chicken."

Eusebio stared at him for a moment. Then he laughed. "What, of El Ajillo?"

Frank lowered his head and glanced at his shoes. A torrent of shame came over him like a child caught in a terrible lie.

"Coño, you're crazy. Why don't you just ask me to murder El Caballo." Eusebio waved his hands in the air. "Frank, my friend, you're asking for something that is absolutely impossible."

"What about Quesada?"

"Quesada who?"

"The owner."

"The State owns the restaurant."

"But Nestor Quesada was the original owner. He knows the recipe. Maybe—"

"I don't know any Nestor Quesada."

"He's my father's uncle."

"Frank—"

"It's his recipe."

"There is no Quesada at El Ajillo, Frank. No. This is impossible."

"But Justo said you could get it for us."

"Justo doesn't know shit. It's stealing. It's illegal. And you're not talking of just any recipe."

"But it belongs to my family—"

"No." Eusebio waved violently. "You sound like the capitalists with the Foundation in Miami, living the good life while they wait for things to change here, like fucking vultures. What the exiles left behind, they abandoned. I'm not going there with you, Frank."

"But Eusebio—"

"If this man Quesada left, he gave it up."

"He didn't leave," Frank said. "He stayed. He trusted Fidel. But he was tortured."

Eusebio stared at Frank, his dark eyes wide, angry. "You know that for a fact?"

"No." Frank said quickly. "No, but my mother implied it. How else would the State get his recipe and reopen the restaurant?"

"Exile propaganda." Eusebio waved.

"But what about Maduros?"

"What about it?"

"We need the recipe—"

"No, Frank. It's impossible."

"Por favor." Frank pressed the palms of his hands together as if he were praying. "We're going to lose it. We'll be left with nothing."

"We should not even be talking about this." Eusebio looked nervously around the garden and in the direction of his neighbor's house.

"It's our only chance."

"No." Eusebio placed a hand on Frank's shoulder. "That recipe is so well guarded, they say only one person knows the full recipe. And he's with the State."

"We can pay."

Eusebio laughed. "Believe me. There's not enough money in your Fort Knox. I had to pay almost two thousand dollars just to get a job there. It's the busiest restaurant in La Habana. I bring home sixty, sometimes eighty dollars a week. Coño, Frank, in Cuba, that is a rich man's salary. I don't want to jeopardize my job. And believe me, neither will anyone else at El Ajillo. Besides, they would also risk going to prison and ending up like your uncle."

"There has to be a way."

"No, no. Absolutely not."

Deep down he had known it would be like this. And in a strange way he felt relieved. His desperation dissipated into the pale sky. Maduros would close and he would be condemned to live a life like his father's.

"There's Huracán baking now. Las mujeres must be back with the beer and perhaps a nice ham steak." Eusebio slapped him on the back and rubbed the palms of his hands together.

But Frank was compelled to push it one last time. "Just tell me you'll look into it."

They could hear the women in the kitchen, opening the beer and talking of summers in Pinar Del Río.

"I'm sorry, Frank," Eusebio said with finality. Then he turned to meet Guajira and Marisol who were coming out on the patio with a beer in each hand. "Por fín, something to cool us off."

They raised their beers in a toast.

"¡A la familia!"

"Yes, Pepe loved rice and beans.
I am not sure I know of anyone who doesn't like them
with a little diced onion and a dash of vinegar."

—Carmen Z. de Martí
widow of José Martí during an interview
with the Mexican newspaper, *El Imparcial*, 1903

The taxi sped along the Malecón. After they passed the Hotel Nacional, Marisol leaned forward and pointed out her building for the driver. "It's the blue one at the curve, before the Deauville."

Frank glanced out the window. "Your apartment overlooks the ocean?"

"Please. It's not as glamorous as you think."

"You can't imagine what that would cost in the States."

"Yes, Frank, but this is Cuba."

They had taken a taxi from Eusebio's and driven along the Malecón to Marisol's apartment. At the front step of the building, an old lady holding three packs of Popular cigarettes raised an eyebrow at Marisol. "Niña."

Marisol nodded. "Señora Peña."

"Y él, does he want any cigarettes?"

"No, Mami. Gracias."

She led Frank up the broken marble stairs. The building was textured by years of neglect. Exposed, tangled wires hung from rusted nails and ran along the length of the crumbling walls. In another life it had been something exclusive.

They reached the third floor. Marisol banged on the large wooden door. "Eulina. Yoselin. ¡Coño!"

"Marisol." The neighbor poked her head around the hallway. "Mira, El Chino came by. He says he has shampoo for two dollars for a big bottle like this. I told him to come back. He might want to trade. And who is this—Italiano?"

"Yuma," Marisol said proudly.

"Yuma, really?" the neighbor smiled at Frank.

"Have you seen Eulina?" Marisol asked.

"She's in there, but she's scared. That hijoeputa Chuck Norris came by last night and scared her half to death."

"Eulina. Open the door, it's Marisol!"

Finally the bolt turned and the door opened. Eulina's eyes were bloodshot.

Marisol caressed her cheek. "Dios mío, niña, what happened?"

"When I came home last night, Chuck Norris was waiting for one of us. He grabbed me by the neck and told me he knew what we were up to and that we were going to be arrested for peligrosidad and that we were a bunch of dirty putas."

"¡Hijoeputa! He has no right to do this to you. Are you okay?"

"Uh huh."

"Did he do anything else?"

"No. He just pushed me against the wall. I hit the side of my head. Then he left."

Frank touched Marisol's shoulder. "Who's Chuck Norris?"

"He's the plainclothes policeman in charge of the neighborhood. He's a short guy with a bad attitude who's always beating up on everyone. Last month he beat up my neighbor's twelve-year-old son for selling avocados in the street."

Eulina glanced at Frank. "¿Italiano?"

"Americano."

"Really? Miami?"

"New York."

"Americano." She smiled. "I have two brothers in Miami."

Frank laughed. "I'm not surprised."

"They took a raft in '94." Eulina turned to Marisol. "By the way, El Chino came by. He says he has shampoo."

"Serenita told me."

"And la vieja from next door has garlic and onions."

"How much does she want for the garlic?"

"Tres pesos. She didn't say about the onions."

"¿Y nada de Yoselin?"

"Not since I saw her dance away with an Italiano."

"Mira." Marisol handed Eulina five dollars. "If the Chino comes back, get some shampoo, okay?"

Frank followed Marisol into her bedroom. It was small and cramped with a single bed, a plain wooden night table, and a tall antique mahogany dresser that had no doors. The walls were flaking with old paint and the ceiling was covered in brown spots. A large frameless mirror with a long crack rested against the wall by the door. On the dresser there were a couple of perfume bottles, a small stuffed animal and a dozen tattered books. A poster of Che Guevara from the famous Korda photograph looked over the room.

"I'm not much of a communist," she said, "but you can't deny he's handsome. Maybe one day I can get a poster of Brad Pitt or Enrique Iglesias."

"I didn't say anything."

"But I saw you looking. You're an exile, Frank. I know how you think."

"I'm not an exile." He had never longed for Cuba. To him, Cuba was a word spoken in occasional newscasts. It was violence. And it was that eerie quiet that surrounded his childhood home.

Marisol opened a pair of large wooden shutters. Frank stepped onto the balcony and looked out toward the ocean across the avenue. The sun was low on his left, far in the distance, past the ocean, behind Miramar. To his right he could see the Morro Castle turning pink. A soft breeze carrying the scent of the Cuban childhood he did not have came and went in subtle waves that left him wondering if it was real, if he had truly smelled it. He rested his hands on the wrought iron rail that had been rusted and shaped by a hundred years of salt and wind. The texture of the wall, the exposed cement and stone of the building, bare under a wash of blue like the part of the sky that was closest to the sun, framed the view that had become a simple memory for thousands of brokenhearted exiles. His stomach twisted and his throat itched with a heavy melancholy he didn't understand.

"Quizá," he whispered without turning from the view that had captured his defenseless nostalgia. "In a way, maybe I am an exile."

Marisol stepped behind him and wrapped her arms around his waist. She rested the side of her face against the back of his shoulder. "Maybe," she said softly, "we're all exiles in our own way."

He didn't know what she meant by it. But in her eyes he recognized his own sadness, a quiet, simmering melancholy he always thought he'd been born with—in all the family photographs he never smiled. He thought perhaps she felt oppressed. Lost. And yet, he didn't feel she would be better off in Miami or Spain. If she accepted the simplicity of Cuba, she could be happy. But that was naïve of him. Maybe she was happy. He knew nothing of her life. Besides, he was focusing on the wrong thing. He was here for the recipe. He had to find another way to get it.

They stayed that way for a long while, absorbing the sounds of Havana that swept in gusts: the broken exhausts of cars and the pedaling of Flying Pigeon bicycles buzzing like insects below the window. The sky slowly turned to fire, covering Havana in gold dust. A group of children marched on top of the seawall in a broken line. Couples held hands as they walked past. From somewhere, the sound of a lone trumpet playing the morose notes of a bolero pierced through the tepid evening.

"Ven acá." Marisol pulled Frank away from the window and onto her bed. She undressed him slowly—slowly like the setting sun turning a darker shade of amber.

This time it was different. Marisol lay on her back with her eyes open, watching him, looking into his eyes. Frank kissed her lightly as if she might break. He moved without urgency. He spoke to her with his touch. Goose bumps followed the pattern his fingers traced on her golden skin. He noticed everything about her—her small sighs that broke between the rhythm of her breathing, her subtle movements from muscles he didn't know existed, her hands pressing against his back, her nails digging lightly into his flesh, the white of her eye as she looked up, then sideways, the shine of her lip as they kissed, her foot tangling around his, her breath against his ear. And the secret Lucumi words she whispered went straight to his heart.

*"Some of the men complained that the rice
was always undercooked. I didn't mind so much.
We were on a campaign. We were fighting a revolution.
We were lucky to have the food we had."*

—Ernesto Che Guevara
La Habana, 1959

Later that evening they walked down the Malecón to the Máximo Gómez monument, up Calle Tacón to Calle Cuba, and into the heart of Habana Vieja. Ancient colonial buildings loomed over narrow cobblestone streets. In open doors and windows, blue lights flickered and glowed from Soviet-made televisions tuned to the same government channel.

On Calle Empedrado, they turned into La Bodeguita Del Medio and pushed their way into the crowded bar that Hemingway had made famous. Frank whisked a couple of drinks from the bartender who had a revolving line of mojitos prepped along the length of the counter to appease the thirsty tourists. At La Bodeguita nobody drank anything else.

They stood pressed against each other, sweltering in the heat of the overcrowded bar. A short dark man with an old guitar sang that son about a man who cries black tears for his woman who did him wrong—he's doomed to love her even if it kills him.

Marisol seemed hypnotized by the music, her eyes focused at infinity as if she were trying to recall a lost memory. Frank wondered if she was remembering a lover she'd left back in the provinces. He was surprised at the punch of jealousy that jabbed his gut. It had been a long time since he'd felt the anguish that accompanies affection.

"Entonces," he said trying to bring her back to him. "Who's your favorite writer?"

She stared at him as if mulling over the question. She said, "There are too many. Alejo Carpentier, Cabrera Infante, Cervantes, Neruda, García Márquez…"

"So mostly magical realism."

"I don't see it so magical," she said. "Just look around you. Reality's pretty crazy around here."

"Good point."

"Besides, it's very difficult to find books here. With complicated novels, I can read them over and over and every time it feels like I'm reading something new. Like with William Faulkner. I seem to follow a different character every time I read him."

"At least you didn't say Hemingway."

She laughed. "Ay, Frank. You really are Cuban." She placed her hand on his arm. He looked away because it felt good. But it also made him nervous. He was afraid of her. When he saw her in that light, the bare bulbs casting shadows, sharp like machetes and curving along the contour of her face, her skin warm and smooth like fired clay, her eyes moist with laughter, and all the mojitos twisting everything just enough for the benefit of perfection, he saw her beautiful. He saw her more than he had seen her before, because he had not really been looking then. He saw so much more in the darkness of her almond eyes, more in her lips that formed crescents at every angle, more in her small expressive hands with the cheap pink nail polish from the dollar store, and the thin fake gold bracelet that encircled her delicate wrist, little golden hearts resting at the joint.

He pressed gently against her side and took in the smell of her perfume like sugar and vanilla. For the first time in a very long time, he felt the joy of a future filled with possibility. He wanted to breathe her in and take her deep inside him. His desire for her took him by surprise. He swallowed hard and looked away, his fingers pulling gently at his chin. He reminded himself there would be no chicken recipe, no Maduros. But there was Marisol.

They were led through the maze of dark hallways and half-lit rooms marked, drawn and carved with slogans and the names of customers, to a secluded nook in the center of the restaurant.

Marisol shrugged. "I don't see the charm of this place. It's always hot and the waiters are arrogant."

"They say the food's good, no?"

She reached across the table and took his hand. "Any Cuban mother can cook this food. It's in the blood, chico."

"Sure, but what if you don't have a Cuban mother?"

"Your mother's not Cuban?"

Frank laughed. "Oh, she's Cuban. She's probably more Cuban than all the other Cuban mothers in New York and Houston. And maybe even Miami." He leaned across the table and whispered, "Can I tell you a secret?"

"Of course."

"I can cook like a Cuban mother."

"I don't believe you."

"When I was little and got in trouble, my father would punish me by making me help my mother in the kitchen. I've cooked it all: picadillo, ropa vieja, vaca frita, arroz con pollo, boliche, ajiaco..."

Marisol covered he mouth and laughed. "¡Ay, no!"

"By the time I graduated from high school, I had peeled and chopped millions of chayotes and onions and plantains and malanga..."

"And boniato and yuca?"

"Absolutely. And so much garlic and batatas and everything else a Cuban mother uses to cook dinner."

"Maybe, if I'm lucky, one day you can cook for me."

He shook his head. "I hate cooking. My poor mother spent her life in the kitchen. But you know, I think that was her link to Cuba. The food made her feel close to home.

"But you enjoyed her food, no?"

"Sí, claro. But imagine me, thirteen years old and stuck in the kitchen all weekend. Por favor."

Marisol raised her glass. "¡A las madres Cubanas!"

He took a sip of his drink and examined the glass. "You think these mojitos taste like the ones Hemingway drank?"

"I think a more appropriate question is why is Cuba's most famous citizen a Yanqui?"

Frank's eyes drifted around the restaurant. This was not the Cuba of his mother's paranoia. He tried to picture his parents on a date at the Bodeguita, sipping mojitos, maybe hoping to get a glimpse of Hemingway or Errol Flynn or some other celebrity back in their day. He ran his hand over the layers of crayon wax and ink that covered the wall like a Jackson Pollock painting. All the individual names and independent thoughts that had been scrawled and carved on the wall, attempting to make a statement, had blended into a single blob that said nothing—each voice drowned out by the others.

"Maybe my parents' names are carved somewhere in the restaurant, encircled in a heart and pierced by an arrow: Filomeno and Rosa forever."

"Are they from La Habana?"

"Oriente." But he really didn't know where in the eastern part of the island, maybe Santiago, maybe another small town. A sugar town. "They didn't talk much about Cuba. I suppose they felt Castro stole it from them."

"I don't believe that. All the exiles that left when the Revolución triumphed gave it up of their own free will. Coño, why didn't they fight him?"

Frank stared at her across the table. He was thinking of when he was nine years old. He was playing in the backyard with Pepe. They had their GI Joes set up in strategic positions around a little fort built of sticks and rocks. For some reason they referred to the battle as a revolution, but it wasn't Castro's revolution. For them it was the Vietnam War. It hovered over them like a foul smell. It was everywhere. Whenever the principal's voice crackled over the intercom interrupting class, calling a student to come to the office, it was a death sentence. Everyone knew it. A father or an older brother would be coming home in a bodybag. It had nothing to do with Cuba.

"And what about the Bay of Pigs?" he asked.

"Óyeme, no." She gestured with a wide sweep of her arm, her hand flapping like a wounded butterfly. "When they saw that this crazy barbudo was going to stay, they got scared and decided to do something about it. But it was too late."

A vicious weight pressed against his shoulders. He had to defend his parents. But he didn't know enough to take a stand. Besides, his parents had done nothing. "At least they tried, no?"

"And what a failure."

It kept ringing in his head: Filomeno did nothing about it. What Frank knew was that his father had run away as far as he could. He left Cuba and never looked back. It was a miracle he hadn't moved the family to Alaska.

"Forgive me, Frank," Marisol said softly and reached across the table for his hand. "I upset you. Maybe you have a relative who was killed at Playa Girón."

"No, no, you're right. My father did nothing. I don't think he cared."

His past hung like the cigar smoke in the Bodeguita, a place steeped in so much history. His father's temper and his mother's sorrow were all over the place. A tight ball of anger rose within his chest. He hated his father for his silence, for turning his back on their Cuban heritage.

It wasn't until Justo arrived in Houston that Filomeno began to soften. And then, of course, there was Maduros.

A waiter took their order with general disinterest. Marisol watched him walk away. "You see that. I bet he doesn't like serving Cubans."

"Maybe you're reading too much into it."

"Pero, ven acá, you don't now how it is here." She glanced around the restaurant. "I bet you anything, that in all these names written on all the tables and walls, there is not a single Cuban name."

"Marisol." He laid it down like a domino. "I really don't want to spend my time with you arguing about politics."

"I'm sorry, Frank, but politics are a part of every Cuban. Even me."

Frank leaned back and crossed his arms over his chest. "Quizá, but I'm not going to argue with you about communism and democracy and all this mierda about what is right and what is wrong for Cuba, because Cubans and Cuban exiles have been arguing this shit for four decades and nothing's come of it. I don't want to waste my time the way they've wasted theirs."

She fell silent for a moment. "I suppose enough people have suffered because of this Revolución."

"Entonces," he said and leaned forward. "Tell me, do you miss your home?"

"In Cienfuegos? Of course. I miss my family and my friends. Sometimes, I think that for us who come from provincia, it's as if we're exiles too. All my family lived in the same neighborhood. I grew up knowing everyone in my street. Here, I don't have any of that. I'm alone. La Habana today, coño, it's a lot of dollars but no love."

Frank reached across the table and took her hand. He looked into her eyes. He wanted to know everything about her. He wanted to make everything all right for her.

But when he opened his mouth, he said, "At least you had that. I never met my grandparents. I had no uncles or cousins. All we had was television."

Marisol waved a finger at him. "That's very American, Frank."

"I am American." But then he really didn't know anymore. In Houston he was forced to defend what little of Cuba he had inside. Now, in Cuba, he had to do it all over again. It was as if his life was a series of dots that never seemed to connect.

The food arrived in a cloud of citrus and garlic—thick slices of roast pork, chunks with skin and fat attached and covered with thin circles of sliced onions and strong garlic mojo sauce. A cup of black beans, white rice, yucca and maduros and a small plate of moros.

Frank studied their meal. "So what do you think?"

Marisol picked at her rice and beans. She took a bite and coughed. A grain of rice projectiled from her mouth and landed on Frank's lap.

"Ay, perdón." She laughed and covered her mouth with her hand. "But it tastes just like my mother's arroz moro. I have never tasted anyone cook it like that." Her eyes became glossy. She took another quick bite as if to make sure she had tasted what she thought she'd tasted. "Pero qué rico. It's just like hers, Frank. She always adds extra bacon and throws in a little canela to give it that special taste. Try it."

The taste was deep and smoky. He picked at the pork. The meat was tender, the flavor fresh. Tart.

Marisol scooped a piece of pork from his plate. "Cuban food is the best. It's like, el corazón de todo. It makes everything better, no?"

Frank nodded and chewed a mouthful of pork, the citrus and garlic infusing his senses. "My God, Marisol. I don't care if you're Cuban or not, but this is the greatest roast pork, and the mojo…"

"It's good," Marisol said, "but I have to tell you. You haven't tasted my uncle's lechón. Every Christmas he butchers a pig in our yard. My father and him start early in the morning. They take all the insides out and pour hot water over the carcass and shave the hair. My mother and my aunt make a mojo with the garlic from our friend Hernando García who has a farm outside the city. She uses bitter oranges and lime to get the perfect tartness. Then they wrap the pig in big leaves from my father's banana trees and cook it all day with marabú charcoal buried under the red clay. It is so good. Frank, you can't even imagine. We have a big party with all the family, the grandparents, the children and even some neighbors. I wish you could be there sometime. Do you think maybe you will come back at Christmas time?"

"I don't know. Are you inviting me?"

"Of course, mi amor. Will you come?"

"Sure." But he didn't believe it himself. Or only half believed it because he was in Cuba. He was not supposed to have come, and he would probably never return. He had four precious days to spend with her. Then it would be over. And what did he have to go back to? A failing restaurant and an empty apartment.

After dinner they squeezed their way out between the mob of tourists, jineteras, jineteros, musicians, taxi drivers and street kids that had congregated at the narrow entrance of the restaurant. They walked down the block to the Plaza de La Catedral. A gentle breeze cooled their skin. The laughter of children echoed along the cobblestones. Couples—Cubans, tourists, Cubans and tourists together—strolled past arm in arm.

The street vendors were packing their books and arts crafts from around the plaza. A group of barefoot, shirtless street kids, their dark skin powdered in the dust of Habana Vieja, strutted around the outer tables of a café seeking handouts and stealing bread from unattended tables.

Frank took Marisol's hand, their fingers laced together like cloth. He wanted her close. He loved the feel of her skin against his. Her smell. Her laughter and the way she seemed to ponder in mysterious silence.

At the Parque Central, a group of homeless men slept under the moon shadow cast by the statue of José Martí. From the cars parked on

Calle Zulueta, the aggressive whispers of the private taxi drivers rose like crickets in the night, "Taxi...psst. Taxi..."

They walked into the Plaza Hotel. A group of jineteras prowled the lobby. The bar was quiet, the piano silent. A pair of drunk-looking European men talked quietly with their Cuban dates. The bartender tapped a rhythm on the counter. The man sitting across from him pulled the cigarette from his mouth and nodded.

"Frank," Marisol said and pointed to where two young ladies and a waiter were trying to capture a stuffed toy with a coin-operated crane. "Can you give me a dollar to play the game?"

Frank ordered a beer and sat. He watched Marisol press her face against the glass of the arcade game. At the other end of the bar, the Cuban girls faked interest in the conversations of their tourist friends. They sat erect, decked out in tight, multicolored Spandex, their faces bright and shiny with sweat and makeup. They smoked American cigarettes, their hands tilted to the side, their movements sexy, flamboyant. But their eyes were empty. Lost.

A jinetera ambled up to him. "Italiano?" She leaned close, the powerful smell of her cheap, too-sweet perfume flooding the table. "My name is Dolores."

Frank pointed behind him. "I'm with her."

The waste was blatant: the girls at the bar, their happiness, their income, their life hanging on the whim of a foreigner. They had no choices, no opportunities, not like in the States. But he had never taken advantage of those opportunities himself. His father had had no ambition other than to fit himself into an American life, like forcing on a hat that was too small for him. He blamed Fidel and communism for his misfortunes. That was what Frank was afraid of—that he would give up, like his father.

But maybe it was already too late. Everything was a mess. Maduros was a mess. His relationships had been a mess—with Julie and with every girl he had ever dated. If he had been honest with himself he would have realized he'd never loved Julie. It wasn't that he hadn't done anything to stop her from leaving. He hadn't done anything to keep her.

He doubted that he had ever really known love. All his life he had sailed in and out of relationships he knew were safe. Even with Lizzy.

He had never opened up. He was afraid to show her who he really was—that he was too much like his father. She had taken his virginity and run away with it to Austin, and he had accepted it with the same complacency that seemed to mark all his relationships.

He'd run away from a girl named Melissa Baker because she was starting to care about him too much. He had followed her from College Station where they had both been attending Texas A&M, and moved together into a small apartment on Dennis Street in Montrose, a block from the Lankford Grocery. When he started feeling vulnerable, he just left. He didn't allow their relationship to develop. It seemed like too much trouble.

It was a pattern, Pepe said. He called it a fear of commitment. When Julie left him, no one was surprised.

Maybe it was a fear of commitment that made him feel unfulfilled. Maybe it had nothing to do with his father or Cuba. It just was. But doesn't everyone lack something inside? Don't people live their entire lives with a hollowness they can't understand—a need that is never satisfied? They just push it aside or camouflage it with money, expensive cars, sports, religion, relationships. Maybe he'd replaced Lizzy with Melissa, and Melissa with a girl named Genny, and Genny with Julie, and one day he would replace Julie with someone else. He was just filling up the emptiness.

But it was different with Marisol.

He thought of his father. It was possible that Filomeno had suffered a similar void where there had once been Cuba. Perhaps it was all part of something that made Frank who he was. Exile was a sickness passed down to the next generation and the only cure was Cuba.

They left the bar just as the voice of Pablo Milanés began to sing about Yolanda.

They took a turi-taxi through the dark empty streets. Frank's mind buzzed with too many thoughts, of what life was supposed to be, of his father and Cuba. And of Marisol. He wanted to learn her mystery. He wanted to keep the moment suspended in this place, in a limbo that was neither with nor without.

But it was impossible. The taxi pulled in front of the dark building.

He leaned over and touched her hand. "Would you like me to walk you upstairs? Tú sabes, in case of Chuck Norris?"

"No, mi amor. Besides, what Chuck Norris wants is to find me with someone like you."

"I had a great time, especially this afternoon. Up there."

She smiled and leaned her head to the side. "Am I going to see you again?"

"Of course."

"Tomorrow?"

He held her chin and kissed her on the lips.

She turned her gaze to the dark ocean.

"I'm sorry," he said suddenly and reached into his pocket. "How much should I give you?"

She grabbed his wrist and stopped him. "No. I don't want it to be like this with you."

"It's okay." He pulled out his wallet and counted out a few twenties. "You have to eat, no?"

"No, Frank. Please."

He folded the bills and placed them in her hand.

But she didn't take them.

"Those were good days.
We would come in from a long day of fishing
the Gulf Stream and dock Pilar and clean the catch.
Then we'd walk to La Terraza for drinks
and the best paella outside of Valencia."

—Ernest Hemingway
Life Magazine, 1955

I
t was almost two in the morning when Frank walked up the steps
of the Sevilla. The clerk handed him his key and a folded piece of
paper.

Frank stepped away and read the message: "Meet me at my house immediately. Important. E."

He froze. Read the note again. Twice.

He ran out of the hotel to a turi-taxi parked on the side of the street, but the driver was gone. He turned to the doorman, "Taxi?"

The man plucked the cigarette from his mouth and wiped his nose with the back of his hand. "Sí señor, un momentico." He walked to the same taxi, looked around and walked back to the entrance of the hotel. "Well, I wonder where this man went?"

"Is there another one?" Frank followed the doorman. "Can we call one?"

"No, no. Don't worry," he said. "We'll find this one. He has to be somewhere, no?"

He went into the hotel, peeked into the patio bar and disappeared behind a door. A moment later he came out and rejoined Frank at the entrance of the hotel. "I found him. He's coming."

"I'm in a hurry."

"Yes, yes. He's coming now." The doorman winked. "You see, he's having a little thing with the night waitress. Sometimes when it's not too busy they take a little break. ¿Tú sabes?" He thrust his hips back and forth and smiled. "La Habana after hours. Candela, eh? Perhaps, you are looking for a girlfriend, señor?"

Frank stared across the lobby.

"I have some friends," the doorman insisted, "medical students. Good girls, not jineteras like you find on the streets. They would be very interested in meeting a handsome and successful man like yourself. Where you from, España?"

Frank noticed movement in the lobby. "Ah, is this him?"

They sped away into the dark night. San Lázaro was deserted all the way to La Rampa, where the lights were bright. People walked out of bars and clubs and started their own party in the street causing minor traffic jams.

Frank watched the lights zoom past like long neon arrows shooting across the night. He thought of Maduros and the first time he went to New York City. He was visiting Pepe who was living in a tiny studio apartment on the Upper West Side. Frank had just turned twenty-two. He had been drifting for the better part of three years, working menial jobs in Houston. Then he enrolled at Texas A&M to study business. His father had insisted.

He and Pepe went up to the roof to smoke a joint. It was cold and windy and they could hear REM playing out of someone's stereo across the street. They leaned against the parapet wall. They could see a tiny dark rectangle in the distance that was Central Park. Frank took a long toke. As he exhaled, he announced his plans to drop out of college.

Pepe said nothing for a while, watching the pigeons huddle together against the cold. They listened to the music, the cars on the street below, a siren.

"And?"

Frank shook his head. "That's it. I'm moving back to Houston."

"To do what?" Pepe took the joint.

He looked out at the buildings, at the clouds and the smudge of light that was a quarter moon. "I don't know. Work."

Pepe looked at him like he was crazy. "And live with Mami and Papi?"

Frank laughed. "I'm getting my own place. With Melissa."

"This is about Lizzy, isn't it?"

"Lizzy's ancient history."

They were silent while they smoked. Finally Pepe said, "So it is about Lizzy."

"It's about Melissa."

Pepe offered him the joint. "You know what your problem is? You avoid reality. It's like you're scared to finish something, to commit, to succeed."

"What the fuck are you talking about?"

"You have this thing about you," Pepe said and waved his hands to demonstrate the image of a cloud hovering over him. "Every time something is going well for you, you hop off the bus. Why don't you finish school? It's only two more years."

"Who cares? You never even went to college."

"That's not the point."

"I love Melissa."

"So? It's not as if Houston's that far."

Frank turned away. He didn't admit it then, but Pepe was right. And he didn't really love Melissa. He didn't love anyone. It was an illusion. It was what he was supposed to feel. What he was supposed to say.

After a moment Pepe stepped closer. "Did you tell Papi?"

Frank took a long toke and held it.

"You're gonna have to tell him."

Frank let the smoke out and passed the joint to his brother. "I never wanted to be an Aggie or study business," he said, his voice loaded with tension. "That's his dream, not mine."

Pepe stubbed out the joint and flicked the roach over the parapet wall and into the night.

"All my life I watched Papi come and go to work." Frank crossed his arms and hunched his shoulders. "I want more than that. You know?"

"So you're dropping out of college. That's brilliant."

"You don't get it," Frank said. "Remember Nicole Schwartz? She just opened a little art gallery on Westheimer. She's doing great."

"So you want to open an art gallery?"

He didn't know what he wanted. He just didn't want to be doing the same thing over and over again. He wanted more.

"You know," Pepe said suddenly. "We should open a restaurant."

"What, in Houston?"

"No. Here."

And that was that. They said nothing more. Frank thought the idea would simply dissipate in a cloud of marijuana smoke along with all the dreams they'd ever shared. But the idea stuck with them for years. And then, seven years ago, when Pepe had come back to Houston for the Christmas holiday, he and Frank sat with their father in a booth at the Ninfa's on Navigation Boulevard and connected in a way they never had before.

"I'll be honest with you," Filomeno said with a gentle wave of his finger. "I know nothing of restaurants. Your mother and I rarely eat out."

"All we're asking for is a loan to get started," Frank explained. "We have everything set up. Justo has even agreed to be the chef."

"Is he going to quit his job?"

Frank nodded and leaned forward on the table. "And La Palma is one of the most popular restaurants in New York right now."

Filomeno smiled. "I'm glad to hear you boys are working together. It makes me very proud." He took Frank and Pepe's hands and held them tight. "It's important to me that you boys stick together—"

Frank looked down at his father's hand holding his as Filomeno went on and on about the family with overbearing sentimentality. Frank shifted uncomfortably in his seat. He glanced at his brother who gave him a look as if signaling him to be patient.

After what seemed like forever, Pepe interrupted Filomeno. "Papi, about the loan?"

"Óyeme bien," Filomeno said. "I am not going to make you a loan. I am your father, por el amor de Dios. Loans are for banks, not families. Claro, unless you're Italian." He laughed by himself. Then he pushed away the plate of fajitas that had stopped sizzling and bowed his head. "I worked every day since we came to this country. Thirty three years at the refinery. All of it for you boys."

"Papi..." They'd heard it before. They'd heard it when Pepe left for New York two years after he'd graduated from high school instead of going to college, and then six years later when Frank left to attend Texas A&M. It was as if the old man did not want them to leave and seek out their own lives. But it was Filomeno who had always been absent, lost in a drowsy haze of rum and Cokes.

"Let me finish, Frank." He slowly raised his eyes and looked at his two sons. "I will give you the money."

Pepe smiled and spread his arms.

"I have some savings," Filomeno explained. "And you can have it all. But I have to ask two things of you."

"Whatever you want." Frank leaned forward.

"I need you to promise me you will take good care of your mother after I die."

"Coño, Papi, don't talk like that."

"Listen to me, Frank. I want you to promise me that you will take care of her. You have to promise me that."

"Of course we will. Always."

Filomeno stared at his sons' eyes for a long while. He nodded, glanced at Pepe and back at Frank. "The other condition is that you make Justo an equal partner in this restaurant."

"Justo? But Papi..."

"Promise me, Frank. I don't think it is too much to ask."

"Sure, Papi, we promise," Pepe said.

"You, too, Frank. You have to promise me."

"But why?"

"He's my godson," he said quietly. Then he looked down at his hands and whispered. "I owe it to him—and to his family."

"Fine." Frank waved his hand in a vague, half-hearted gesture. "I promise."

"¡Coño!" Filomeno banged his fist against the table so the plates bounced up and the people in the booth behind him turned to look. "Promise me!"

Later, Frank imagined his father had said that because he already knew he was dying. He'd been limping for months. He was breathing differently, and his eyesight was beginning to falter. Maybe Filomeno hadn't wanted anything until now. The way Frank saw it, his father wanted to be reassured that they would stick together after he was gone. And the restaurant was the way to do it.

"We promise," Pepe said and kicked Frank under the table.

Frank nodded and kissed his thumb crossed over his index finger.

The day they opened the restaurant, people came from all over the city. Every table was taken. Frank and Pepe stood against the back wall looking over the dining room, listening to the sweetest sound they had ever heard: silverware scraping plates, a hundred conversations going on at once.

When Frank arrived at Eusebio's house, Guajira greeted him at the door.

"Am I late?"

"No, qué va, chico. Come in." She led him past a room where Eusebio and three other men were slamming dominoes against a table. Frank peeked inside. Someone yelled and then a hard slam was followed by another as they furiously set down their fichas. Then someone shouted, "¡Coño!"

"They'll be finished soon. Do you like CNN?" Guajira took his hand and led him into the living room. They sat on the sofa in front of the large TV. Guajira leaned forward, elbows on her knees, chin on her hands. "I love to see what the women wear and all the different countries. My wish is to one day have the opportunity to travel."

Frank was speeding on adrenalin. He sat erect, his knee bouncing up and down, and stared straight ahead at the television.

"I would go to so many places. Paris, Rome, wherever." Guajira waved as if tossing out all the countries before her. Then she leaned sideways on the sofa and looked at Frank. "You know, before we could travel to the Soviet Union or any of the communist block countries, but not anymore."

"Now you have CNN."

She laughed and stared at the glossy image on the screen.

"It's funny," Frank said. "When I was a boy I loved watching the documentaries of Jacques Cousteau. I always thought I'd do something that would take me to exotic places—the Galapagos Islands, the Great Barrier Reef..."

"And have you gone?"

"No, qué va." He had wanted to travel, to become a photographer or an artist. He'd had so much hope for his future, but time had played nasty tricks on him. One day the world seemed wide open and full of possibilities, and the next he was adding receipts in the back office of Maduros, stuck in a loveless relationship and committed to a marriage he didn't really want.

He turned to Guajira and forced a smile. In her eyes, he could see the innocence and hope he'd lost long ago.

"So, which are your favorite shows?" he asked, trying to clear his mind of the clutter of the past, of time and its ugly habit of moving too fast.

She laughed. "I like them all. Do you know *Gilligan's Island*, about these poor people stranded on an island and they can't leave? It's so frustrating, but very funny."

Frank thought of his father. He loved any show with a laugh track except the *I Love Lucy Show*. He hated Desi Arnaz because Desi reminded him of Cuba.

The voice of the CNN anchorman was drowned by a burst of shouting from the other room. Guajira turned to Frank. "He takes his dominoes very seriously."

"Do they always play this late?"

"He just got off work. He picks up as many shifts as he can. He's very ambitious." She leaned closer and whispered, "Le gusta mucho el guaniquiqui."

"Who doesn't like money?"

A roar of laughter came from the other room. Chair legs scraped the floor, followed by footsteps, boisterous yelling. The group shuffled slowly into the living room.

"Coño, Frank, discúlpame," Eusebio said. "I'm sorry to keep you waiting."

"No problem, I was in good company."

"Compañeros," Eusebio said, "you will have to excuse me for a few. I have my cousin here from Miami. I have to talk with him about some very important business up on the roof. Por favor. Make yourselves at home. Guajira, bring some rum for the muchachos."

Frank followed Eusebio outside and up a spiral staircase to the roof. Huracán barked at them. Eusebio shouted a command and approached the dog. A homemade harness was strapped around the animal's compact, muscular chest and neck. It was tied to a set of cement weights he dragged behind him.

"He's in training." Eusebio adjusted the harness, petted the dog and turned to Frank. "Entonces, let me explain the situation. There is a man. Un viejo from Matanzas who they say used to be a cook at El Ajillo many years ago, before the Revolución. They say the owner of the restaurant cut his tongue out so he could never pass the recipe to anyone."

"Coño. You think my father's uncle—"

"I doubt it. It's probably just a rumor, Frank. But listen to me. I tell you this only to let you know what it is you are dealing with. The State is almost bankrupt. Most of the foreign money they bring in comes from tourism. And El Ajillo is a cash cow, ¿me entiendes? The old man, well, if it's true about him, he's probably dead. We are not going to go to Matanzas in search of a nameless mute. But this is serious business."

"I understand, Eusebio, but what about Quesada—"

"You were right about him. The State forced him to close the restaurant two years after the Revolución. He lived in a big house in Miramar. And then, in 1966, he disappeared, just like that."

"Perhaps he moved abroad."

Eusebio grinned. "It doesn't work that way. Cubans don't disappear abroad, they disappear in prisons. But I like your optimism."

"So there's no way to get to him."

Eusebio shook his head. "Listen to me." He lowered his voice and leaned close to Frank. "The chef at El Ajillo is absolutely untouchable. He's with the State. What they will do to him if the recipe gets out is something so terrible that even the thought of it gives me goose pimples." He raised his arm and showed Frank the bumps. "See? La piel de gallina.

"But," he continued, "the chef has a few helpers who have access to the kitchen. Only they are not allowed to work together, and they are assigned only a specific portion of the recipe. I know—like anyone who works there and pays attention—that the chicken is marinated and baked. Entonces, one set of helpers makes the marinade while the other prepares the batter and places the chicken in the oven. Are you with me?"

"Sí, claro."

"Okay then. This is the tricky part. The chef mixes the spices in secret. The kitchen help call it Aché. Nobody other than the chef has knowledge of the full recipe. And that is our problem."

"Okay, but—"

"Ah." Eusebio raised his hand to stop him. "I know what your question is, and I will tell you: I don't know. We can try, but I really don't know. A waitress tells me there is a cook, a viejo, who is a maricón. She says he likes to dress up as a woman. Apparently he talks with her about clothes and makeup and all that shit maricones like to talk about.

"There is another who is with the Partido. That's how he landed the job at El Ajillo. And there is a skinny Hungarian. We might be able to bribe him, I don't know. I am still looking for other possibilities. But even if we get the two parts of the recipe, we still need to know what's in the Aché, otherwise we have nothing."

"How do we—"

"'Pérame, Frank. I'm not finished. I'm looking into this, and I'm willing to help you if I can, but however we approach this, it cannot be traced back to me."

"But Justo said you would—"

"No. Justo's wrong. I'm willing to help you, but I'm not stealing it."

"But—"

"We can use Michi and Orlando as go-betweens. Whatever we do, it cannot come back to me, or I will lose my job and probably end up in Combinado del Este."

"I understand."

"I do not enter into this business lightly. You are stealing something. This is illegal. A crime. And when you live in a dictatorship you exist at the whim of a dictator. If you get caught, you could go to prison. Or worse."

"But the recipe belongs to my family."

Eusebio frowned. "Trust me, the State will not see it that way. Also, I will need something from you in writing with your signature. I know that between us our word is enough, but the world has become a complicated place, and things need to be done within certain protocols so they can be validated. I don't like it any more than you do, but what can I do? I am only a poor Cuban waiter, eh?" He laughed and patted Frank on the back. "What I would like in return for my help is to be a partner with you and Pepe and Justo. I would need you to write up a contract agreement making me an owner of your restaurant in New York. Okay?"

"Sure, but—"

Eusebio raised his hand. "You will wire me whatever money is allowed by the bloqueo. The rest you can put into a savings account for me. This thing" —he waved his hand— "is not going to last forever. Maybe one day I can go and cash in that account. Meanwhile what you send me will help me live well. Besides, in Cuba they don't let you live like you have money. If you have more than your neighbor, they hit you with the Ley Maceta and take it all away. One day soon, perhaps you and Pepe and Justo will move to Cuba, and our children will play together in the backyard of our house on Miramar while we sit drinking Heinekens, watching the sun set and laughing all the way, eh?"

Frank smiled. "It sounds great, Eusebio, but I need to check with Justo and Pepe, tú sabes?"

"Coño, absolutely. And if your brother and Justo decide they do not want to make me a partner in the restaurant, that would be better. We can forget about this business, butcher a pig and have a party."

"Sure, but if they agree?"

"Ah, that is another thing. I will send you instructions on how to proceed. Right now I have no idea how we're going to do this. I am not the kind of guy who likes to force things out of people. I don't want it in my conscience that we had to injure an innocent man just to get a chicken recipe, tú sabes?"

Frank stepped back. "You think we'll have to be so drastic?"

"Coño, do you want the recipe?"

He turned away and ran his hand over his hair, his fingers pulling hard at the roots. He was gripped with a wave of nausea, like he might vomit. This had not been the plan.

Eusebio stared at him for a moment. "Not a word about this

to anyone. In Cuba you cannot even trust your own family, do you understand?"

"Of course."

"We will send all our messages in sealed envelopes." Then he waved and patted him on the back. "Now let's go downstairs and celebrate with a drink of rum. ¿Qué te parece?"

Frank started to go, but Eusebio caught him by the shoulder and turned him toward the street. "And one more thing. You are going to have to forgive me, but whatever happens, I cannot have you come to my house again. You see that white Lada parked at the end of the block?"

A small white square car sat in the dark two houses down.

"MININT. Police from the Ministerio del Interior. It seems our government is keeping an eye on you."

"What? Why? Why would they be following me? I haven't told anybody anything."

"Don't worry, sometimes these things happen. This is Cuba. But my problem is that I train fighting dogs. I live in this house, which I acquired through a questionable exchange with Capitán. And, well, then there is this little business of yours which is very touchy. So I have to ask you not to come here directly. Contact me only through Michi and Orlando. We can always get together at your hotel, or we can go out somewhere, a bar or a paladar. I just don't want them near my house."

"I don't understand. Why are they following me?"

"No sé, chico. It could be anything. It might have to do with your father."

"But he's dead."

"Maybe they don't know that."

"But why? He left after the Revolución. He never got involved with exile groups."

"Calm down. This kind of thing happens all the time. I don't know if your father did anything after he left Cuba, but my mother told me he worked with Frank País in Santiago."

"Who the hell is Frank País?"

Eusebio rolled his eyes. "Coño, Frank, don't worry about it. Let's go get that drink." He led Frank back to the kitchen where he rinsed out a pair of glasses and poured the rum. "Ice? Water?"

"No, nada, gracias."

Eusebio handed him a glass and held his own up in the air. "Salud."

Frank took a long drink and stared at his glass. "Eusebio, what did my father do? Why would the government be interested in him?"

"I only know what I told you."

"Coño. That's more than what I know." Frank took another long drink. "Why would they be following me?"

"Frank, never mind those hijoeputas, they're probably sleeping anyway. This is not the time to get paranoid, okay? Now, how are you going to get back to your hotel?"

"I'll get a taxi."

"Coño, this is not New York. You can't just get a taxi here in the street at four in the morning." He peeked into the living room, "Ernestico, un favor." Then he turned to Frank, "Ernesto will give you a ride."

When they arrived at the Sevilla, Frank stepped out of the car. "Ernesto." He leaned in through the window. "Have you ever heard of Frank País?"

Ernesto shifted the car into reverse and leaned over the seat. "Of course. He's one of the martyrs of the Revolución."

Frank woke just before noon. It hit him slowly like a terrible hangover. This had not been the plan. He was only willing to steal the recipe because the Cuban government had stolen it from his family. Or at least that was what he believed. Castro had taken too many things from them and from thousands of other exiles. So many Cubans had lost everything because of Fidel and his revolution. Stealing was one thing, but what Eusebio was proposing was something else altogether. He didn't want anyone hurt. He didn't want anyone having his tongue sliced off. He didn't want anyone tortured.

But maybe they wouldn't have to go that far. Eusebio had no plan. Not yet. But they would have to move fast. It was already Wednesday. He had only four days left.

He placed a call to New York and in vague terms explained Eusebio's business proposal to his brother.

"Is he crazy?" Pepe cried.

"It's the only way. This thing is what everyone says it is and more, but you and Justo need to agree."

"Hold on. Let me get Justo." In a moment he was back on the line. "Frank?"

"Yeah?"

"Justo agrees. I'll go along if you're okay with it. You sure you feel right about this?"

"No. As a matter of fact, I don't. But I'm here. And like you said, we have this one chance, right?"

"So you're not in?"

"Oh, I'm in. I just don't know if it'll turn out well."

"Why not?"

"Mami was right about her uncle."

"Jesus."

"Please tell her I love her." There was a long silence. "Did you hear me?"

"Yeah, sure," Pepe said. "You okay?"

"Did you ever hear Papi mention a guy named Frank País?"

"I don't think so. Why?"

"Nothing. Never mind."

Later, Frank went downstairs and found Michi and Orlando sitting at a table by the broken fountain in the patio of the Sevilla.

"How are you, Frank?" Michi said. "It's good to see you again. You know, Eusebio told us we should come see you. We have been here since, when?" He glanced at Orlando. "Ten o'clock?"

Orlando nodded and raised three fingers. "I've already had three cafés."

"I'm sorry. I was up until four last night."

Michi leaned forward and gave Orlando a high five. "La mulatica, no? What was her name again?"

Frank signaled the waiter to bring him a coffee. He looked around the bar. His eyes skipped over all the characters—the tourists, the prostitutes, the hotel employees and the young hustlers prowling the lobby like hungry cats. He had never actually seen a government agent or a plainclothes policeman. He didn't know what to look for.

"¿Entonces?" He sat back on his chair and rubbed the palms of his hands together. "You guys hungry?"

"Bueno, well, maybe a little something." Michi moved the small spoon around his empty coffee cup so it rang like a little bell.

"A Cuban sandwich," Frank told the waiter. "¿Y ustedes?"

Michi glanced at Frank and up at the waiter. "Me too."

"Cuban sandwich," Orlando said. "And a Tropicola."

Michi raised his hand. "Me too. Tropicola."

When the waiter walked away, Michi leaned forward. "So, how are you liking it here in Cuba?"

"Fine." Frank kept scanning the lobby, still trying to spot the MININT agents. "I feel good here."

"Perhaps you belong here. I mean if you're a relative of Eusebio's, you must belong here, because ese negro," Michi said and waved his finger, "is the most Cuban guy I know."

"Did he send you to get something from me?"

"As a matter of fact, he did. He commissioned us as couriers. He also mentioned you would be buying us lunch."

Frank laughed.

"That's what he said. No es verdad, Orlando?"

Frank got some stationery at the front desk and wrote out a simple letter agreeing to give Eusebio a quarter partnership in Maduros. He signed it for himself, Pepe and Justo. Then he folded the paper, and turned it over to Michi. "I need both of you to sign as witnesses. And write your name and address under it."

"Coño, Frank," Michi said, "let me see what it says."

"This is between Eusebio and me."

"Sure, but my signature on a piece of paper—"

"What am I going to take from you, your tennis shoes?" Frank pointed to the bottom of the paper with his pinky. "Read it here, it says you're only a witness."

They both signed. Frank folded the paper, sealed the envelope, and handed it to Michi. "This is private business, eh?"

"Frank," Michi said taking the envelope, folding it in three, and putting it in his fanny pack, "What do you think? Eusebio and us, we go way back."

"I just wanted to make it clear."

The waiter brought the food. Frank was ravenous. He took a large bite of his sandwich and chewed with his mouth open.

Michi glanced at Frank, but addressed Orlando, "Just yesterday he was so timid, now suddenly he's Yames Bond."

"And another thing." Frank pointed at Michi with his sandwich. "If you bring me any messages from Eusebio and you can't find me, wait for me here. Give nothing to the clerk at the front desk, you understand? Nada."

"Coño," Michi said, "what is it about Cuba that makes people so paranoid?"

"I'm serious."

"Don't worry, Frank. We're professionals."

Frank sighed. "That's what I'm afraid of."

F rank took a taxi to the gray building on Calle Concordia in Centro Habana. He stood under the balcony and shouted for Esperanza. A woman with a huge afro poked her head out. "¿Quién es?"

"It's Frank Delgado, a friend of Justo Rocha."

"¡Ay!" she screamed. "Coño, chico, come on up. It's number seven on the third floor."

Esperanza greeted him with a long hug and a kiss on the cheek. "Pedrito told me you came by." She spoke quickly and moved her hands along the sides of her faded blue cotton dress. She was skinny in legs and arms, but had a huge pregnant belly.

"I was wondering if you were going to come by again. ¡Alabao! I am so happy to meet you. Please, come in, don't be shy, chico."

She took his hand and led him through the living room to a pair of patio chairs set by a large window where a pleasant breeze did its best against the hot day. The apartment was sparsely furnished. The walls were a collage of peeling paint. Laundry hung like festival decorations on a line going from the middle of the living room to the balcony. In a corner was a pile of two by fours and a small hill of cement. "Please excuse the apartment. Things in Cuba are not as easy as one would think. And getting material for construction, well, you can imagine how that goes."

Frank handed her a bag with a few presents. "They're from Justo. Mostly for the twins and Pedrito."

"¡Ay!" She peeked into the bag. "Justo is such a sweetheart. He's always taking care of us, ever since he was a little boy. ¿Sabes?" She opened one of the presents. A pair of pajamas for the twins. Another present had Pedrito's name, and she set it aside for him. She opened another one for the twins. "Ay, thank you Frank..."

"No, no. Thank Justo."

"Óyeme, but what am I thinking? Let me go and make some coffee."

Frank watched her waddle to the kitchen. She looked worn and tired. He wondered if it was Capitán or Cuba that had loaded the years upon her.

He looked out the window at the gray building across the street. It was large and invasive. On one of its balconies, he noticed a beautiful woman leaning out, looking down at the street where someone was calling for her. He thought of all the open windows and doors in the city. It seemed someone was always looking in on someone else. On another balcony, an older woman was staring at him.

"You take it with sugar, no?" Esperanza called.

"Sí, por favor."

She returned to the living room and handed him a small cup. Then she reclined on her chair, a pillow supporting her lower back. "Ay, Frank, what a shame," she said and ran her hand through her unkempt hair. "You caught me in such a state. With Capitán gone, I don't pay much attention to myself. Es una lucha, chico. There is always something."

"So I'm finding out. When are the twins due?"

"The doctor says July. Maybe on the twenty-sixth, could you imagine? I think it will be sooner than that though. I feel as big as a cow."

"And Capitán?"

"Unfortunately, he's in Pinar del Río. He had to take some reports and quota goals to the warehouses. That man is always traveling. He might be back by the weekend if he finds transportation. They make a car available to him, but there is no gasoline so he ends up having to find his own way, ya tú sabes." She laughed and leaned forward and placed her hand on his knee.

A voice rose from the street, "¡Yuca! ¡Tengo yuca!"

Esperanza pushed herself off the chair and ran to the balcony.

"How much?" She shouted down to the old man who carried a basket of yuca under his arm.

"Cinco pesos."

"Show me." Esperanza squinted at what the old man held up for her to inspect.

"Give me two." She put a ten-peso bill in a plastic yellow bucket tied to a rope and lowered it down to the street. The old man took the money and placed two of the large roots in the bucket.

"Gracias, puro." She pulled the bucket back up and set it on the floor and sat back on her chair. "Disculpame, Frank. I just saved myself a trip to the mercado. What a relief."

"Esperanza, I wanted to ask you something."

"Claro. Frank, whatever you want."

"I was talking with Eusebio—"

"What a capitalist, eh? He has done very well for himself."

Frank stared at the empty coffee cup in his hand. "He mentioned something last night about my father from the time before the Revolución. It was just in passing. My father never talked about his life in Cuba. I was wondering if maybe you could help me."

"I think Justo might know more about it that any of us. He's the oldest."

"Eusebio mentioned a man. Frank País."

Esperanza looked out the window for a moment. "Frank País was a school teacher in Santiago who fought in the Revolución. He was killed early on. He's one of the martyrs, everyone in Cuba knows about him. But I know nothing about your father's relationship with him. Filomeno, right?"

Frank nodded and wiped the sweat from his brow with the back of his sleeve.

"You should visit my tía Hilda. That vieja is full of stories. She knows everything."

Frank glanced at the line of laundry. Esperanza's eye followed his gaze to a shirt that had come loose from one of the pins. She stood slowly, pressed the sleeve between her hands, and pinned it back on the rope.

Frank stepped out on the balcony. He looked up and down the

street. As he turned to go back inside, he noticed a white Lada parked on the corner of Calle Concordia, across San Francisco.

"Esperanza," he said quickly, "I have to go."

"Well." She took his arm and walked him to the door. "Hilda lives in an old house behind the Partagás Cigar Factory on Calle Amistad, almost on the corner with San Martín. It's the only house on the block with two large wooden doors, and it has a window with green iron bars. If you don't find it, just ask for Hilda."

"Is there a place where I can get a taxi around here?"

"Mira, go two blocks up Concordia like this." She gestured with her hand to aid her with the instructions. "Follow San Lázaro to the Habana Libre. It's only a few blocks."

When he walked out of the building, he crossed Calle San Francisco and took a quick glance at the Lada. There was no one inside. He followed Esperanza's directions until he came to the corner where the Habana Libre Hotel rose in thirty-two stories of green glass and pale concrete. A long line of turi-taxis were parked along the side of the road.

"He (Hemingway) enjoyed the paella very much. Personally, I like the palomilla steak. All my life I have been eating fish. I enjoy meat too, you know."

—Gregorio Fuentes
Cojímar, 1994

F rank jumped out of the taxi in front of the Partagás Cigar Factory and ran into the Casa Del Tabaco store. It was like being inside a giant humidor, cold and quiet, with the intense smell of fresh tobacco and cedar. Montecristo, Romeo & Julieta, Cohiba, Flor De Cano were displayed in pretty decorated boxes. They had them all: Coronas of various sizes, Torpedos, Panatelas, Claros, Maduros. He strolled casually from the back of the store to the front. He paused by a display of Cohibas stacked by a window and shifted his focus to the street. The white Lada.

He slowly backed away from the window, searching desperately around the store. Hilda's house was only a few blocks away. He bought a five pack of Montecristo Numero Cuatro. Then he walked out and crossed the street. As he passed, he glanced at the driver of the Lada. He was sitting back with the window rolled down reading the latest edition of Granma. He had a large square jaw and a thin mustache and a complexion that had been scarred by acne.

Frank walked quickly down Calle Industria and turned on San Martín. A pair of elderly women were sitting in front of an apartment building selling slices of cake and cups of coffee from a plastic thermos.

He stepped behind the women and asked for a cup of coffee. He glanced up and down the street. One of the women handed him a small cup. He moved back as far as he could into the recessed entryway, his back against the wall.

The women stared at him. The white Lada cruised slowly down the street. Frank hid behind one of the women.

"Compañero," she asked, "are you all right?"

He froze. The Lada passed.

He poked his head out and watched the car travel down the road until it turned and disappeared on a side street.

On Calle Amistad he found the two tall wooden colonial doors and knocked. A small door cut out of one of the tall ones opened and a short, old black woman peeked out of the darkness of the house. "¿Diga?"

"Hilda?"

"¿Sí?"

"Are you Hilda, the tía of Esperanza?"

"Yes, that is who I am. And also the tía of Eusebio. And who are you, chico?"

"I'm Frank Delgado, a friend of Justo's from the United States. Esperanza told me—"

"Justo?" The old lady's eyes lit up. "Pero dime, how is that boy? He left here after his mother died, and we have not seen him since. Has he grown? Is he eating well?"

"Yes, he is." Frank laughed. "And he's married too."

"Yes, of course. We do get letters from him. Sometimes he even sends money. Ay, chico, but come in, pasa. And Esperanza? I have not seen her in almost a week. How is she managing with that stomach of hers? No, but chico, tell me more about Justo, it has been too long. You say you are a friend?"

Frank followed her past the open living room to a small courtyard which was set in the center of the house in the typical Spanish colonial style. In the eighteenth century, the house must have been a mansion, but now the building was in ruins. Despite what appeared to be multiple attempts at renovations, nothing had been done recently to stem the decay. The rock and mortar were crumbling.

"Yes," Frank said. "We own a restaurant in New York."

"¡Ah!" Hilda took his hand. "You are one of the Delgado boys." She wielded a finger at him. "I did not make the connection right away. You said your name, but I was only thinking of Justo. ¡Alabao! It has been a long time since anyone mentioned that name of your father: Delgado. Pero que gusto, chico. What a surprise. And I thought I would die and never see any trace of your father's family."

They sat at a small iron table in the patio. Frank leaned forward. Hilda held his hand, squeezing it lightly and shaking from old age.

"Esperanza tells me you knew my father."

"Of course I knew him. He lived up there." She pointed to the side of the house. "He rented the room above the kitchen. Of course, the house was not in this condition back then. No, chico, it was never much, but now it is falling apart. This patio had a beautiful garden and furniture. But I have been forced to sell it poquito a poco."

"Hilda," he said, "can you tell me about him?"

"About your father? Sure, chico. What would you like me to tell you?"

"He never talked to us about Cuba and—"

"Ay, Filomeno." She laughed and rubbed her temples with the tip of her fingers. Her dark skin was marked with wrinkles. Her hair was soft and white. "But where did I leave my manners. ¿Quieres café?

"I just had one Hilda, but if you want one—"

"Never mind then, we will have one a little later." She shifted on her seat to face Frank. "Your father. When was it that he came into our lives—'56 or '57? He came from Niquero. Or was it Santiago? Anyway, they came from somewhere in Oriente to attend the University."

Frank nodded. "My mother always said they were from Oriente."

Hilda waved. "It has been a very long time. My memory, well, I am an old woman. It was late summer and the fall session at the University was getting ready to begin. I think your father was studying to be a—"

"An engineer."

"Claro, an engineer, verdad," Hilda affirmed. "And Abel was in the school of medicine."

"Abel who?"

"Filomeno's brother."

Frank drew back. "My father's brother?" His gaze fell behind Hilda.

"That is what I am telling you." Hilda petted his hand. She nodded and waved a finger at him. "Filomeno and Abel came to La Habana together."

"But Hilda." Frank stood and gripped his hair above his ears as if he might pull it out. "My father never told us he had a brother. Are you sure we're talking about the same person?"

"Of course I'm sure, but I never met Abel." Hilda waved impatiently. "But let me tell you. Siéntate."

"It's just that—"

She motioned for him to sit. "Celia told me they were attending the Universidad de La Habana, but I later discovered that was not the truth, at least where it concerned your father. And this was, in effect, the cause for his crossing paths with my sister."

Hilda went on to tell him how Celia had been working with the Directorio Revolucionario, one of the many revolutionary movements of the time and how Filomeno was part of a different group, the Movimiento Nacional Revolucionario in Oriente. "This was after García Bárcena's people joined Fidel's 26 de Julio," she explained and squinted at the sunlight. "Many years after your father left Cuba, Celia confessed to me the true reason your father came to La Habana was to make contact with the people of the Directorio. She said his mission was to maintain communication between the different revolutionary groups in La Habana and the 26 de Julio. She said his orders had come directly from Fidel."

Frank stood. His eyes searched the patio for an answer, for his father's confession, for the answers to the questions he had never asked. He dropped back on the chair and pressed his hand against his forehead and closed his eyes.

What he knew of Cuba and the Revolución had been reduced to his mother's romantic tales of a storybook life in Oriente before the Revolución and the horror stories of how terrible things were after Castro came to power. Her nostalgia was divided in two sections: Before Castro and After Castro. His father's silence had not contradicted any of this. It had only served to confirm the stories his mother had told them.

"You see, at the time there were many different groups trying to overthrow Batista, and Fidel's plan was to unite them. He was very isolated up in the Sierra Maestra, and he feared loosing control of the urban groups in La Habana."

"Hilda." Frank glanced at the floor. "I really don't think we're talking about the same man."

"But we are. Filomeno Delgado. Tall, handsome, and always very well dressed. When I first met him, I was struck by his confidence. He stood out from the rest of Celia's friends. There was something different about him. I could tell he was someone of significance. And Celia could tell too. She was so beautiful. Did you know that at one time she was going to become a dancer at the Tropicana? But the Revolución changed everything. You cannot imagine." She paused and seemed lost, staring at the space between them as if searching for a distant thought.

Frank turned away. Hilda's words kept ringing, "The Revolución changed everything," only it sounded more like, the Revolución changed Filomeno.

"Frank?"

He blinked and stared at her. "What about my mother?"

"Ay, sí claro. Rosita. How is she, is she keeping well?"

"Yes, she's fine. Thank you. My brother Pepe lives with her."

"She must miss your father very much." She said it with so much honesty. For the first time since his father died, Frank considered Rosa's feelings as a woman. All his life he had seen her succumb to his father's wishes, tiptoeing around his silence.

He wanted to declare something important, about how Rosa had been their emotional anchor, about how much she missed Filomeno, about how she had raised him and Pepe, about how she missed Cuba, about how she'd found solace in the church, about how he wanted to do something good for her and make her happy because it seemed to him that her life had been filled with too much yearning and melancholy. But all he said was, "She's a strong woman."

"Even the strongest women are weak when it comes to matters of the heart," Hilda said bluntly.

Frank stared at her small dark eyes. He felt insignificant. What did he know about sacrifice, love, heartbreak? About dying for a political cause, for freedom and dictatorship?

Hilda leaned back on her chair and squinted. "Well, life has been tough for all of us. And back then, it was much worse for young people with political inclinations. Every day bodies would turn up hanging from lamp posts or floating in the Bahía de La Habana or on the side of the road with their throats cut."

"This was during the Revolución?"

"This was early on. At the time they did not call it that, it was just people trying to overthrow Batista. Your father was very intense and idealistic. I knew when I met him that he and Celia would fall in love. With those two, it was unavoidable."

"So my father dated Celia?"

"Of course. They were enamorados. Sometimes they would even take me along on their dates to Playas del Este for a picnic on the beach or to the Vento Drive-In to see the latest movie from the United States. Your father loved John Wayne."

Frank laughed. "I know."

"Back then, Filomeno used to drive to Santiago every month. I always thought he was visiting his father who suffered from diabetes. But years later Celia told me the truth. Your father was in fact smuggling weapons and money for the 26 de Julio in Santiago. He would make his deliveries to Frank País, who would then arrange for the local guajiros to carry the weapons and supplies to the rebels in the Sierra Maestra."

Hilda told him how Celia's friends with the Directorio and members of the 26 de Julio and other opposition groups raised money and gathered arms in La Habana and Mexico and Miami. Filomeno would usually arrange for the weapons to be transported to Santiago, but sometimes he would do it himself. He would hide the guns and the money in a compartment under the back seat of his Ford and deliver them to his contacts in Oriente.

"Hilda, I'm sorry to interrupt you." Frank took a deep breath and wiped the sweat from his brow with the back of his hand. "It just doesn't sound like my father. I really can't see him gunrunning and fighting revolutions. And a brother? And who is Frank País?"

"Frank was one of the leaders of the 26 de Julio in Oriente. Filomeno and Frank were very close since childhood. Celia told me it was your father who introduced him to his fiancé América Telebauta."

Frank covered his face with his hands. "I can't believe this. There is no way my father could have done any of this. He was just a quiet...he never showed any passion for anything."

"Frank," Hilda said gently, "you have to understand. At the time, many of the young people of the middle class were involved with what was happening. Your father was not the only one smuggling arms across the island. People were being killed every day. This had been going on for years, even before Batista. It was a different time. Celia herself was very lucky. She had planned to go with the other members of the Directorio when they attacked the presidential palace, but Filomeno was supposed to make contact with a foreign journalist at Sloppy Joe's, so he asked Celia to go with him as a cover. Can you imagine if she would have joined that attack? Those were her good friends that were killed there."

Frank ran his hands through his hair. His father was nothing like that. He was just another suburban dad. He had erased Cuba from his conciousness. He cussed in English and complained about paying his taxes just like any non-revolutionary father. "But if this is true, why did he leave Cuba after Castro came to power?"

"I don't know," Hilda said quietly.

Frank sighed. They shared a long silence. "So what happened?"

Hilda laughed, and her eyes lit up. "When Fidel rode into La Habana, chico, that was the most beautiful moment in the history of Cuba. I cannot describe it. It was more emotional than when the Pope came. And mira, I'm a Catholic!"

"But Fidel—"

"None of us knew what was going to happen. Things took a life of their own. All that mattered then was that Batista was gone. Fidel and his boys were our salvation." Hilda leaned forward and whispered, "Fidel, for all his faults, always manages to say the right thing. And back then, chico, he was so strong."

Frank took a deep breath and leaned back on the chair.

"But I am getting ahead of myself." Hilda made a quick gesture with her hand as if dismissing a thought. "Before the Truimph, things got worse for everyone, but I suppose that is what always happens. I mean, it was a war after all. As the Revolución advanced, everything became more complicated and dangerous. One day Filomeno drove a carload of weapons to Santiago and hid them in the place where they had instructed him to make the delivery. Then he went to see his cousin. The police learned of the weapons, and they went from house to house searching for them. Your father had to hide in a tank of water in the roof of a house. Imagínate, with water all the way up to his ears. They didn't find him, gracias a Dios, but they found Frank País who was supposed to receive the weapons. Bueno, you know the history books, they took him out on the street and shot him. Your father was very affected by this. He would not admit it, but I swear I saw him cry."

Frank did not look up. His eyes traced the cracks in the floor, trying to find a memory that might help him understand.

"Would you like me to continue?"

He nodded slowly.

"Well, the misfortunes were far from over. When the university closed for the Christmas holiday, your father stayed in La Habana so he could attend a meeting with the different anti-Batista groups. He loaned his car to Abel so he could go home and spend the holiday with their father. Ay, chico. On his way to Santiago, Abel got killed outside Las Tunas. The police said he was speeding and that he refused to stop at the roadblock."

"Why didn't my father tell us any of this?"

"He blamed himself."

"But it wasn't his fault."

Hilda stood. "Come with me to the kitchen. We will make some café."

"I don't understand him. I don't think I ever did."

"Frank, your father was very conflicted." She poured the coffee grounds into an old Italian espresso maker with a bent metal pipe attached by a nail as a handle. "Can you close this for me? My hands. It's the arthritis."

Frank closed the coffee maker and set it on the burner. "What you're telling me sounds crazy. I mean, Filomeno. He was just your average angry exile. He pushed Cuba aside and lived his life waiting for Castro to die. He was so stubborn. He didn't even go see the doctor for his diabetes. That's what killed him, you know? Not the diabetes, it was his stubbornness. If he had gone to the doctor, they could have treated him." He threw his hands up and his lip trembled. "He could be alive today."

"I remember him being very headstrong. Eso sí. He had his principles, and he could be difficult when he had his mind set on something. You know, he reminds me of another very stubborn Cuban." She stroked her chin as if to indicate a beard. Then she pointed to a shelf behind Frank, "Can you pass me two cups, hijo."

The espresso maker made a spitting sound as the coffee traveled up the center stem filling the kitchen with its pleasant fragrance. Hilda added sugar to each cup. Back in the patio the afternoon had progressed, bringing a slightly cooler temperature and a more agreeable smell.

"Do you like it? Does it need more sugar?"

Frank smiled. "No, it's fine, gracias. Let me ask you, Hilda, why would he want to keep all this a secret from his own family?"

"I cannot get into your father's head. He was in his twenties then. He was very idealistic. Celia was the same way. I'm certain the events going on around them were a big influence. They thought they could change the country. And they did."

"I'm not saying there's anything wrong with what he did. I just wish he would've talked to us about it."

"No sé, Frank. All I can do is tell you what I know. Perhaps when you go home you can ask Rosita about it. I can only tell you from what I saw with my own eyes and what Celia confessed to me later, after your father had left Cuba."

"Yes. I'm sorry. I wasn't trying to—"

"Está bien, chico. Do not concern yourself." Hilda sipped her coffee. She placed the cup on the table and wiped her lips with the tip of her index finger.

Frank's eyes were blank, distant. He drank what was left of his coffee and forced a smile. "The coffee's good, Hilda."

"Gracias, hijo. I have to mix it with peas, because there's never any coffee in the bodega."

"I can bring you some from the dollar store if you like."

"That is very kind of you, Frank, but you do not need to bother yourself with that. I am so used to the flavor, I actually like it."

Then her expression turned grave. She ran her hand back and forth over the armrest of her chair. "After Abel's funeral, your father was a changed man. He stopped coming by the house. The few times I saw him, he never smiled. It was as if something inside of him had died. Celia said the same thing. It was after that that he became engaged to your mother."

"Where had she been all this time?"

"In Santiago, I suppose."

"That sounds a lot more like my father, keeping secrets from the people he loved."

Hilda stared at him for a moment, as if she might be thinking of something to say. Frank thought perhaps she was judging Filomeno for his infidelity.

"He came to get his things after the new year. He stayed for a week." Hilda paused and looked at the sky for a moment. "No," she said. "It could not have been a week because my father was back at sea. Maybe it was just a couple of days. I didn't see him though. He came in and locked himself in his room and when he came out, he left. Celia later told me that all he did was cry."

"Where did he go?"

There was a knock on the door and they both turned. "Please excuse me, un momentico." Hilda stood and went to door.

Frank's eyes followed the pattern of the bougainvillea that grew at the corner of the patio. He traced the curves of its branches and the cracks on the pavement where the wall touched the floor, all the way up one of the columns of the arcade to the ceiling. He wondered if his father's stoicism was rooted in his guilt for the death of his brother. Maybe his silence was shame. The ideas turned and twisted in his mind like the branches of the bougainvillea. He could hear Hilda's voice somewhere in the distance and then her slow, dragging steps as she came back to the patio.

"Frank, you are going to have to forgive me. My friend Mildred is just out of the hospital, and her daughter is here to take me for a visit." She leaned closer and whispered, "She had a hip operation. They still don't know if she will be able to walk again."

They walked together to the front. "If you will visit me tomorrow, we can continue our conversation."

"Sure, gracias."

"It has been wonderful to finally meet you."

"Hilda." Frank gave her a kiss on the cheek. "Can I bring you anything from the store?"

"No, qué va chico. Just come yourself. That is all I need."

"I always slice the garlic lengthwise.
If I have to dice it, I first take out the center stem.
It takes away any bitterness. It's very subtle,
but it can make a big difference in your sofrito."

—Sonya Corona
Housewife, Centro Habana, 1998

F rank left Hilda's house and turned on Calle San Rafael. He walked to the Parque Central in a daze. He couldn't help suspect Hilda was lying or exaggerating. Or that in her old age she had gotten the facts wrong. It was as if his father had not been his father. He did his best to put all the pieces together. Much of what she said could possibly explain his father's behavior in Houston. Perhaps Filomeno had clashed with the Revolución. Many people had. There had been attempts to fight Fidel—and not just during the Bay of Pigs. Maybe it explained his father's angry, silent demeanor.

He felt a thin thread of pride. Whatever had caused his father to leave Cuba didn't matter anymore. Filomeno's life was finally making sense to him. The pieces were coming together like a puzzle. Filomeno had believed in the revolution, but the revolution had betrayed him. His best friend and his brother had been killed. It was clear to Frank that he just wanted out. It made sense. And it explained his father's need to assimilate and become a full-blooded American.

He walked along Prado's center esplanades as the evening turned to night, trying to picture his father, the urban guerrilla. He imagined Filomeno racing around the country, arming Fidel and his rebels.

It was a relief to think of him that way, instead of as the potbellied refinery worker who wasted his evenings sitting on a plaid easy chair watching television.

Frank crossed the street and turned the corner to enter the Sevilla. Opposite the hotel, on Trocadero, was a shiny white Lada. He hid behind one of the wide columns that lined the sidewalk. There was no one inside or near the car. He waited. Then he snuck into the hotel behind a group of German tourists.

"What a miracle." Michi and Orlando were sitting at a table in the patio. "We have been waiting for you for almost three hours."

"Since four o'clock," Orlando said.

"I apologize." Frank took a quick glance around the lobby. "I had things to do."

"Your mulatica?" Michi asked cheerfully.

"No, something else." Frank gestured, trying unsuccessfully to catch the waiter's attention.

"Chico, I would rather it had been the mulata. But anyway, here we are. Would you like to buy us a beer?"

When the waiter brought the beers, Frank popped one open and drank it in a few long gulps. "Do you have something for me?"

"Now that you mention it." Michi unzipped his fanny pack and pulled out a red envelope. "From our friend."

Frank read the letter—

I am glad to hear our brothers have agreed. Michi will take you to the house of Hugo, el Sordo. Do not mention my name, and do not allow Michi and Orlando to hear your conversation with him. Offer Sordo money to get the recipe from a man named Granudo who resides in the Playa neighborhood. Make sure you tell Sordo not to shake up Granudo's wife and children. Sordo has terrible penmanship so make sure Granudo writes down the recipe. He will ask for a few hundred dollars. Do not haggle with him but give him only a third of the money in advance. Tell him to seal the recipe in an envelope and deliver it to Michi. He knows to take this directly to you. Destroy this as soon as you are finished reading it. Suerte.

Frank folded the note and stared at his beer. His hand was trembling. He unfolded the letter and read this section again—

Make sure you tell Sordo not to shake up Granudo's wife and children.

He thought of his brother and Justo telling him how simple it would be to get the recipe. It wasn't supposed to be like this. This was not stealing. This was a nasty, dirty business he didn't want to be a part of. He was terrified of what they were setting in motion. His gut spasmed. He dropped his head in his hand and shut his eyes. He told himself this was not happening. He could give up. Go home. Forget about the restaurant. Forget about Cuba. But there was also Quesada. It was quite possible he was tortured to death by Castro's agents. The recipe had been stolen. He was just stealing it back. It all went around in a circle that ended back at Maduros going into bankruptcy. Everything gone. He thought of what Hilda had revealed about his father. Perhaps he was experiencing the same turmoil, the two of them living the same dilemma forty years apart. But he couldn't put aside those ominous words that kept ringing in his head: *do not shake up, do not shake up. Do not.*

He shrugged his shoulders and shuddered, glancing across the table at Michi. "And when do we go?"

"¿A dónde Sordo? Let's go then."

"I need to run up to my room for a moment." Frank pushed his chair out and stood. "Meet me on that big street..."

"Prado?"

"Right. Wait for me on the other side of the esplanades, okay?"

"Sure, whatever you say."

In his room he reread the note one more time. Then he burned it over an ashtray and used the dying flame to light a Montecristo. He picked out a few hundred dollars from the pages of *Crime and Punishment* and paused. He didn't have to do it. If he went back to New York without the recipe, he could make up some excuse. No one would know.

No. There was too much at stake. He was here. It had to be done.

Instead of leaving by the main entrance on Trocadero, he walked the path between the shops and exited on the Prado side of the building. He crossed the esplanades and jumped into the back of the Moskvitch. "¡Vámonos!"

Michi gave Orlando instructions. Then he turned back to Frank, "You and Eusebio, you have a little business going, eh?"

Frank lay low on the seat. "I can't talk about it, Michi. So don't ask. When we finish this little errand, I'll buy the mojitos, okay?"

"Coño, Frank, I knew from the moment I saw you calling for Eusebio that working with you was going to be full of intrigue."

The streets were dark and busy with traffic. At the intersection with Vía Blanca, they had to wait at the same light through two changes. Michi cursed the congestion. Frank remained low on the back seat and out of sight, occasionally stealing glances behind them in case of a tail. But there was no way to make out the Lada with so many oncoming headlights.

Once they took a left on Luyano, the traffic was lighter. A few blocks up the road Michi pointed to a street, "Es aquí, take a left here."

They turned on Calle Rosa Enríquez, crossed a couple of streets and pulled over in front of a simple yellow cinder block house not much different from the others.

Frank looked back, then forward and pointed ahead. "Orlando, park up there, near the corner."

"Coño, Michi," Orlando said as he parked the car. "He's a secret agent."

Michi laughed. "Verdad que sí. Frank, you sure you're not with the CIA?"

But Frank said nothing. He stared at the earth-colored cigar trembling between his fingers. His heart was racing, beating like an engine against his ribs. Sweat dripped down his temples.

"Michi tapped his knee. "You okay?"

He glanced at Michi. He set his cigar on the ashtray and took a deep breath. It was all or nothing. "You two wait here."

"But, coño, Frank, what if you need my help? I know how Sordo can be—"

"I can handle it." But he had no idea what he was doing, what he was going up against, what he was setting in motion. He was out of his element. He lowered his head and swallowed his fear.

"Bueno, but if you need backup, give us a shout."

Frank stepped out of the car and stumbled. His legs were weak. He tapped lightly on the door. It opened a crack and a small woman, her face marked with the kind of wrinkles that don't come from age, poked her head out. "¿Diga?"

"I'm looking for Hugo."

The woman pushed the door open and stepped aside. Frank walked in. A large man with bluish-black skin and a shiny bald head stood at the end of the hallway, his huge arms crossed over his bare chest.

Frank offered his hand. "Hugo?"

"Sordo," he said in a deep, flat baritone.

"Of course. Yes, Michi...he recommended you for a job."

Sordo made a motion with his finger and led Frank to a small cement patio.

"Michi mentioned you might be able to help me." He glanced at an altar set on a small table with various statues, small primitive masks and plastic flowers. "I need to get some information from someone who doesn't want to share it with me."

Sordo smiled. A gold-capped tooth caught the reflection of the single light bulb that hung on a wire near the door. He followed Frank's gaze to the altar. "Yemayá."

Frank nodded. "Very nice." His eyes bounced from Sordo to the altar and back. "I have a name and an address for you—"

"Momentico," Sordo interrupted. "First of all, why don't you tell me your name?"

"Right. I'm sorry, Frank, Frank—"

"That's fine, Frank. Now, relax. Take a deep breath."

Frank stared at him.

"Come on. Like this. Do it with me." Sordo placed his hands on his chest and inhaled and exhaled dramatically. "In-and-out. In-and-out."

Frank did as he was told.

"Again, come on."

Frank breathed long and deep: in and out. His heart slowed and his shoulders relaxed.

"Better, eh? Now, tell me about it."

Frank hesitated.

"It's not political, is it?"

Frank shook his head. "It has nothing to do with that."

"A girl?"

"It's a recipe."

"A recipe? No me jodas, chico."

"I'm serious. It's like a grandmother's secret recipe."

Sordo smiled. "And you want me to juice it out of the old lady, eh?"

Frank stared at Sordo's dark empty eyes. His heart started racing again. Sweat dripped from his temples. "No. It's a cook. A man. But I really don't want you to hurt this person."

"How bad do you want this recipe?"

Frank was trying to regain perspective, breathing deep and slow. His mind repeating the words: *Do it. Do it.*

"If he doesn't give it to me, I might have to hurt him a little," Sordo explained.

Frank shuffled his feet. "What I mean is, what kind of methods do you use? I really don't want this man hurt. I don't want any injuries."

"¿Que fué? Michi didn't tell you what I do?"

"He wasn't specific."

"You're thinking I will torture the man, eh?" Sordo smiled and waved a finger. "No, that's not what I do, chico. That kind of work is for Doctor Maceo. He's the one who does the real torture. He works for MININT and freelances on the side. With things the way they are in Cuba these days. Hay que resolver. Even the ones who work for the government need a few dollars to survive."

"But what about your methods?"

Sordo shrugged. "Intimidation. Sometimes I use the wife or the children. That works best. I fondle them and the man caves in like that." He snapped his fingers. "Sometimes I do fingers or eyes. I might even do a knee or an arm. It depends."

"You break them?"

"Of course I break them." Sordo laughed. "What do you think, I kiss them? ¡Coño!"

Frank averted his eyes. His gaze bounced from Sordo's glossy, hairless chest, to the bare gray walls, to the altar, the colorful statuette of the virgin with the baby, the small decorated plates, the rotting fruit.

"No te preocupes, chico. This happens to everyone on their first time. Fea!" He called, "Bring me a bottle. Now listen to me, Frank. I will tell you a little secret about my work. Most people spill the goods before I even touch them." He brought his index finger to his lips. "But that secret is only for you and me, entiendes?"

Frank nodded.

The woman appeared and handed Sordo a clear bottle with no label. "Ron a granel," he boasted, "not that Havana Club shit you people drink."

Frank smiled nervously and watched the bubbles rise as Sordo took a long swig of the rum. He wiped his lips with the back of his hand and offered him the bottle. Frank took it. He threw his head back, tilting the bottle over his lips, and drank. The rum was like sand in his throat. It ran down to his stomach like fire. He coughed and grimaced.

Sordo laughed. "Better?"

Frank nodded and took another long drink. It went down easier.

"I like you, Frank. I can see this is not your game. But yet, here you are. Like in Cuba, a man has to do what he has to do. Even if he doesn't like it."

"Hay que resolver."

Sordo pointed at him. "You have to survive, that is the truth, coño." He took the bottle from Frank, drank, and passed it back.

"Well?"

"I will try not to hurt him. But if I have to, what should I go for first, a finger?"

"Well, no, not a finger. He's a cook," Frank said and took a drink. "He needs his fingers. How about an eye? Or no. I know, why don't you ask him?"

"What?"

"Yes." Frank took another long sip from the bottle and passed it back to Sordo. "Ask him what he would rather lose, a finger or an eye. See what he says."

Sordo rubbed his chin and looked past Frank. "I never tried that before."

"It might work to intimidate him, no? He might just give it to you."

"That's good, Frank. That's very good. You surprise me."

Frank laughed and reached for the bottle. It was almost empty. The rum was getting him high. He was feeling mighty.

"What about the wife and children?"

"No." He waved furiously. "Don't touch them. Definitely not."

"Coño," Sordo complained, "why don't you just do the job yourself."

"No, no. I couldn't do this." He was losing his grip. His body was feeling loose, his movements exaggerated. "Anyway, I have to give you the details."

His body swayed forward and back as he wrote out the information on a piece of paper.

"When do you need it?"

"What's today, Wednesday? Two days at the latest."

"How do I contact you?"

"Take it to Michi. But wait." He was suddenly aware of his drunken state. He rubbed his eyes and pointed at Sordo. "Listen, I need Granudo to write down the recipe."

Sordo laughed. "Michi told you about my penmanship, eh?"

"I'm serious. And another thing, make sure you put the recipe in a sealed envelope, okay? I don't want Michi to know what it is."

"It's just a stupid recipe."

"Hey!" Frank raised his voice. "I'm paying."

Sordo frowned. "That rum is making you cocky, amigo."

"I'm sorry." Frank stepped back and raised his hands. "I'm sorry."

"What about the money?"

"Ah, yes, the money. How much?"

"Six hundred dollars."

"Six hundred?"

"Didn't Michi tell you that I don't haggle?"

"I wasn't haggling. I wasn't. I was only making sure."

"In advance," Sordo said seriously.

"Two hundred in advance. Michi will give...he'll give you the rest when you deliver."

"No, Frank. I need it all now."

He was losing it. He made every effort to concentrate. "I don't have it now. Besides, Michi told me..."

Sordo stared at him. Then he laughed and waved a finger. "Coño, Frank, you're okay. We have a deal. I will deliver by Friday."

"Very well. And...and listen, Sordo. This man, Granudo. He works nights. You can get to him in the—"

"No worries." He glanced at the note. "You have given me plenty of information."

Frank pulled out his wallet and held it close to his face. He squinted and counted out the money.

Sordo took the cash and put it inside his shorts.

Frank was nauseous. He searched for something to hold on to, but there was nothing to lend him support. He blinked and squeezed the bridge of his nose with the tip of his fingers. "Coño, I have to go. That rum of yours is getting me drunk."

"Óyeme." Sordo put his heavy arm around Frank's shoulder and steered him in the direction of the altar. "For your own protection, leave a little something for Yemayá."

Frank held a dollar bill over the altar uncertain of where to place it. Sordo took his wrist and guided his hand over a plate of coins and candy and a small rotting orange.

He walked quickly out of the house and stumbled down the block to the blue Moskvitch and plopped himself on the back seat.

"Coño, Yames Bond." Michi gave him thumbs up. "How did it go?"

"Let's get out of here."

Michi slapped Frank on the leg and laughed. "Sordo got you drunk on that chispa, eh?"

Frank's eyes rolled back in his head. The inside of the car was blurry. Everything turned.

"I guess no mojitos tonight, eh?"

He didn't answer.

Michi laughed. "That rotgut really does a job on your brain."

Frank sat up and leaned his head out the window.

Orlando glanced at him through the rearview mirror. "You want me to pull over?"

Frank didn't answer.

Orlando pulled over and Frank spent the next twenty minutes vomiting on the side of the road.

As they drove back to the Sevilla, Frank drifted in and out of consciousness. In the distance, he could hear Michi and Orlando disagreeing about an umpire's call against Los Industriales in a game with the team from Santiago.

It was still early when they dropped him off at the hotel. The lobby and the patio bar were busy with tourists. He could feel their eyes following him as he walked sideways across the lobby. In the distance, a voice called, "Señor Delgado. Señor Delgado." A bellboy caught up to him and handed him a folded piece of paper.

Frank swayed past the bar to the elevators. He leaned against the wall and focused on the note.

Frank, mi amor:

I would love to see you again. Maybe tomorrow?

Muchos besos,
Marisol

"Many people prefer ajiaco for a Sunday meal,
you know, to cure the hangover.
My favorite hangover meal is a big plate of vaca frita.
I add a little vinegar and a lot of pepper.
It always makes me feel better."

—Beny Moré
La Habana, 1961

F rank awoke to the foul stench of his own vomit. It was smeared all over his shirt and pillow and caked on the side of his face. The room was turning, his head pounding like a batá drum calling for Ochún.

He showered and swallowed a couple of Advils. He had not shaved in two days. His eyes were swollen, bloodshot with dark, half moons hanging under them like a pair of dirty hammocks.

He imagined a terrified Granudo screaming in pain as Sordo twisted his fingers, the cartilage popping as he pulled them out of their socket. Sordo's sinister laugh echoed all over the room. Then he saw himself passed out over his own shit in a damp Cuban jail, his face bloody, his fingers bent out of all proportion.

Everything had changed. The old Frank Delgado was dead. He was someone else now. The word for what he was doing ran over him like a curse: criminal. Criminal. Cri-mi-nal.

But he was doing it. He, Frank Delgado, had placed everything in motion and there was no stopping it now. He sought solace imagining the State torturing his uncle Nestor, as if it had been true, as if two wrongs made a right. He thought of the stories his mother had told him of her father's farm in Oriente and all they had lost to Castro and the revolution. He thought of all the exiles in Miami and New York. He was doing it for all of them.

But that was a lie.

He was living a nightmare of his own invention. And there was no going back.

He cleaned up and went downstairs. Michi and Orlando were in the patio bar, their arms crossed over their chest, empty little coffee cups on the table, bored expressions on their faces.

"To me," Michi complained, "someone says he'll get the mojitos, entonces, he gets the mojitos. Someone says be here at ten, and I am here at ten. Frank, I don't know exactly how it is you do things back in Nueva Yor', but in Cuba, por favor, chico. All we ever do is wait for you."

"I'm sorry, Michi." Frank searched the lobby and out the windows along Trocadero. No white Lada. "Let me have a coffee. Then I'll buy you guys lunch, okay?"

Michi glanced at Orlando and leaned forward. "But tell me, how did it go with Sordo? Because last night you were in no shape—"

"I know." Frank rested his elbows on the table and rubbed his temples with the tip of his fingers. "And believe me, I'm paying for it now."

"Coño, that shit's going to kill that negro."

"He seems to handle it pretty well."

"It doesn't matter how he handles it," Michi said. "He drinks a bottle of that mierda every day."

"Listen to me. Sordo's going to be in touch with you tomorrow. He'll have an envelope for me. I'm going to give you some money for him."

"What's in the envelope?"

Frank waved. "That's not important."

"But I should make sure that it's inside the envelope, no?"

"No. We're going to have to trust Sordo."

"But what if he tries to trick you?"

"I'm paying him good money. Besides I don't think he's that smart."

"Coño, Frank—"

"Trust me," Frank said with finality. The smell of burning bread was turning his stomach.

"And after Sordo gives me the envelope?"

"You give it to me. Eusebio might get in touch with you for another errand."

"Pero Frank," Michi whispered, "what are you two up to?"

Frank signaled the waiter for a coffee. "Nothing."

Michi stared at him for a moment. Then he grinned and rubbed his hands together. "Y, any word from your mulatica?"

Frank smiled.

"¡Candela! Eso sí, in New York or Miami or in the North Pole, a Cuban is always a Cuban!"

The waiter served them coffee and recited the menu: ham and cheese with or without bread, cheese pizza, and peanuts.

Michi waved him away. "Frank, in the bar of the Hotel Inglaterra they serve a very good pan con bistec."

"It's punta de filete," Orlando said.

"Whatever," Michi said. "It's a good sandwich with beef and onions."

They drove up Prado to the Inglaterra and sat at one of the vacant tables near the hallway. The bartender was shaking up a martini at one end of the long wooden bar. At the other end, a small elderly man sat on a tall stool between two lean black women who took turns caressing his shiny bald head.

"El Cubano," Michi pointed out, "the one that lives here in Cuba, he doesn't get to eat beef very often, no señor."

Orlando watched a group of tourists waiting for the elevator.

"What happens," Michi explained, "is that the State is the owner of all the cattle. The guajiro in the country who tends to the cattle, he can't just kill a cow to feed his family and maybe sell un poquitico to a friend or at the local farmer's market. Me, I love beef. I would love to go to the Burger King. Do you have those in New York?"

"Sure," Frank said. "One day they'll be all over La Habana."

"I don't think I have ever seen beef meat like that in Cuba, tú sabes, coming out of the grill like that."

"You haven't seen any beef meat in Cuba, y punto," Orlando said.

"Coño, that's not so. Before the periodo sometimes they had beef at the bodega."

Orlando waved him off. "That meat they provided at the bodega could just as well have been horse meat."

The waiter served their sandwiches, bread rolls stuffed with small pieces of marinated beef and diced onion and sweet red peppers mixed in gravy heavy with Worcestershire sauce. It was like stew on bread.

"Tell me," Michi said with a mouth full, "do you serve beef steak at your restaurant?"

"Sure. We serve a thin breaded steak, tú sabes, empanizado, and with onion, the palomilla. But the real king of steaks is the ribeye, el ojo de la costilla. You can get it as thick as you like. That piece of meat is so perfect, full of little veins of fat. We don't even marinate it. We just sprinkle a little salt and pepper. When you cook it medium, it's a nice pink color on the inside, and it's juicy..."

"And tell me," Orlando said. "How do you find this sandwich?"

"It has a nice flavor. But you're right, it's not great beef."

"I tell you, and with all the sauce they put on it, it could just as well be pork, no?"

"Or dog," Michi put in.

After lunch they drove back and parked on Prado just past the Sevilla. Frank leaned forward on his seat and counted out the money. He sealed it in an envelope. Then he glanced out the window toward the hotel and passed it to Michi who shoved it in his fanny pack.

"Michi, don't you have a better place for that?"

"What's wrong with it?"

"That's a lot of money. What if you get searched?"

"By whom?"

"I don't know, the police?"

"Why would they search me?"

"I don't know. Maybe because we're doing something that is illegal."

Orlando glanced out the window, then he turned to Michi. "Maybe he's right."

"So where should I put it?"

"I don't know. How about inside your shoe?" Frank suggested. He stepped out of the car and leaned in on the passenger side. "When Sodro gives you his envelope, you give him that one. Okay?"

"Sí, claro."

"Now go straight home. I don't want you to lose that, entiendes?"

"Sí, Frank, take it easy."

"I'll relax when you come back with Sordo's envelope."

"Right," Michi said. "And you buy the mojitos."

Frank smiled. "And I'll buy the mojitos."

"I remember my grandmother used to make a coconut custard
that was out of this world. It was white and creamy and sweet,
and she would add little shavings of toasted coconut on top.
Back in the good old days when I worked for Mr. Lansky,
I used to bring some to the Riviera. The fellas loved it."

—Armando Jaime Casielles
Meyer Lansky's driver and bodyguard, later the public relations director
of the Conjunto Folklorico Nacional, Havana 1972

Frank lay on his bed and stared at the ceiling fan. He tried to sleep but every time he closed his eyes, he saw Sordo crushing Granudo's fingers with a Stilson wrench while Granudo's wife and daughter cowered in a corner, crying, holding each other, begging for mercy.

Then the telephone rang.

"Frank?"

"Sí?"

It was Eusebio. "I would like you to come to a little party tonight in the penthouse of the building next to the Sierra Maestra choppin. Bring your mulatica if you like. And Frank. Don't bring the Lada."

Marisol. He had a sudden irresistible urge to see her. But he also wanted to see Hilda. There was so much he wanted to ask.

He left the room in a hurry. When he stepped out of the elevator in the lobby, he almost crashed into Marisol herself, coming around the corner.

He grabbed her by the waist and pulled her close and pressed his lips against hers. He closed his eyes and took in her sweet smell, her taste, her warm body against his, breasts pressing against his chest. For an instant he felt safe—at peace.

Then he opened his eyes and saw the white Lada parked across the street from the exit. The MININT agent with the wide jaw sat on the hood with his arms crossed, looking at the hotel.

Frank turned away. Three hotel security guards stood by the other exit.

Marisol touched his face. "What's the matter?"

"No, nada." He forced a smile. "What a coincidence."

"Did you get my message?" she asked.

The MININT agent was showing himself, getting closer. There was no way out of the hotel. Not without the Lada following. "I was just going to look for you. Do you want to go swimming?"

"But I didn't bring my swimsuit."

Frank put his arm around her shoulder, and they walked into the hotel's boutique to buy one.

The pool area was sandwiched between the hotel and an old building. The security guard at the street entrance held the gate slightly ajar so curious pedestrians walking down Prado might get a peek at the foreign men and the beautiful Cuban women splashing in the cool water.

Frank lay back on a recliner. The sky was blue, innocent. White puffy clouds moved slowly with the breeze, changing shapes, traveling toward Miami.

From the building on the Ánimas side of the street, rows of balconies decorated with hanging laundry and aloe plants overlooked the pool like box seats at the opera. He was on display. And all the unsmiling eyes in Havana focused on him alone. Paranoia and insecurity crept up his spine. Then he caught sight of Marisol walking out of the changing room wearing a blue and white striped bikini. The MININT agents, Granudo, Sordo, Filomeno, Abel, Frank País, the revolution, Maduros, the recipe, Huracán, Pepe, Michi, Fidel and the stale heat and stink of Havana vanished in the flash of her absolute beauty. His heart sped with every step, her hips swinging, her arm swaying freely like a runway model, her breasts bouncing lightly, hair flowing with just the right effect. Whatever she was—jinetera, prostitute, student, lover, friend, girl, daughter, woman—she was perfect.

"Mi amor," he smiled nervously. "You look...fantastic."

She smiled and took a long look around the patio. Frank followed her gaze. The bartender, the security guard, the other tourists in the pool area, the girls in the pool, the group sharing a pizza, they all stared at her.

Frank and Marisol lay on recliners taking in the sun and breeze and the smells of chlorine and coconut sunblock and the exhaust of cars driving on Prado.

Then she began to hum.

It was a soft melodic song, a son without words. Her voice rose and fell slow and easy from the depth of her throat. Frank closed his eyes, relaxed. His hand touched hers like it was a safety net. He felt completley at ease. Her presence erased all the madness that swirled around his pathetic life. She made him feel as if everything was all right with the world. Even when it wasn't.

When her voice faded into the breeze, he opened his eyes. His gaze traveled lazily along the rows of balconies and the windows of the building above the patio. A pair of children, their heads resting against the top rail of the balcony, ate bread rolls and looked down on the pool area.

Then he noticed the guard at the street entrance staring at him. When their eyes met, he turned to the street. He was talking with someone who was out of sight on the other side of the fence. He thought of the Lada. His nerves began to tighten. At the opposite entrance, a man in blue slacks and a light-colored guayabera strolled across the patio. He sat at the bar and nodded at a figure who quickly disappeared inside a doorway.

Frank sat up. He clenched his jaw. His legs were ready to sprint, but there was nowhere to run.

Marisol stood and adjusted her bikini bottom around her hip and buttocks and dove into the pool.

The guard at the door lit a cigarette. He seemed oblivious to the activity in the pool. And the man sitting at the bar was eating a sandwich and drinking a beer. Suddenly, none of it appeared suspicious. Frank glanced at Marisol floating belly up in the middle of the pool, her arms extended, her wet skin glowing under the Caribbean sun. She wasn't innocent. And neither was he. Nobody was. In this world, in Cuba, it was impossible to remain pure.

He dove into the pool and surfaced where Marisol was floating. He took her in his arms. "You know—" He paused. He didn't know how to take it further. He dipped under the water and resurfaced.

She smiled and caressed his hair.

"—you're wonderful." He wanted to say more, but he kept crashing against a wall of his own creation. He felt her skin against his, rubbing like a kiss. Their legs entwined, their flesh like fish. His arms moved like wings under water. They kissed and he was lost, floating in a cloud far away in the blue.

*"The Cuban lobster is not like the one from your country.
Ours is a spiny lobster. It doesn't have claws like the one
you find in the United States. I usually tear the tail off
and cut it in half, lengthwise. I sprinkle a little olive oil,
some salt and pepper. And if I have any, I also put
garlic and oregano, then I place the tails meat side down
on the grill for a few minutes."*

—Rubén Castillo
Fisherman, Matanzas, 1999

That night Frank and Marisol arrived at the Sierra Maestra shopping plaza where the Malecón ended and Miramar began. One block down, on the ocean side of the street, a dark gray building with shattered windows rose twelve stories high.

Marisol took his arm. "It looks abandoned."

Frank stared at her. Everything in Havana looked abandoned.

The penthouse was a maze of rooms that had been converted into galleries. Electric extensions ran along the ceiling and single bulbs were set a few feet apart to illuminate the art on the walls. The crowd moved in and out of rooms as if they were searching for something specific.

"Look." Marisol pointed at a painting, her fingers inches from the abstract landscape. "It's the Cienfuegos of my youth."

Frank stared at the colorful swirls, bright greens, orange and blue. Deep in the canvas he saw the shape of a thousand butterflies. "Do you think it's the place that changes? Or is it us who change?"

"Time," she said quietly, her eyes hanging at the fringe of the painting. "It changes everything. Innocence is a gift. We spend our young lives trying to lose it, trying to grow up, but when we're older we long for those days of innocence."

He blinked and the butterflies disappeared. "We can't win," he said, thinking of his efforts to find his own place where it all came together, where he could look at his life and appreciate the memories, enjoy the present and dream of the future. He wasn't old—not by a long shot, but he felt as if his life was already overflowing with regret.

Marisol laid her head against his shoulder. He kissed her hair and took in her smell of fruits and flowers.

"I wish you could see the old Cienfuegos. The one in the painting," she said.

"Maybe it will look that way to me."

She pushed him away and shook her head. "It's not like that anymore. That painting was done from memory. It's homesickness."

They moved on to the living room. People danced. Two women moved together on a tabletop, following the rhythm of a conga drum. The crowd mimicked their moves. Then someone shouted something about justice in music. The DJ scratched the record. A deep bass hit like a mortar shell, rattling ribs. Hip-hop turned to salsa, and back to hip-hop. Everyone moved together and the party became a single organism moving to the same steady rhythm.

A tremendous wind blew through the broken windows in the rooms that faced the ocean. In the large kitchen, a banquet with grilled lobsters, an entire baked swordfish, a lechón, chicken, beans, rice, and yuca had been laid out for the guests.

"Frank!" Eusebio cut through the crowd. "What do you think? You like it? A magnificent party, no?" He kissed Marisol on the cheek and led them to where Guajira stood on a terrace overlooking the Florida Straits.

Guajira and Marisol leaned against the balcony. The wind flirted with their hair, their skirts. Eusebio put his arm around Frank's shoulder and led him back inside.

"Look at this kitchen. Just look at the size of this place, eh? It doesn't have the original appliances, but look at the tile work and this butcher block. Coño, you know this had to be the penthouse of someone rich like Meyer Lansky or a Rockefeller. This is a perfect example of how the aristocracy that Fidel chased out of this country used to live. While they were having their cocktail parties with prostitutes and generals, all the guajiros and negros toiled away cutting the cane that sweetened their fucking drinks."

They went from room to room, Eusebio pointing out the details of the apartment. "I love Fidel. I know, I'm probably the most aggressive capitalist in La Habana, but coño, I love that man. What he has done for the people of Cuba no other man has done for any country in the world. The difference with him, I think, is that he genuinely cares.

"Look at this. Another kitchen. What kind of people lived here that they had the need for two kitchens? I think the problem with Cuba is that we, Cubans, we're capitalists at heart. El Cubano, coño, el Cubano inventa for everything. Take me for example." Eusebio moved closer to Frank and lowered his voice. "I put together this little party with a couple of friends. Any artwork that sells, I will get a percentage."

"Eusebio," Frank said, "how is everything going?"

Eusebio ignored the question and led him into another room. "Look, all those windows there, they all face the ocean. And on that side, where that little terrace is, you have a perfect view of the Malecón."

But all Frank could see in the dark reflection was Granudo. Torture, pain. And Sordo's golden tooth catching the light in his perverted smile. "Yes," he said quietly and looked away. "It's very impressive."

"That's putting it mildly, chico."

They went to the bar that was built into the living room wall adjacent to the dining room. "What are you drinking, ron?"

"Sure, thanks."

"Give us some of that añejo," Eusebio said to the bartender. Then he ran his hand over the carved wooden columns that separated the bar from the dining room. "Pure Cuban mahogany. This shit doesn't exist anymore. The hijoeputas cut it all down. Some poor guajiro in Pinar spent years carving a bar he could never take a drink from."

"It's beautiful."

"But it's falling apart. All of it is falling apart: the six rooms, four bathrooms, two kitchens. The bar. And the big terrace, all of it is in disrepair. Coño, Frank, it makes me want to cry."

"Eusebio—"

"You know, there's a part of me that respects the fact that someone was rich enough to own such a penthouse. Then there's another part of me that hates the fact that such a thing even exists. And you know what? There is also a part of me that wishes I could own it."

"You're contradicting yourself."

"Yes, yes, I know, but this is Cuba, the land of a thousand contradictions. It's like Fidel. I think he truly loves the Cuban people, but he dines on lobster while the rest of us sit down to a plate of picadillo de soya. Have you ever tried that shit?"

"So what is this place now?"

"A group of artists live here. I used to live here for a time but there was no water. We had to hire someone to haul it up in buckets. Twelve flights. More contradictions, no? We paid rent for a rich person's penthouse that is in ruins and has no water. Coño, this balcony has a better view than the Hotel Nacional. You know something Frank, you could buy this place."

Frank laughed, "I don't think so."

"Well, technically no. Besides, there is already a rumor going around that some Argentineans are buying the building. That's why everything is in ruins. What is the point of fixing something that might be sold from under you like that? What we need is more capitalism in Cuba. Tell me, how do you like that rum?"

"It's excellent."

Eusebio pointed to a painting of Che Guevara. "I hate Argentinos, starting with that hijoeputa right there."

"You were just saying how you loved Fidel."

"Fidel, yes, but not that arrogant motherfucker."

They walked out to a balcony where a group was sharing a joint. "Eusebio," Frank said quietly, "Do you know if it went well with Granudo?"

"I know nothing." Eusebio waved. "Don't ask me that, because I don't know. I wouldn't know. And I don't want to know. Talk to Michi when you see him."

"When am I going to see him?"

"Coño, Frank, how would I know?"

Frank stared at the darkness. "I'm afraid Sordo might hurt this man Granudo."

"And what, you think I'm not? You think I'm a criminal?" He lowered his voice and spoke close to Frank's ear. "I have never done anything like this. Don't believe for one minute that I don't care what happens to Granudo. Coño, when I go to work tomorrow night, I will have to face the poor man. And I am praying to all the Orishas that he doesn't show up with bandages on his fingers or with an eye patch. Or even worse, that he does not show up at all."

Twelve flights below there was a large pool half full with brown water. Beyond it, the ocean, dark and furious, the waves illuminated by phosphorescence and a half moon rising in the east. This and the darkness that surrounded them compounded Frank's fear and guilt. He turned away.

Eusebio grabbed his arm. "Come on. Let's go check on the dogs."

They walked along the edge of the terrace. The dogs were in cages set at opposite ends of the patio. Eusebio kicked a cage.

"Is that one yours?"

"They both are. Some gusano from Miami is coming to buy them."

"Really?"

"I get them as puppies from the guajiros who fight them in the countryside. But I train my own. Those brutes just throw them in a pit and let them kill each other. Can you believe that? ¡Animales! I fight mine a few times. If they win, a buyer shows up. They're mostly from around here or provincia, but every now and then someone shows up from Miami."

Frank knelt and studied the dog. His ears were clipped aginst the skull and his skin was marked with old scars. He looked sad. "How much do you get for them?"

Eusebio scratched his ear and looked down at his shoes. "I want two thousand for Huracán. He has a very good reputation. But I tell you, if he offers me fifteen hundred for both, I'll let him have them."

"What about the embargo?"

"¿El bloqueo? Coño." He waved his hand and laughed. "Dog fighting is illegal, drugs are illegal, el bloqueo is illegal. And here we are."

Frank stood and took a short sip of rum. "What are the dog fights like?"

"No sé chico. I never go. I only train them. My socio takes them to the fights. I know you won't believe me, but that's gambling. And I don't gamble. Don't ask. It's one of my things. Maybe it has to do with my respect for Fidel and some of the better things the Revolución has done for us. Besides, my interest is in making money, not losing it. How do you think I was able to pay for the job at El Ajillo? Come on, I think it is time for you to meet Jabao."

Frank looked at his glass. "And get another rum. This sure beats the crap Sordo gave me."

Eusebio laughed. "You've been baptized with chispa, eh?"

They went back into the living room and refilled their glasses. Frank leaned close to Eusebio and whispered, "This thing with the MININT, it's really making me paranoid. Do you think I'm safe, I mean with what we're doing and all?"

"To be honest with you, Frank, I don't like it. But they were following you before we started on this business of the recipe."

"Yes, that's true. But it's making me very nervous."

"Something like that would make anyone nervous."

Frank took a long drink of rum and watched two women and a midget walk past them. "By the way, I visited your tía Hilda."

"How did it go?"

"You think her stories are true?"

"Coño, of course. Hilda has lived a long hard life. My grandfather was a sailor. He was always away. My mother and Hilda, they had these shitty jobs before the Revolución. My mother worked at El Encanto and Hilda worked as a seamstress for private clients in Miramar. But after the Revolución, they volunteered to cut cane during every safra until the seventies. And Hilda, who had only a sixth-grade education, went to the university and obtained a degree in history and became a teacher. That's why I admire Fidel, tu sabes? I mean for her, life became much better after the Revolución. Claro, until the periodo especial. Now, if Justo and I didn't give her a little help—"

"I didn't know..."

Eusebio shrugged. "Óyeme, let me explain to you what is going to happen before it gets too late. This Jabao is a homosexual—and like everyone else—a jinetero. You will go with him to La Casa de Lola and look for this viejo who knows the other half of the recipe. He will be dressed as a woman. I was told he'll be wearing a red dress. He calls himself Verónica. Here." Eusebio handed Frank a small plastic camera. "Take this Kodak. Jabao will engage Verónica, and when they're in the middle of it, Jabao pulls the wig off and you snap the photo."

Frank looked at the camera. "Why?"

"So you can blackmail him."

"For being gay?"

"Or you can hire Sordo to beat it out of him if you prefer."

"No, no."

"Yes, that's what I thought. I went to the choppin, but they were out of film. But it doesn't matter, just make sure the flash goes off."

"But there's no film."

"Coño, Frank, he won't know that."

"Okay, red dress. And calls himself Verónica."

"That's right. Now let me try and find this Jabao so you can meet him. You don't have to be at La Casa de Lola until after midnight. And Frank, no Marisol, okay?"

"Coño, Eusebio. I can't just leave her here."

"Frank." Eusebio spread his arms. "She's a grown woman. She was doing fine before you came to Cuba, okay?"

"I can't do that."

Eusebio grabbed his arm and pulled him close. "Listen to me. This is not just about you. It's about me. And Michi and Orlando. We could all go to prison. You can't speak to her or anyone else about this. This is Cuba. Trust no one. You understand?"

"I love my grandmother's Fufu de Plátano.
It's so good, it's erotic."

—Cuban-American gay porn actor Damian Cruz
during an interview with *El País*, 2006

A strong breeze laced with the scent of perfume, marijuana, garlic, rum, and that peculiar and sensual wisp of sweat traveled in and out of the rooms. Frank took a long sip of rum and thought of Marisol. Just knowing she was there, in the same room, made him feel queasy with the kind of excitement he had not felt in years. But he had to find a way to tell her of his immediate plan—that he was going to have to leave the party without her.

"Mi amor." She came to him from behind.

He turned to face her. "I was just thinking about you."

"I'm here," she said, her eyes half closed, an easy smile on her face.

He touched her shoulder, ran his hand along the arch of her back and up her neck.

"Do you have parties like this in Nueva York?"

In the glory days of Maduros, there was always a party somewhere. But it was different. New York was full of flash and pretention. Cuba, this party, the people—there was something real here. It made sense. The New York social scene had been a waste of time. It was how he had met Julie. She had come on to him at one of those all-black events in the Village where people spoke in whispers and bragged about their real estate investments in Brooklyn.

He should have come to Cuba years ago. Marisol ran her hand slowly along the contour of his face and down his chest. "What's wrong?"

"Nothing."

"You look worried."

He smiled. "I'm fine."

"Relax, mi amor." She moved her hand around and down the length of his back to his crotch. She fondled him. "Why don't we find a dark corner and, tú sabes..."

"Marisol." He kissed her on the lips and pulled her hand away. "Not right now. Please."

She reached into his pants and pushed him back toward the wall. "Anda. Let's make love."

"Here?"

She pushed herself against him, her hand gripping his penis which was quickly reshaping itself in her hand.

He backed way and looked over her at the guests, but they ignored them. "Marisol—"

"Frank." She unzipped him. "Nobody will see us." She pushed him farther into the corner and lifted her leg. She held him, led him inside.

Her warmth took him. They wedged themselves into a dark corner between an open door and the living room.

She put her arm around his shoulder, her lips against his ear. He pushed himself farther inside. Her face glowed with the mist of sweat. He bit into her neck and pushed himself harder against her.

"Marisol..." he whispered as he let go of himself and everything went blank and beautiful and his body filled with the slow tingling of an approaching orgasm.

"I'm yours," she whispered in his ear. "Te quiero."

And those words, te quiero—I love you—shook him to the core. He thrust himself forward. Her fingernails dug into his neck. A jolt like electricity ran through his body.

"Frank!" Eusebio's voice called over the music. "Frank!"

He pulled out and looked back. Eusebio's head was poking above the crowd and coming toward them.

"Frank..." She pulled him back. "What's wrong?"

"I have to talk with Eusebio." He zipped up.

"But Frank—"

"Marisol. Wait here. Please understand. I have to do this," he said backing away, his hands gesturing, telling her to stay.

He left her alone in the darkness, the palms of her hands facing the ceiling. Her face contorted as he disappeared into the sea of people.

Eusebio met him in the living room and put his arm around his shoulder. "Coño, I've been looking all over for you. That Jabao is here. Let's go find him. You're going to have to leave soon."

"What does he look like?"

"Blonde, mulatto, very attractive. Tall..."

"Is that him?"

"No, black features, light skin...Ah!" Eusebio pointed. "There he is in the corner, talking to that little maricón."

"The one with the green shirt?"

"That's him. Introduce yourself and talk to him in private about your little business. And, Frank, don't mention me, entiendes?"

"Sure. Listen, how much should I offer him?"

"Qué sé yo. A hundred dollars? You have the Kodak?"

He touched his pocket and nodded. Then he walked across the room to where Jabao was talking with a teenage boy. "Perdón," he said, "can I speak with you a moment?"

Jabao's eyes shifted from the boy to Frank. "Do I know you?"

"No. But I need to talk with you. In private." There was a long silence. Frank looked at the boy and then at Jabao.

Jabao leaned forward. "What's so private? Three is still company."

"Por favor."

Jabao sighed. He glanced at the teenager and made a motion with his shoulder. "Give me a minute, Charlie."

"But Bibi...," Charlie complained.

"Wait for me at the bar. This will only take a minute. I promise."

Charlie glared at Frank and stomped away.

"Children." Jabao laughed and placed his hand on Frank's shoulder. "Amigo, this better be worth my while."

"I need your help."

"My help? I don't even know you."

"A friend told me you might be interested—"

"What friend?" Jabao moved closer so their noses almost touched. Then he glanced past him at the bar where Charlie was leaning against a wall with his arms crossed, staring at them.

Frank was rigid, his arms flat at his sides. He could smell Jabao's breath, mint and alcohol and a cologne that was trying to pass as Dior. "He didn't want me to say."

"Mierda." His eyes were on Charlie.

"It pays a hundred dollars."

Jabao focused on Frank again. "Go on."

"It's about going to La Casa de Lola."

Jabao nodded. "And?"

"There is someone there who likes to dress up as a woman. I need you to seduce him, take him to a dark corner so I can catch him in the middle of an act."

"Fucking?"

"Sucking."

"Me his?"

"He yours."

"A hundred dollars?"

"That's right."

Jabao crossed his arms. "I don't know. Why?"

"Does it matter?"

"It does to me."

"A hundred dollars says it doesn't."

Jabao smiled and scratched his chest.

Frank's eyes dropped from his face to his hand and back.

"When?"

"Tonight."

"What?"

"It has to be tonight."

"No, no, no. I don't think so. See that pretty boy over there. He wants me. I want him. Look at him. Qué culo."

"A hundred and twenty."

He looked at Frank. "Why are you doing this?"

"It's personal."

Jabao sighed and shifted his weight. He glanced at the bar and back at Frank. "About the money—"

"That's all I have. One-twenty."

Jabao nodded toward the bar where Charlie was waiting. "Does that look like a hundred and twenty dollar culo to you?"

"I don't know. But you'll get a blow job out of it."

Jabao pushed him. "Who the fuck are you?"

"What?"

"Are you gay?"

"No."

"Bi?"

"No."

Jabao grabbed him by the shirt and pulled him in and pressed his lips against his, forcing his tongue inside his mouth.

Frank stiffened. He could feel Jabao's tongue pushing between his teeth, trying to get in, the taste of rum and mint invading his mouth. But he didn't draw back. He just stared at Jabao's eyes looking back at him like a circus nightmare.

Jabao released him and rolled his eyes. "Can we take the young one with us?"

Frank wiped his lips with the back of his hand. "Sure."

On the street, people were hanging around cars parked along the street, smoking, passing bottles. A stereo was playing the Gypsy Kings' cover of *Hotel California.*

Charlie clapped his hands above his head and tapped his feet on the asphalt. "I love this song. La la la la la la-California..."

On the following block they found a taxi, a beat-up '49 Cadillac. Jabao ran his hand along the curve of the low tail fin. "I would love to do it in a car like this."

The Cadillac's electric window controls had been substituted with window cranks from a Lada. The seats had been reupholstered with bright blue vinyl, and the chrome details had been torn off. The car turned its engine and moved slowly up Primera, bouncing and rattling with every pothole.

They drove up Paseo, around and behind the Plaza de la Revolución, the towering Martí monument looking down on the patched white Cadillac as it turned down Boyeros and came to a stop at the corner with 19 de Mayo.

"I have a theory," Jabao said as they left the car and walked down the dark empty street. "I think all Cubans are homosexuals. I think that's the reason why they're so afraid of homosexuals."

"You know what your problem is?" Frank said. "You either think everyone is gay or antigay. There's no in between."

Jabao pointed to an official looking concrete buildings behind tall walls. "Those are the offices of the Central Government. You know, where Fidel does whatever it is he does. Over there is MININT, where they torture homosexuals and dissidents. And over here—" He turned into a narrow alley where a group of men and women were crowding a doorway. "—is where Habana's most decadent gays do their thing."

"Bibi!" Charlie screamed and ran ahead of them. "La Casa de Lola. I love it!"

Frank paid the cover and followed Jabao down a set of narrow stairs that led to a large basement-like space lit by red, blue and black lights. There was a long narrow bar a few steps above a large dance floor. Burgundy velvet drapes hung from the ceiling giving the club the atmosphere of a European cabaret from the 1920s. Techno music blasted out of speakers. The dance floor was full of half naked men and women moving like a single person—up-down, up-down—to the rhythm of the music.

"By the way," Jabao yelled over the music. "Just so you know. All the women here are men."

They made their way to the bar on the far side of the dance floor and lost Charlie to the crowd. Frank gave Jabao money for the drinks. Then he leaned back against the bar and scanned the dance floor for someone who might fit Verónica's description. All eyes seemed to be on Jabao.

"Do you see her?" Jabao handed Frank a glass with rum and a dash of Coke.

"No, not yet."

Jabao took a long sip of his drink and smiled. "This is how I imagine heaven is like."

"Doesn't that go against the Bible?" Frank asked.

"It doesn't matter. Jesus was gay."

"Coño, to you everyone's gay."

Jabao laughed. "It's the truth."

"What about Fidel?"

"Of course. And Che too. The Revolución was all a big love triangle. Che and Fidel were in love. Then Camilo showed up and Che had a thing with him. When Fidel found out, he became furiously jealous and had them both killed. Crimes of passions. Te digo, Fidel es candela."

Jabao laughed and moved his body to the rhythm of the music. "Do you ever go to bars like this, Frank?"

"No."

"I can imagine the bars you go to. Everyone looking very proper, showing off their money, talking on their cellular phones, drinking martinis and all that pretentious mierda."

"You exaggerate." But it annoyed him because it was true. In the States, everything was dressed up and labeled. Cuba, on the other hand, was naked.

Jabao's eyes narrowed. "Tell me, how did you meet that mulatica of yours?"

"At my hotel—"

"Was it easy?"

"Well, yes. But I had no intention—"

"Come on, Frank." Jabao spread his arms. "I know the game. You have a wife back in Miami, and you're here having an affair with a mulata who is everything your wife is not. And you have nothing to worry about because this will never get back to her. Coño, I experience the same thing, only from the other side. I receive the tourists who come to La Habana to live out their fantasies. Most of them are in the closet. Even married. Emotions are not a part of life here. In Cuba, there is no love, only sex.

Frank crossed his arms over his chest and looked away. "That's your opinion."

"Please, don't tell me you're in love with her?"

Jabao's words were like a hammer to the back of his head. He saw Marisol lying on her bed, the sun caressing her skin and her dark eyes looking at him with complete sincerity, exposing everything—like Havana without all the gloss of the hotels and restaurants.

"Look at Charlie." Jabao said. "The Canadians are going to have a party with him. They'll screw him until his culo turns purple. He's going to make a killing in Varadero when he goes out strutting that tight, sexy body on the beach. But love? No chico, he'll never find it there."

"You can't speak for everyone."

"Yes, I can. I know what I'm talking about. Here, love is a figure of speech, not a feeling. Coño, Frank, you can't love if you expect to survive."

Frank pointed at him with his glass. "You're a pessimist."

"What would happen if that mulatica fell in love with you?"

Frank turned away. He hadn't thought of that.

"When you go home to your country, you will break her heart. After that, it becomes harder for her to fall in love again. Then she meets another one. Because you know she will. And if she falls in love and loses him, she'll become more cynical, more professional. Pretty soon her heart will turn to stone."

Frank stared at the ice floating in his glass. He was angry with himself. He had not considered her feelings or her future. He had only focused on Maduros and the recipe. He was angry for how he had treated her, for abandoning her at the party, for not saying anything, for not being honest even with her, with himself.

The music stopped and a deep voice broke in. "Bienvenidos y bienvenidas, todo el mundo..." The lights dimmed and a bright spot isolated a robust woman at the corner of the club. As people walked off of the dance floor, she walked to the center, the tail of her long yellow gown dragging on the floor behind her.

"Yes, we have a fantastic lineup for you this evening as we do each and every Thursday night here at La Casa de Lola. We will be graced with some wonderful singing and acting."

There was a brief applause. Someone yelled something. The woman at the center of the dance floor raised her hand. "Please, let's begin tonight, like we do every Thursday, with a fine performance by our talented and very dear friend Verónica. So let's hear it for this sultry lady in red who will be performing an old classic by the great late Mexican singing star, Chelo Silva. Ladies, Verónica!"

An older, slightly heavyset transvestite wearing a red dress and shoulder-length blonde hair stepped out from behind a curtain.

Jabao winced. "What a hideous dress."

The music started. A light tropical beat, almost a danzón, and the high-pitched scratch of an old vinyl record. Verónica bowed and looked at the ground. In a deep, masculine voice she said, "Como un perro." Then she began to sway her body to the rhythm of the music. She slowly brought the microphone to her mouth, and began moving her lips to the words as Chelo Silva sang, "Por tener...la miel amarga de tus besos..."

When she finished, the crowd gave her generous applause. She made a flamboyant curtsy and strutted proudly off the dance floor.

The next number was introduced and the crowd roared as a dance troupe from Baracoa took the floor—four black men wearing g-strings, their bodies glazed with Vaseline, moved to the frantic rhythm of congas.

Jabao stared and moved his torso to the beat.

Frank set his drink down and nudged Jabao with his elbow. "Come on."

Jabao twisted with the music. "They're fabulous, no?"

"Let's get to work."

They walked across the club. Jabao took Frank by the arm. "Go to that bathroom over there. I'll take her into a stall. We'll do it in there."

"You want some money—"

"Por favor." He laughed. "It's her privilege."

The bathroom was small and stank of shit and urine and mildew. There were four toilet stalls on one side and a line of urinals on the other. Two men stood by the sink going through the motions of an arcane transaction. Another man leaned against the wall, writing something over a urinal.

Frank walked to the urinal farthest from the entrance. A moment later, the door flew open and Jabao marched in with Verónica tagging behind.

Jabao kicked open a stall and pulled her in.

Frank heard the unzipping, Verónica's giggling and some vague comments about Jabao's size.

The drumming went on. Fast. Frank's hands trembled as he pulled the camera out of his pocket and turned it on. The flash made a whizzing sound as it charged. The orange ready-light blinked. He moved toward the stall, his knees weak. He took a deep breath and pulled the stall door open.

He was not prepared for the sight of Verónica kneeling on one knee with Jabao's erect penis in her mouth, her head moving forward and back in a single smooth motion.

She turned to look at him, but continued working on Jabao as if having an audience was perfectly natural. Frank slowly brought the camera to his eye.

Jabao pulled the wig off.

Verónica screamed.

Frank was paralyzed.

Verónica reached for the wig, but Jabao held it up. She paused for an instant, then turned back to Jabao's penis.

Then the drumming stopped and Frank woke from his trance. "¡Oye!"

Verónica turned. Frank pressed the shutter button and the flash filled the bathroom with a burst of white light. Someone outside the stall cheered. Jabao moved quickly out of the way and Frank stepped into the stall with Verónica. Two men were trying to look in, but Jabao shut the door. "No, nothing," he said, "It's my friend's turn, qué fue?"

Verónica stared up at Frank. She was sweating. Her eyes were dark, confused. Jabao tossed the wig over the stall and it landed on the floor.

Verónica picked it up and held it against her breast. Her lipstick was smudged around her mouth and chin. She touched her hair and wiped her face with her hand. Then she began to weep.

"The recipe for the chicken." Frank's voice came out a whisper.

"¿Qué?"

He coughed and raised his voice. "The recipe for the chicken."

"I didn't do anything," Verónica whimpered.

"Listen to me." Frank leaned forward. "I want the recipe for the chicken. You understand me?"

"I don't know," she covered her face with her hands and receded to the small space between the toilet and the side of the stall.

Frank grabbed her by the arm and pulled her out. He was shaking, riding on adrenaline. "The recipe. I need the recipe."

She shook her head.

"Tell me."

"Please. They'll fire me. I'll go to prison."

Frank wielded the camera in front of her. "I'll take this photograph to your boss. Your wife, your children. They'll know everything."

Verónica's face twisted with fear. She turned away and started to cry. "Tell me!"

She cowered and shielded her face with her arms. "I can't."

"I swear. I'll tell everyone."

Her cheeks were black with mascara. "But I only do the batter."

"Tell me what you know."

"For...for every cup of flour, you mix a tablespoon of minced garlic and a teaspoon—"

"Wait, hold on." Frank reached into his pocket for a pen and fumbled the camera. It fell on the floor and broke open revealing the empty chamber.

"There's no film!" Verónica cried. She lunged at him, hands at his throat.

Frank grabbed her wrists and held them against his chest. "Please, just tell me."

"¡Hijoeputa!"

Frank tried pushing her away, but he was pinned against the side of the stall. He had no leverage.

Jabao stormed in. He shoved Verónica back down on the toilet and slapped her with one hand, front and back, two-three-four-five times. "Start talking, comemierda."

"I'll go to prison." She dropped the wig and covered her face with her hands.

Jabao slapped her again. "Talk!"

Frank pulled Jabao back. "That's enough."

Jabao smacked her again.

"Stop it!" Frank pulled him back.

Jabao's eyes were on fire. He was shaking. Frank pushed him out of the stall.

Verónica was crying, her hands on her face.

"Just tell me the recipe," Frank said. "Please."

"I can't."

"The State stole it from my uncle." His voice was almost gentle. "They tortured him."

Verónica stared at Frank. Her lower lip began to tremble.

"They took his restaurant. They jailed him and tortured him for the recipe. I'm only trying to get it back."

"They tortured Xavier. They took him away. They beat him and tortured him. They did many ugly things, so many terrible things. He hung himself with a belt."

Frank stepped back.

Verónica shook her head. "He was my lover. The love of my life."

Frank's entire body lost its power. His shoulders slouched and he bowed his head. "I'm sorry."

Outside, someone was singing a rendition of Gloria Gaynor's disco hit, *I Will Survive.*

Verónica lowered her head. Then she began to speak in a quiet monotone. "You mix the first ingredients and cover the chicken with them. Rub them in. Then you sprinkle the salt and pepper. A teaspoon of pepper and a teaspoon of salt and a tablespoon of pimentón..."

Frank woke as if from a dream. He scrambled for his pen and wrote down everything she said.

"A tablespoon of dried thyme for every pound of chicken."

"Wait. You're going too fast. A teaspoon of salt?"

Verónica sighed. Her hands fiddled with the wig on her lap. "But this has to be in proportion, entiendes?"

Frank wrote it all down. "And that's it?"

Verónica wiped the sides of her mouth and nodded.

Frank stared at her for a moment. He was overcome by her story, and by the sadness he'd witnessed all over Havana. He reached into his pocket and offered her fifty dollars.

"Why?"

"I'm sorry. I'm sorry for all this."

"You know, you're going to need the rest of the recipe. And the Aché. No one knows what's in the Aché. You can't make the chicken without it."

"I know."

"Are you going to open a paladar?"

Frank shook his head. He stared at her for a long while. He could see the beard stubble and the age lines around her eyes and mouth. He was ashamed, embarrassed. Sick. "I'm sorry," he whispered.

She stood and made a dismissive gesture. "Hay que resolver." Then she placed the wig on her head. "Can I ask you something?"

"Sure."

"Did you like my show?"

Frank smiled. "Sure."

She wiped the mascara from around her eyes. "So it was just okay?"

"No, no, it was good. Really good."

Verónica blushed. "You're not just saying that?"

"No. I really enjoyed it."

"Thank you." She smiled as they walked out of the stall. "You know, you should see me when I do Edith Piaf. I'm really great then. I can do the French accent just like her."

"I suppose the toughest part is the food,
eating in restaurants all the time.
Nothing can compare to a home-cooked meal."

—Rubén González
during an interview with the *Houston Chronicle*
while touring with The Buena Vista Social Club, 2002

O n the drive back to the hotel, large waves pounded the seawall and sprayed across the Malecón. When he arrived at the Sevilla, Frank found Michi and Orlando sitting at a table in the patio drinking Cristal from the can. Michi turned to Orlando and asked for the time.

Orlando glanced at his wristwatch and rolled his eyes. Then he showed Michi four fingers.

"Since ten thirty." Michi waved his finger. "Ten thirty!"

Frank sighed. He plopped down on a chair, his body slouched forward on the table and ordered a round of mojitos.

"I thought we were going to have a good time working with you, Frank."

"I'm very sorry. I had other business. But now I'm here. Let's have a mojito—"

"Claro. You think mojitos are going to make everything better."

Frank rested his elbows on the table and rubbed his eyes. It had been a long day—a long night. His nerves were wound tight. And he had a terrible headache. "They make everything better for me."

"¡Coño!" Michi smacked the table and turned away.

"Look," Frank said, and offered his hand across the table. "I didn't know when you were coming. I apologize."

"Well." Michi shook his hand. "At least you showed. I'll give you that."

"At least, no?"

"I told Orlando, but he didn't believe me. He assured me you had gone back to Miami."

"New York," Frank said.

"Sí, New Yor', I know. But Orlando said Miami."

"It wouldn't be so bad," Orlando said, "if we didn't have to come and go all the time. The seguridad in this hotel is very abusive. If they don't see us with a guest, they kick us out. We've been coming and going from this bar like a puto yo-yo."

Michi reached under the table. He pulled an envelope from his sock and handed it to Frank. Orlando sat back on his chair. Michi fished the yerba buena leaves out of his drink.

Frank read the note. As his brain processed the words, sounds and colors and smells were sucked out as if by a vacuum.

"Coño, Frank. ¿Que fue?" Michi said.

He stared at the empty space between them. Then he slammed his hand hard against the table. "That comemierda wants more money."

"I gave him the envelope you gave me."

"You didn't open it?"

"You told me not to."

"¡Hijoeputa!" Frank drained his drink and stood. "You two wait here. I have to run upstairs. We're going to Sordo's."

"Now?"

"Yes, now. Don't worry, I'll pay you."

"Coño, Frank, we're in this together. We'll take you. No problem."

Frank ran up to his room and took two hundred dollars from the pages of *Crime and Punishment*. Then he threw the book against the wall. He began to pace. He couldn't believe it. He was so close. Sordo. Damn him.

He took out the piece of paper where he had written Verónica's side of the recipe and looked at it. He was surprised at his own shaky handwriting.

Orlando parked the Moskvitch down the block from Sordo's house. Frank stepped out of the car and looked up and down the street. The neighborhood was silent.

"Frank," Michi said, "maybe I should go with you."

Frank shook his head and gestured for him to wait. He marched up to the yellow house and banged on the door with his fist. A dog across the street started to bark. He banged on the door again. "¡Sordo!"

"Coño." Sordo opened the door. He was naked except for white underware and blue plastic flip flops. "¿Pero qué fue, chico? It's almost four in the morning. What's the matter with you?"

Frank pushed his way inside. "You know damn well what's going on. You have my recipe."

Sordo grinned and picked the lint from his belly button. "Yes, I have it, but it's not yours. Not yet. When we made the deal, I didn't know what you were getting from this fellow Granudo." He stepped past Frank and closed the door.

"We had a deal."

"That recipe, coño, it's worth gold."

"But we had a deal, Sordo."

"Yes, I know, but things change. This is Cuba, tú sabes. Things don't always go the way they're supposed to. Hay que resolver, chico."

"Óyeme, hijoeputa." Frank waved a finger in Sordo's face. "Give me that recipe or else—"

"Or else what?" Sordo's eyes grew wide. "I don't like your tone, Frank. You can't come in here like that, calling insults at my mother."

Frank took a step back. "Coño, Sordo—"

"Frank." He smiled and made a gesture with his hand. "I could squeeze you like an orange."

"I need that recipe, Sordo. You don't understand—"

"I have it here for you. But I am going to need a little more guaniquiqui before I can hand it over. I know what I have, and it's worth a lot more than the six hundred you gave me."

"Coño." Frank ran his hands through his hair. "We had a deal. You can't do that."

"I can do anything I want. I can sell this recipe to a fellow I know who has a little paladar in Guanabacoa. He will pay me very well when I tell him I have the recipe for the chicken of El Ajillo."

"Don't be stupid, Sordo. That's not the complete recipe. It's only the marinade. Besides, I know for a fact that neither Granudo nor anyone else has the recipe for the condiment mix. You can't cook shit with what you have."

"What are you talking about?"

"It's not the whole thing."

"Don't lie to me, Frank. Granudo gave me a very long recipe."

"Granudo's job is to marinade the chicken. You're only holding half the recipe."

"I don't believe you." Sordo crossed his arms over his chest.

Frank recognized the doubt in Sordo's eyes. He stepped closer and waved a finger at him. "I know you're a smart guy, Sordo. Listen to me, why would the restaurant let one man hold the entire recipe? It would be too easy for us to do what we did. There's more to making that chicken than what Granudo knows."

"And who has the rest of the recipe?"

Frank smiled.

"¡Coño!" Sordo stared at Frank. Then he flashed his gold tooth. "Now I know you're lying. How did you get it?"

"I hired someone else for that job. I knew something like this might happen."

Sordo tapped the side of his head with his finger. "You are a smart one, eh?"

"You know how it is—trust no one."

Sordo was quiet for a moment. "But the recipe you have is useless without this one."

"That's true. But you can't sell the one you have because it's not complete."

"A thousand dollars."

"What?"

"On top of the six hundred you gave me."

Frank laughed. "Coño. I will give you a hundred. The longer it takes for you to make a decision, the lower my offer will get, entiendes? Give it to me now for a hundred or bring it to Michi's tomorrow for free. This game you're playing is not going to benefit your reputation. Word will get around. Trust me."

"That's not right, Frank. Give me five hundred dollars, and I'll give it to you. I have it right here." Sordo pointed over his shoulder with his thumb.

"Sixty dollars. Take it."

"I can get a few hundred for it somewhere else."

"Coño, Sordo, any experienced cook will take one look at that recipe and know it's incomplete. Besides, if a paladar served a chicken like the one at El Ajillo, the State would close them down in a second. No one in La Habana will want to touch that recipe. It's too dangerous." Frank moved to the door and turned the knob. "If I walk out this door, I will offer you nothing."

"Fine. I'll take the hundred."

"Twenty."

"Coño, Frank, por favor. I have a sick child in the policilinico and the medicine is very expensive. I have to buy the pills at the choppin. You know how it is."

"Twenty."

"Coño, Frank..."

"Okay, forty. That's it."

They stared at each other for a moment. Frank was drenched in sweat. His hands were trembling.

Sordo nodded and slowly shuffled down the hall and disappeared.

The silence in the hallway was eerie, like a prison cell. Suddenly, Frank imagined Sordo coming back with a club or a knife. He opened the door.

A moment later Sordo came back and held up the envelope. "Fifty."

Frank reached for the envelope, but Sordo pulled it away.

"Sordo."

"Fifty." He offered him the envelope again.

Frank moved his hand slowly. Sordo didn't move. Frank took the envelope. His eyes locked with Sordo's. He opened it and read the recipe. It was in good penmanship and professionally explained. He folded the paper and put it in his pocket.

"Fifty, right?"

Frank nodded and stepped out of the house.

"Frank..."

"The money's in the car. You know, just in case."

They stood staring at each other: Frank outside and alone, engulfed in the dark night, Sordo boxed in the hallway like a giant toy. A rooster crowed, and they both blinked. Sordo looked past him at the street and back. Then he nodded.

Frank walked slowly to the corner. That short walk, from Sordo's doorway to the Moskvtich, changed everything. Each step made him more aware of his surroundings, of his own potential. His confidence soared. For the first time in his life he had done something with complete resolution. He had absolute control. Triumph was a beautiful thing.

He hopped into the back seat of the Moskvitch. "Let's go."

Michi turned around. "Did you get it?"

"Of course."

Orlando turned the key and they drove off, leaving Sordo standing in his underwear in the threshold of the yellow house on Calle Rosa Enriquez.

Michi asked, "How much?"

"Free."

"Really? Coño, Frank, how did you do that?"

Frank leaned back on the seat and smiled. "I said please."

"Cuban cuisine is very unique.
It is a blend of the Spanish, African and Arawak influence,
but it also has a more modern Caribbean influence, and even
a North American influence. What we need to do now, in
modern-day Cuba, is to take those influences and push them
further, the way they have done in Mexico and Perú.
We need to develop a new Cuban cuisine."

—Chef Eddy Fernández Monte
President of the Federation of Culinary Associations of Cuba, 2004

L ate the following morning, Frank sat up in bed and read the recipes. If what his mother had said was true, he was the first person outside El Ajillo to hold the famous recipe. He would save Maduros. Pepe and Justo would recognize him as a hero. The chicken was their future, and he held it in his hands. Uncle Nestor, wherever he was, would be proud. Avenged.

But his excitement didn't last. His mind flooded with fear. He imagined Granudo and Verónica confessing to the police. But Verónica had given him the recipe of her own free will. Besides, she would go to jail too. And Granudo didn't know he existed. Eusebio had planned well. Sordo.

He hopped out of bed and began to pace, his fingers pulling at the tip of his chin. He tried to look at it from every angle, searching for loose ends. Sordo didn't know where he was staying. He would go after Michi. He would have to warn him. No. Sordo would accept the loss. He had nothing to gain by going after Michi. They had made a deal. Sordo was a professional. He would let it lie. It would ruin his reputation if anyone knew he extorted one of his own clients. Besides, it would be embarrassing for him if people knew he had been outsmarted by a rookie. And a foreigner at that.

And then there was the MININT agent. He had no idea what he was after, but he had to take precautions.

He searched the room for a safe place for the recipes. He pulled out the insole of his shoe and wrote down the ingredients using his own abbreviations. Then he wrote the preparation instructions on the inside margins of *Crime and Punishment*. When he finished, he set the originals in the ashtray and burned them to an ash.

Marisol. He thought of what Jabao had said about jineteras. At the party she had said, "Te quiero." Was it true? Perhaps she still retained enough innocence to fall in love. And what did Jabao know anyway? Besides, she hadn't taken any money from him. She'd said she didn't want it to be that way between them. He had been the one keeping all the secrets. She was the one that kept him believing that love was possible.

It was a dark, gray morning. Rain fell in heavy drops over the city. At the entrance of the hotel, rain-soaked Cubans congregated, trying to shelter themselves from the weather. The patio bar was closed and only a few tourists lingered in the lobby. Everyone seemed lost without the sunshine.

Frank took a taxi to the Malecón and ran across the street to the blue building where Marisol lived.

Eulina opened the door and smiled. "Marisol! Your Yuma's here to save you from this deluge."

Yoselin poked her head out of her bedroom and waved at Frank. "Hola amigo." Then she turned to Eulina. "Coño, niña, hurry up and get me a bucket before we get washed out to Miami."

Eulina rolled her eyes and stomped into the kitchen. She came back with a pair of small plastic buckets. The living room was littered with colorful containers: glasses, plastic bowls, buckets and cans, catching leaks from the brown spots in the ceiling.

"¿Entonces?" Marisol came out of her bedroom and faced him, her hands resting on the sides of her waist. "To what do I owe this miracle?"

"Marisol..." But he couldn't find the words.

Marisol raised her hand. "I'm busy."

"Look." Frank gestured, trying to form the words in the air with his hands. "I'm sorry."

"Not now, Frank." She turned away and grabbed a can from a side table and replaced it with an empty one. "Can't you see we're getting flooded?"

He could see the hurt in her eyes. "I'm sorry, Marisol. It was an emergency."

"You know why I'm angry?" She pointed at him with the can, water splashing on the tile. "It wasn't that you left. I have no control over what you do. But how you left. You didn't say anything. You just...you just left." She turned away and placed the can on the ground where it caught a slow drip.

Yoselin poked her head out and looked at the two of them standing at opposite ends of the living room. "Marisol, empty the ones in the bathroom."

"I know," Frank said, "and I'm sorry. Please..." He moved closer and reached out to the space between them. But Marisol rushed into the bathroom.

Frank lowered his head, his chin against his chest. He had to tell her something. The truth. He could see her in the bathroom where she was dumping water down the sink and replacing the containers. "I came to Cuba to do business with Eusebio. I didn't know he was going to drag me out of the party like that. I swear I didn't know. I'm sorry. I asked Eusebio to make sure you got home okay."

She came out of the bathroom, a large red plastic bowl in her hands. "I don't need you or anyone to take care of me."

"Marisol, please..."

She bit her lower lip. "I just thought it was different with us."

He ran his hands desperately over his hair. "Please understand—"

"What does it matter anyway?" she said flatly. "We don't owe each other anything. In a few days you'll be back in New York, and it'll be business as usual for the both of us."

"Marisol!" Yoselin yelled from her room. "More pots. Hurry!"

Marisol shook her head and walked past Frank and disappeared into Yoselin's bedroom.

Suddenly, the recipe, Maduros, Pepe, and even his father didn't matter. It was only Marisol at the center of everything.

"It's under control over here," Euilina called from the kitchen.

Frank peeked into Yoselin's bedroom. "Can I help?"

Yoselin laughed. "Can you stop the rain?"

"I would if I could," Frank said.

Marisol set an empty bowl on the bed and met Frank at the entrance to the room. "You're soaked," she said and took his hand and led him into her bedroom. She handed him a towel. "Did you walk from your hotel?"

"I had to go to this place..." Frank began, but there was nothing more he could say. Eusebio's words kept echoing in his head: trust no one. Trust no one. "There's so much I need to tell you."

She placed her hand on his lips. "You don't owe me explanations. We don't owe each other anything. I have no right."

"But you do." He met her gaze and caressed her cheek. "You have every right."

She helped him take off his wet shirt and handed him a dry T-shirt, a green one with a logo for Callahan Auto Parts. Then she reached past him for a bowl that was overflowing. She tossed the water out the window and replaced it under the leak.

He took her in his arms and they kissed. "I'm sorry."

The leaks in the roof dripping into the different containers filled the room with an arcane symphony of plips and plops. In the background, the panicked voices of Yoselin and Eulina came and went as they hurried to control the flooding.

"I'm afraid you'll leave, and I will never see you again."

"But you will," he said. "I promise."

They sat on the bed. She took his hand. "Last year I came to La Habana because there was nothing in Cienfuegos. I didn't know what I was going to do. But I knew that if I stayed there, I would just waste away, maybe marry someone, have children. I know it sounds stupid, Frank. But I want more than that."

He caressed her face, kissed her tears.

She leaned against him. "I watched my parents working and sacrificing all their lives. Sacrificing for Cuba. Sacrificing for Fidel. Sacrificing for everything. It's not fair. None of this is fair."

He thought of his father wasting away in Houston. "It will be different for us. I promise."

"I didn't come here to become a jinetera. It's just how things turned out. The trourism school has a long waiting list. There is no work. Nothing to do. It's all we have."

"It's okay."

"Frank. I hate to think that you're leaving soon."

His stomach burned with fear and excitement and so much more that he didn't understand. "I'm not leaving you, Marisol."

"But you're going back to New York."

"I know, but I'll come back. Our story is not going to end like that. I want to be with you." He didn't know where to take it, what to promise, which promise he could keep and which one he could not. He only knew what he wanted: Marisol.

She let out a nervous laugh and turned to the window. "This rain reminds me of my mother."

He hated that he couldn't offer her anything tangible. He clenched his jaw and held her, pressing her tightly so he could feel the beating of her heart against his chest.

"She always cooked masitas de puerco whenever it rained. But instead of mojo, she made a sauce with lime and mango. We'd all sit together and eat and watch the rain. I used to love rainy days."

"You miss them, don't you?"

She bit her lip and buried her face in his chest.

"Maybe you should go home and visit them."

She shook her head and her voice cracked. "I have to help them. They need me here."

"I'll help you, Marisol. I'll do everyting I can." The promises he had been keeping in check came down like the rain. "I'll find a way to help. I'll send you money. I'll come back, I promise. Everything will work out. Please. Trust me."

She chuckled and wiped her eyes with the back of her hands, but didn't turn around. "When I was little and things got difficult, my father used to take my sister and me to the botanical gardens. We would sit by this big bamboo. The wind would blow and the bamboos would tap against each other. They made a strange sound, like a chime, and my father would make up songs to the rhythm of the bamboos." She laughed and turned to face him. "They were always funny songs, chistes, really. He invented them as he went along. He was very aware of how much we were suffering."

He held her in his arms and looked out the window where the rain had erased the ocean. She leaned against him, and the way she pressed the side of her face against his chest told him more than she could ever say in words.

"Mi amor," he whispered. "Let's go out on a date tonight like real novios."

She pulled back and curled a strand of hair behind her ear. "Really?"

"Where would you like to go?"

She shrugged and looked away where a bowl was beginning to overflow.

"Isn't there a place you've always wanted to go?"

"Wherever you prefer, Frank."

"But I don't know La Habana."

She looked away. "NG La Banda is playing at the Palacio de la Salsa. Maybe—"

"Good. We'll go there."

She raised her eyes. "Really?"

"Claro, if that's where you want to go."

"Ay Frank, that would be wonderful. But listen to me." She smiled and waved her finger at him. "We have to arrive early, otherwise we won't get in."

"Sure. Tell me at what time, and I'll be here."

"At nine, after the novela, okay? I'm going to wear my red dress. You're going to love me in my red dress."

*"I first marinate the pork in a sweet sauce, then I smoke it.
That's my trick, this is why my fried rice
is the best in the neighborhood."*

—Food vendor Horacio Chang
Centro Habana, 2001

W hen Frank made it back to the hotel, he found Michi sitting alone on one of the sofas in the lobby of the Sevilla, carefully wiping mud off his tennis shoes with a paper napkin.

"Chico." Michi looked up. "You don't know how glad I am to see you. I thought I would end up waiting here all afternoon."

Frank's eyes focused past Michi to the MININT agent with the thin mustache. He was standing at the far end of the lobby, looking out the window.

"You're not glad to see me?" Michi asked.

Frank stepped back and hid behind a column. "What?"

"Do you like arroz chino?"

"Sure, but I was—"

"Good. Go put on something dry and we'll go."

"Right now?"

"Por favor, Frank." Michi tapped his wrist with his index finger. "We have an appointment."

"With who?"

"With Eusebio, who else?"

They snuck out the side entrance and took a taxi up Prado. Frank glanced at the road behind them and back at Michi. The Lada was nowhere in sight. "What happened to Orlando?"

"Nothing. He just decided to take the day off."

Frank laughed. "What's wrong, he doesn't like capitalism?"

"This isn't capitalism. At least not yet."

"I suppose you're right. In Cuba, you can still control it. Real capitalism controls you."

Michi told the driver to take a right on Calle Dragones and pull over at the corner with Calle Manrique. From there, they walked down a short street that was blocked off to traffic. It was crowded with merchants who had braved the rain to sell bottles of soy sauce, ketchup, tomato sauce, and box lunches.

Eusebio stood on a door stoop at the end of the alley. "Frank. I hear everything is working out for you."

They shook hands and huddled under a narrow roof to shelter them from the rain.

"Michi mentioned Sordo tried to pull a fast one on you."

"He tried, but it turned out fine in the end."

"I'm glad to hear that. But tell me, how do you like our little Chinatown?"

Only a few Chinese details marked the architecture. Except for a couple of red lanterns, there was nothing Chinese about the neighborhood.

"It's not bad."

"Thank you, Frank." Eusebio gave him a gentle pat on the back. "It's a shitty little place, full of bad magic and stingy merchants. But thank you. You know, in the days of our parents this neighborhood was a lot worse, full of wild pornographic shows and adventurous prostitutes."

Michi laughed. "Sounds like a great place to me."

"Michi." Eusebio handed him five dollars. "Go get us some fried rice. I need a few words with Frank."

Michi ran off in the rain toward the market. Eusebio took a plastic photographic film canister from of his pocket and handed it to Frank. "This is what you were missing. Aché."

"Coño, Eusebio, mil gracias. How did you get it?"

"I had someone pay one of the dishwashers to collect it from what spills on the counter. There's not much, but maybe it's enough for Justo to find out what it's made of."

"I hope so."

Eusebio waved his finger. "I hope to hear from you very soon."

"Don't worry. You're going to be the richest man in Cuba."

"Coño, Frank, don't joke about that. I just want a fair deal like we agreed. My interest is only in a humble salary. They have a saying here. They say once a Cuban emigrates to the United States, he drinks the Coca Cola of forgetfulness. I don't want you or your brother Pepe or Justo to drink that Cola and forget what happened here this week."

"No te preocupes. Besides, I don't even like soda."

Eusebio smiled. "I like that, Frank. That's good."

"Did you sell your dog last night?"

"Qué va." Eusebio gestured. "That hijoeputa never showed up. I got word today that he might come next week. All I know is that it better be soon because people keep challenging me to fight Huracán."

"I hope it happens for you."

"Óyeme, if this little business of ours works out, my next dog will be a Chihuahua."

They were quiet for a moment. The sound of the rain falling on plastic tarps and the street seemed to get louder. Frank imagined the victims of their crimes. He looked at the gray sky with sad disgust. "You think Granudo's okay?"

"I don't know. But let's not talk about that. It's over. Let's put it behind us."

"It's not easy."

"No, chico, no es fácil. Not for anyone."

The rain slowly let up to a drizzle. Michi arrived with three warm little cardboard boxes. When they opened them, the aroma and steam of the fried rice, of garlic and soy and salt flooded their nostrils.

"Coño." Michi sighed. "It smells good, no?"

"I love arroz frito." Eusebio tore a piece off the top of the box, folded it with his fingers, and shoveled the rice into his mouth.

Frank followed his lead.

"A Chino once told me the secret is to fry it twice."

Michi picked at his box. "I wish it had more little shrimps in it."

"Is it anything like the rice you get at the barrio chino in New York?" Eusebio asked.

"Not at all. But it's good."

"I can't imagine it any different," Michi said with a mouthful. "How do they make it taste so good?"

"Maybe it's the cardboard," Frank suggested.

Eusebio laughed and licked his fingers. "We Cubans are used to the cardboard taste. Here, everything is served in a cajita."

"It's too bad Orlando isn't here," Michi said.

"Lazy hijoeputa. And by the way, Frank, your mulatica was very upset that you abandoned her last night."

"I know. I just saw her."

"And, did you fix it?" Michi asked.

"I hope so."

"Because if it doesn't work out for you, Frank, I know this pretty girl who—"

"Michi, I'm only interested in Marisol."

"Sure, but—"

"I'm serious."

Eusebio stared at Frank. "Coño. Don't tell me you're in love?"

Frank ate his rice. He used his fingers to pick a small piece of fried pork and put it in his mouth.

Michi laughed. "¡Alabao!"

Frank looked away. But it was true. He could feel it over every inch of his body.

"Entonces," Eusebio said, "are you going to take her back with you or what?"

"Coño, Eusebio. I can't do that."

"Why not?"

"Well, because..." The thought of New York repulsed him—the grayness, the rush, the cold, and the incessant anonymity. It was better in Cuba, where he was himself, where he felt truly free. This was where he belonged. This was where he wanted to be—with her.

"They do that shit all the time here," Eusebio said. "Cuba's third largest export is women. ¿No es verdad, Michi?"

"It's true."

Frank stared at the street with a melancholy expression. He would be with Marisol tonight. And then what?

It stopped raining. The clouds began to part, and the sun came out over half the city. Above the buildings of Chinatown, past the dome of the Capitolio toward the harbor, a rainbow appeared in the sky.

"Look." Eusebio pointed.

"Coño," Michi said, "will you look at that? They say there's a pot of gold at the end of the rainbow."

"Where the hell did you hear that?" Eusebio asked.

Michi scratched his arm. "En los muñequitos."

"In the cartoons?" Eusebio laughed and turned to Frank. "What kind of shit is that?

"I'll tell you the truth," Michi said. "At the end of all Cuban rainbows is a place called Miami."

"Miami is not the end of a rainbow," Frank said.

Eusebio glanced at him. "It is for the Cuban people."

Michi stepped out on the street and looked at Frank. "What would be the end of the rainbow for you?"

He didn't even have to think about it. He could smell her on his skin. And somewhere in a future memory, he saw himself with her, together in the Cuba that he loved. The Cuba that was raw and honest and beautiful. "You know," he said at last, "maybe one day the end of the rainbow will be Cuba."

"Coño." Michi turned away. "Que mierda. I don't understand that about foreigners. They all fall in love with Cuba. But look at this dump. It's falling apart. We stand in line for everything, we can't travel, there are no jobs, no money. Cuba is not the end of a rainbow, it's the bottom of a fucking toilet."

"Michi, I'm speaking of the future."

"Only foreigners and little children dream of the future."

"Forget it, Frank," Eusebio said. "You can't argue with Cuba's disenchanted youth."

"Oye." Michi waved his finger at Eusebio. "And what the fuck do we have to look forward to if it's not Miami?"

Eusebio picked his teeth with the corner of a piece of cardboard. "Tú resuelves bien, Michi. You could be worse off."

Michi shrugged. The rainbow was fading.

Eusebio turned to Frank. "I hate to make this little cajita of Chinese rice our farewell dinner, but I think it would be better if we don't see each other again until, tú sabes."

"I understand," Frank said. "Thank you for your help, Eusebio."

"I hope to hear from you before summer," Eusebio said and stepped away. "I want to get an airconditioning unit for the bedroom before the heat settles in."

"Don't worry."

"And Frank, before you leave, make sure you take care of Michi and Orlando."

Frank watched Eusebio walk away, down a narrow street, in the direction opposite the rainbow. He turned to Michi. "¿Entonces?"

"Back to the Sevilla?"

"I have to visit Hilda. Let's meet tomorrow night. My last night in La Habana. We'll do something fun."

"¿Mojitos?"

"Mojitos."

"The funny thing is, I don't like chocolate.
I like pastelitos with fruit fillings like the ones you find
in the neighborhood bakeries all over La Habana."

—Boxer Eligio Sardiñas, (Kid Chocolate)
during an interview with *Ring Magazine*
after knocking out junior lightweight champion Menny Bass, 1931

F rank knocked on the large wooden door and called for Hilda, but there was no answer. "Compañero." An elderly woman sitting on the front step of a building across the street waved. "She's not here. She went to the church. Fue a buscar Cáritas."

"Do you know when she'll be back?"

"Who knows, chico. That's all the way to Vedado." The woman shrugged and looked at the sky. "And with this weather..."

"You think she'll be here tomorrow?"

"Tomorrow?"

Frank stared at her, trying to recognize something in her face. She was Havana, marked with holes and cracks, her eyes saturated with life, sadness, frustration and infinite patience.

"Chico, what's wrong?" The woman's voice brought him back to Calle Amistad and to a man sitting on his bicycle, arguing with a woman who was leaning out of a window on the second floor of the building.

He turned to the old woman and his eyes fell on the Popular cigarettes she was holding in her hand.

"You want to buy a pack?"

He shook his head and walked away towards Prado. The people on the esplanades were silhouetted by the sun. The wet ground shone like polished silver. The scene was exactly like a picture he had seen as a child when his mother took him to an exhibit of photographs of Cuba at the Museum of Fine Arts in Houston. The black and white images of the city were etched in his memory. All through his life, when anyone mentioned Cuba, he saw those panchromatic scenes. Cuba was a gelatin silver print.

He took in the sweet smell of the wet laurel trees and the spice, a hint of cooking and exhaust fumes mixing with damp stone. It was the smell of memories, the smell of a childhood he had never known.

He paused at the center of the promenade and shoved his hands in his pockets. He closed his eyes and soaked in the feeling that maybe at long last he was home. For the first time he did not feel divided or separated or categorized as anything more than what he was—Cuban. He wanted to find out about his father and Rosa. He wanted to travel to provincia and visit Oriente and try and find uncles and aunts and cousins—an entire population his parents had refused to talk about. Their silence had finally broken.

He turned on Trocadero and froze at the sight of the white Lada parked in front of the hotel. It took him back to the other Cuba, the one where jineteros tried to chat up tourists for dollars, where an elderly couple sat on a bench looking exhausted and bored, waiting for the Camello that would take them home to La Vibora or Cerro or some other overpopulated neighborhood, the woman still holding a plastic shopping bag over her head in case the rain came back.

"¡Amigo!" A black, shirtless boy held out his empty hand. "¿España? Give me one dollar, pa' comer chico."

He brushed him away and turned down Calle Refugio in search of sanctuary. He came upon the Museo de la Revolución where the Granma was displayed in better condition than it had been the day the ship delivered the apostles of the revolution to the shores of Oriente.

He browsed the grainy black and white photographs hanging on the walls. The bearded rebels and their weapons looked like toys. Had all this really happened? The people looked happy. Everyone was trying to touch Fidel and Che and Camilo. One of the photographs showed the rebels dressed in their fatigues, Fidel at the center, his arms around another rebel and a man in a pale guayabera, a wide smile on his face. There was something about the man's eyes. Frank placed his finger over the bottom half of the face to cover the smile. It was his father. He was younger, thin, happy. And he was standing next to Fidel Castro. He had the same haircut Frank remembered from when he was a child, the same deep-set eyes. The same heavy brow.

He walked out of the museum. A couple of blocks away a line of people waited at a bodega for their quota of oranges. The line had stopped moving. "Pero, compañero," a man complained to the one weighing the fruit. "These oranges are green."

"This is how they came," the man replied. "If you don't want your quota, you don't have to take it. Someone else will."

Suddenly, the faces of the people in the open windows and leaning over the balconies of all the buildings looked as if they had been holding their breath for forty years. At the corner of Calle Aguacate a group of people were talking about a building in the neighborhood. "Se derrumbó, chico, I'm telling you, it just came down like that."

"But where?"

"On Calle Porvenir."

"Was anyone hurt?"

"Qué se yo, the whole front half of the building came down."

The sky was bruised, turning purple and black. Frank crossed Calle Obispo, Obrapía, Lamparilla and Amargura. The streets of La Habana Vieja were empty. The same intense dialog spilled out of open windows as the Mexican novela fed the citizens of Cuba their weekly quota of drama.

He thought of Marisol. She lived this. She lived in this place, with these problems, this poverty, this anger. He started back for the Sevilla determined to make this night perfect for her.

"You know, they say all these terrible things about Raúl,
but he is really a pussycat. You should see him after dinner.
We sit out on the terrace and enjoy a flan or arroz con leche."

—Vilma Espín Guillos
wife of Cuban President Raúl Castro
during an interview with *The New York Times*, La Habana, 1966

L ater that night Frank stepped out of the Hotel Sevilla for his
date with Marisol when a man grabbed his arm. "Señor Delgado,
come with me, please."

Frank pulled his arm away, but the man tightened his grip. "Do not
be alarmed. It is only a formality."

"What's going on?" Frank glanced across the street. Tourists and
Cubans went about their business like nothing was happening.

"I am Inspector Palacios with the Ministerio del Interior. We would
like to ask you a few questions."

A wave of heat surged through his body. His legs faltered. He jerked
away, but the white Lada pulled up and Palacios pushed him into the
car. In an instant, he was crammed in the back seat between Inspector
Palacios and a foul-smelling man wearing a Mickey Mouse T-shirt. The
Lada sped away, past Prado and into the maze of Centro Habana. His
mother's nightmares were suddenly as real as the stink in the car.

There were four of them. They drove fast, turning left and right
again and again. Frank imagined Sordo confessing to the police. And
Verónica, wearing a black tight-fitting dress pointing at him in a police
lineup. "Yes, that's the monster!"

In a moment, he'd lost all sense of direction. He sat with his hands
tucked between his legs, his shoulders pressed against Inspector

Palacios and the one with the Mickey Mouse T-shirt. He swallowed hard, his throat dry. Sweat dripped down his temples.

He regretted everything. Coming to Cuba. Stealing the recipe. This whole enterprise had been a fool's errand.

"What—" His voice cracked. He coughed, cleared his throat. "What do you want with me?"

"We have a few questions. It is a matter of routine, a formality," Palacios said matter of factly.

They came to a stop in front of a plain block building at the corner of Calle Virtudes and Soledad. They pushed Frank through a doorway and into a small, windowless room with a single bulb hanging on a wire at the center. There was a simple wood table and two metal folding chairs. The man in the Mickey Mouse T-shirt shoved Frank onto one of the chairs.

Inspector Palacios opened a vinyl portfolio and set it on the table. The man who had been driving the car sat on the chair across the table from Frank. He quietly shuffled the paperwork and laid it out in his own particular order. He pulled out a pencil from the breast pocket of his guayabera and wrote a few notes on a sheet of paper.

Then he glanced at Frank. "Could you please state your full name as it appears on your passport?"

"What did I do?" Frank spread his arms. He glanced at the men standing in the shadows. "I want to know what I did. Why am I here?"

"Señor," the man said and tapped his tooth with the pencil. "This is simply a matter of routine. Please answer the question."

"But why, what am I being accused of?"

"If you will just answer the questions, we will finish this and we can all go home, and you can go back to your hotel."

"But what did I do?"

"That is what we would like to know. We have a few questions about your activities in La Habana."

"What do you mean, activities? I don't have activities. I'm just a tourist. I don't have any activities."

"There is no need to be alarmed."

"You kidnap me to this—this place."

Inspector Palacios began to pace. He pulled out a pack of cigarettes, offered one to Frank, and then took one for himself. "You see we have more privacy here. We are just government employees carrying out orders from our superiors. Do not worry. We will not harm you."

"I want to speak with your superiors. I demand—"

Inspector Palacios laughed. "Señor Delgado, you are not here to make any demands. You are only a tourist, no? Now, I am asking—"

"Are you the police?"

Palacios glanced at his comrades and grinned. "Something like that."

Frank looked to his left and right. The walls and floor were stained with what looked like blood and maybe urine. He addressed the man across the table from him. "Why have you been following me?"

"Señor Delgado," Palacios said. "Think of us as your FBI or your immigration police. We have some inquiries. Answer the Lieutenant's questions, and you can go back to your hotel and enjoy the rest of your stay in Cuba."

The Lieutenant tapped the table with his pencil. "Señor," he said in a low, firm voice. "Would you please state your name as it appears on your passport."

"No."

"Señor Delgado." Palacios moved forward and leaned over Frank. "For the last time."

Frank sighed and hung his head. "Delgado. Frank Delgado Ruiz."

The Lieutenant wrote the answer on a sheet of paper separate of the questionnaire. He glanced at the next question and back at Frank. "Nationality?"

"Americano."

"Date of birth?"

Frank leaned forward and glanced at the paper. "October 3, 1965."

"Place of birth?"

"Houston, Texas."

"Profession?"

Frank hesitated. "Restaurant."

The Lieutenant looked at him. "What, cook? Waiter?"

"Owner."

The Lieutenant leaned back on his chair and sighed. "El dueño. Qué bien. And what kind of food?"

"Cuban food."

The Lieutenant stopped writing. He leaned forward resting his arms on the table. "And why Cuban food and not, say, Italian food or American food?"

Frank turned away. He glanced at the men in the shadows, at the overhead bulb and back at the Lieutenant. He was the same man he had seen sitting in the Lada the day he went to the cigar factory. It was the same wide jaw and the scar around his chin. The pencil thin mustache. The heavy overbite. He looked like Freddy Mercury from the band Queen. "Because, my parents are Cuban," he said with a grin. "It seemed like the thing to do."

The Lieutenant frowned. "Do you find something amusing?"

"No." Frank shrugged. "You look like someone."

"Someone you know, perhaps?"

"Someone famous."

The Lieutenant nodded and glanced at his comrades. "Someone famous, eh?"

Frank looked down at his feet. "From an old rock and roll band."

The Lieutenant's eyes narrowed. "I am afraid that in Cuba we are not fond of rock and roll." He stood and nodded to another man. "Gaspar."

"Let's see." The one called Gaspar took the Lieutenant's place at the table. He traced the line of questions with his index finger until he found the place where they had left off. "Ah, yes, here we are. What are the names of your parents?"

"Filomeno and Rosa Delgado."

Gaspar nodded and wrote down the answer. "And your residence now? Miami?"

"New York."

"Have you ever lived in Miami or el Sur de la Florida?"

"No, never."

The Lieutenant whispered something to the man in the Mickey Mouse T-shirt who promptly left the room.

"Vaya." Gaspar leaned back on his chair. He motioned to Inspector Palacios who handed him a cigarette. "So you are telling me you have never lived in Miami?"

"That's right."

"Señor Delgado." Gaspar lit his cigarette. "I find that hard to believe.

At one time or another, it seems that every Cuban exile spends some time in Miami."

"I am not an exile." Frank raised his voice. "I am an American citizen. I was born in Houston, Texas, and I live in New York City. I couldn't care less about your politics."

"Well, then—" Gaspar exhaled a cloud of smoke in Frank's face. "—what brings you to La Habana?"

"I'm a tourist."

"A tourist, eh? Well, tell me, have you perhaps gone to Varadero? Or to the show at the Tropicana? Hemingway's finca Vigía?"

"Well, no." Frank turned away, toward the men in the shadows. "I've been walking, eating...and...things like that."

"Señor Delgado, we have been watching you. You have been visiting people here in La Habana. You have been to an anti-revolutionary club where homosexuality is practiced. Are you a homosexual?"

"No!"

"Why did you go there?"

"I...I didn't know what it was. Someone..." He looked down at his hands resting on his lap. His fingers fiddled, one over the other like he was playing a game. "A friend took me there. I left immediately."

Gaspar slammed his hand hard against the table. "Don't lie, Delgado. What is the true purpose of your visit?"

"I'm a tourist. I swear."

"Tell me, what is your relationship to señor Acosta?"

"I don't know anyone named Acosta. There must be some mistake."

"Are you telling me you do not know Hugo Acosta who resides at Calle Rosa Enriquez 337 in Luyano. Have you not visited him twice already?"

"Oh, Hugo. Yes, he..." His eyes moved quickly from person to person. He shifted in his chair and raised his hands to gesture, then dropped them on his lap. "He's a friend of a friend. We only had a couple of drinks."

"A friend of a friend." Gaspar studied Frank for a long while. "A friend in Miami, perhaps?"

"No, someone in New York. Someone who asked me to visit him, and—"

"And what?"

Frank shrugged. "And give him his regards, that's all. Saludos."

"You hesitate, Delgado. Tell me, why did you visit him twice?"

"I wanted to say goodbye."

Gaspar leaned across the table. "Are you aware that Hugo Acosta has spent time in prison on charges of peligrosidad?"

"No. No." He twitched and his knee began to bounce. "I didn't know. I was just saying hello from a friend."

"Did you and Acosta exchange any money or information of any kind?"

He shook his head and wiped the palms of his hands back and forth against the top of his thighs. "No."

"Did he give you a list of names?"

"No. We drank some rum, that's all."

"Did he mention any names? Did he speak of his time in prison or say anything against the government? Against the Revolución? Did he ask you for any help, any money?"

"No." Frank lowered his head and wiped the sweat from his brow with the back of his hand. "He didn't say anything like that. Nothing happened."

"We know very well what is going on here, Delgado. We want that list from you, do you understand me?"

"What list?"

Gaspar slammed his hand against the table and waved a finger in Frank's face. "We will have that list!"

"But I'm telling you the truth."

"Who do you work for?"

"Please, I told you—"

"Who is your contact in La Habana?"

"I know nothing of any contacts or lists, I swear."

"We can be here all night," Gaspar leaned back and crossed his arms.

Inspector Palacios stepped forward. He set his hands on the table and leaned over Frank. "Listen, Delgado, we are well aware that this Acosta character has placed in your hands a list of names of individuals who are troubled and influenced by anti-revolutionary thoughts and who are currently detained in our correctional facilities."

Frank searched the ground. A cold shiver ran up his spine. His hands began to tremble uncontrollably. "I swear. I'm telling you the truth."

Palacios glanced at his wristwatch. "We have time," he said and joined the Lieutenant in the corner of the room.

Gaspar set the paperwork in a neat pile. Then he stood and paced back and forth, his footsteps echoing in the hot room that was quickly filling with cigarette smoke. The men whispered among themselves. Hours passed. Frank's back and legs were stiff. He was getting sleepy. He stood to stretch.

The Lieutenant reached for his shoulder and pushed him back on the chair. "We can all go home as soon as you give us the list."

"I already told you. I don't have it."

There was a knock on the door. Everyone froze. Gaspar nodded at the Lieutenant and he attended to the door. The man in the Mickey Mouse T-shirt walked in and whispered something to Inspector Palacios. Palacios nodded at Gaspar. They surrounded Frank.

"What?" Frank's voice cracked.

Gaspar put his finger to his lips. "Shhh."

"What's going on?"

"I am afraid we must search you. Will you please remove your belt, shoes and socks?"

"What? No, no. I have nothing. I swear. No list, no names, nothing. I swear it!"

"We have been extremely patient with you. Please remove your clothing so we can search you. Otherwise we'll be forced to—"

"No!" Frank stood.

The Lieutenant grabbed him by the neck and shoved him against the wall. "Listen to me, maricón. Do as you're told or I will put a cattle prod to your testicles until they shrivel up like prunes." Then he released him and elbowed him on the kidneys.

A bolt of pain shot through his body. He lost his balance, but the Lieutenant held him in place against the wall. "Do you understand me, Delgado? This is not a game."

Frank relaxed his body and nodded. His side throbbed.

Gaspar pointed to the wall. "Remove your shoes, socks and belt and stand with your hands against the wall."

Panic took over. He leaned forward to untie his shoe. Then leapt forward and ran for the door.

The man with the Mickey Mouse T-shirt pounced and struck Frank with a piece of rubber hose across the back. Frank twisted and fell face down. He folded over in pain. The man whacked him again on the side of the stomach. Frank rolled on the ground. The man caught him again across the back.

"Gallego!" Gaspar raised his hand, then leaned over Frank. "We do not want to hurt you, señor Delgado. Por favor, hand over the list."

Frank was numb. He stood and leaned against the wall for support. The room was blury. One of the men took him by the shoulder and guided him back to the center of the room.

A voice spoke from the shadows. "The list."

Frank shook his head. He was covered in sweat.

"I have had enough of this shit," the Lieutenant cried. "Strip him. If he does not hand it over, we can shock it out of him."

Frank raised his hands and nodded. The Lieutenant stepped back. Frank slowly went about removing his shoes and socks.

"Turn around and place your hands on the wall," Gaspar ordered.

Frank complied. Palacios stepped out of the shadows and patted him down. The Lieutenant and Gallego searched the shoes and socks. Palacios took the contents of Frank's pockets and placed them on the table.

Gaspar picked up the plastic film canister. "Interesting..." He opened it and smelled the ocher colored powder. "What is this?"

Frank sighed. "Aché. Usted sabe, for good luck. A friend gave it to me."

"It smells like cinnamon," he said.

Inspector Palacios dipped his pinkie in the canister, lifting a pinch of the powder and took a whiff. "More like cloves, no?"

"Compañeros." Gallego waved the insole of Frank's shoe. "I found something."

Gaspar took the insole and inspected it under the light. "What do we have here?"

Frank glanced back over his shoulder, his hands still on the wall. "It's a recipe."

The Lieutenant took the insole from Gaspar and dangled it in front of Frank's face. "Don't lie."

Frank shook his head. "It's only a recipe. I swear."

"¡Cállate!" He smacked him in the face with the insole.

"I'm telling you—"

"Shut up!" The Lieutenant slapped him on the back of the head.

"Okay, enough." Gaspar took the insole from the Lieutenant and sat at the table.

Frank shook his head.

"It must be in some kind of code." Gaspar stared at the insole. Then he took out a piece of paper from the pocket of his guayabera, unfolded it and examined it beside the insole.

The Lieutenant turned to Frank. "What is the code?"

"There is no code." Frank cowered against the wall.

"Listen, hijoeputa," the Lieutenant whispered. "Have you ever had a cattle prod shoved up your ass? Believe me, Delgado, it is not a pleasant experience. Not even for a maricón like yourself."

"Please." Frank began to tremble. The pain from the beating burned at his back and side. He felt sick.

The Lieutenant turned to Gaspar. "Perhaps we could get Doctor Maceo to—"

"Momentico." Gaspar raised his hand and leaned over the insole.

"But I am telling you, Gaspar, let Gallego get Doctor Maceo. This maricón would not last ten seconds."

Gaspar's eyes moved back and forth from the paper in his left hand to the insole in his right.

Frank looked desperately around the room. The door was at the opposite end. Even if he made it out, he would have to run through the streets. He had nowhere to go. Besides, he could place his friends in danger. The coil in his gut tightened like a vise. Even if they tortured him or put him in prison, he would not talk about Marisol or Eusebio or Michi. He would tell them nothing. He would rot alone in his own silence.

The Lieutenant walked up to Frank. "Don't even think about it." Then he glanced back at Gaspar. "Anything?"

Gaspar was stooped over the table, his head moving from side to side scanning the insole as he took notes.

"I'm telling you. Let me get Doctor Maceo." The Lieutenant grinned at Gallego who looked at Frank and smiled. He was missing his two front teeth.

"Wait a minute," Gaspar said, going from the insole to the paper. "Coño de su madre, I think I got something."

The Lieutenant joined Gaspar and Palacios by the table. They all stared at the list.

"It is so amateurish, look at this." Gaspar held up the insole next to the paper where he had a list of names. "Here." He pointed with his finger. "Look at these letters, now look at our list, Cienfuegos Highway Kilometer 5. Frank Betancourt. That is where we picked up Betancourt of the Democratic Alliance. Now, look at this one, 3 TS BS. It's the Seguro brothers. They're in Las Terrazas. Count three prisons to the west of here. Look, La Habana is one, Mariel would be the second and Las Terrazas third."

"Coño," Inspector Palacios rubbed his chin. He glanced at Frank, at the insole and back at Gaspar.

"It lists everyone, CL. Candelario Lima, PS. Pedro Saldivar, CM. Carlos Maderes whom we picked up only a month ago. Coño, we have it!"

Frank looked at the ground. His knees gave and he slowly slid down to the floor.

The Lieutenant walked over and pulled him up. "You see, there is no need to lie, Yanqui comemierda."

Gaspar folded the paper and placed it in his pocket with the insole. "You can put your shoes back on, only I am afraid you will be missing an insole."

Frank approached the table and put his belongings, and the film canister with Aché, in his pocket.

The men huddled by the door. Frank could hear them whispering like rats. After a moment, Gaspar came forward. "Señor Delgado, you are not to visit Hugo Acosta again or you will be arrested. Do you understand me? Not now, not during the rest of your stay, not ever."

Frank nodded.

"Procedure calls for us to file a report and place you under house arrest and deport you as soon as possible. This has the potential to blow up into a very serious international incident." Gaspar stroked his chin and gestured. "I could not help noticing you carry a considerable amount of cash money on you."

"I can't use my credit cards here. The embargo—"

"Ah, yes, the bloqueo. It makes things quite difficult, particularly for us, the Cuban people."

Frank nodded.

"Perhaps we can come to an understanding. Usted sabe. My compañeros and I could delay our report until you are well on your way back to Miami."

"New York."

"Yes, of course." He chuckled. "You see the situation here, the bloqueo, it is hurting our economy, and well, to put it bluntly, we could all use a few dollars to help us in this time of crisis. Cuban currency these days—"

"I know, I know. No es fácil." Frank pulled out his wallet.

Gaspar laughed. "I see you are well acquainted with our situation."

Frank laid the money on the table.

Gaspar picked up the cash. "I believe your flight leaves the day after tomorrow?"

Frank nodded.

"Señor Delgado," Gaspar said, "allow me to share some advice with you. And I hope you take it to heart. Do not visit counterrevolutionary elements. Do not get involved, simply enjoy your vacation. Go dancing, have a few mojitos and go home. ¿Entiende?"

Frank nodded and moved toward the door.

Gaspar signaled to the man in the Mickey Mouse T-shirt. "Gallego will drive you back to your hotel. And señor Delgado." He brought his index finger under his eye. "We will be watching you."

They had been through his room. His luggage, the drawers, the closet, everything had been disturbed. He sat on the bed and leafed through the pages of *Crime and Punishment*. His money was gone, though the recipe instructions were still there. But without the list of ingredients they were useless. He let the book drop to the floor and lay back on the bed. He ran his finger along his side. The pain from the beating was growing. He lifted his shirt and his fingers traced the long reddish welt that ran diagonally from the top right side of his stomach down across to his left kidney.

He closed his eyes. He yearned for Marisol, her smell, her taste. He wanted to dream of her. But when he woke it was the middle of the day, and he had no recollection of having dreamt at all.

It was a bright day. The downpour had washed away the haze and the film of dust that layered the city.

And there was no sign of the white Lada or the MININT agents. It was as if they hadn't existed and only lingered inside him like a horrible nightmare.

He walked down Prado to the Malecón and paused by the seawall. He watched for a tail. When it was clear to him that he was alone, he crossed the street and walked into the faded blue apartment building.

He wanted to tell Marisol everything—about the recipe, about Sordo and Verónica. About MININT. But the truth was too fantastic. Maybe she would believe him. Maybe not. But he had to tell her. She was all he had left. There was no recipe. There would be no more restaurant, no more New York. He had to place his trust in her. And in Cuba.

He walked slowly up the stairs to the third floor and knocked on the door, but there was no answer. "Marisol!" He knocked again and cried out, his voice breaking. "Marisol!"

"No están." The neighbor poked her head out from around the hall. "They went out."

"Do you know where they went?"

"Chico, I just know they're not home."

He stared at the door for a moment. "Did they leave together?"

"Marisol left early this morning. I don't know about the other two."

Frank looked around the dark stairwell, his eyes searching for what wasn't there. "Do you have any idea where she might have gone?"

"She could have gone anywhere. El choppin or to see a friend or visit her family."

"She doesn't have any family in La Habana."

"Maybe she went to see a friend."

"Which friend?"

"Chico, and how would I know?"

He thought of everything Marisol had said to him, every word, every sentence, every expression, searching for a name or a place. But he came up empty.

"Did she ever mention a friend or a place she likes?" he asked.

"No, not that I can recall."

"Por favor."

The neighbor shook her head. "But she's been out a while. Maybe if you came back a little later."

"Can you do me a favor? Can you please tell her I was here. Tell her Frank was here. The Yuma. Tell her I'll come back in an hour or two." He pressed the palms of his hands together like he was praying. "Tell her to wait for me. Please—"

"Sí, chico." The neighbor smiled. "Don't worry, I'll tell her."

"I love boliche. Think about it:
who would ever think of stuffing a
round beef roast with chorizo? It's incredible."

—Artist Aristides del Valle
La Habana, 1945

W hen he left Marisol's apartment, Frank went around the
back of the building and down the street in the direction
of Concordia. He walked quickly, pausing at every block,
looking behind him, watching for the Lada. He didn't notice the children
playing tag in the ruins of an old building or the men playing chess on
the sidewalk or the woman weeping at the entrance of a building. He
stopped at the corner where an old man offered him a pair of oranges.
Someone called for Yulia. The smell of fruits and of beans cooking
somewhere came and went and mixed with the humidity that was rising
from yesterday's rain and the afternoon heat.

He walked down Concordia and around the corner where the blue
Moskvitch was parked on the shady side of the street. A group of boys
were gathered around Michi who sat on the hood of the car preaching to
them about the finer points of the life of a jinetero.

"Coño, Frank." He glanced up and shooed the boys away. "What
are you doing in this neighborhood? Be careful that you don't get
mugged."

"I needed to see you."

"¿Trabajo?" Michi perked up.

"No, we're all finished with that." Frank leaned against the side of the
Moskvitch and crossed his arms over his chest. "Just to settle accounts."

"And the mojitos?"

"We're going to have to postpone it until my next trip. I have a little problem I need to patch up with Marisol."

Michi hopped off the hood of the car and pressed the palms of his hands against his chest. "Coño, so it's true? Amor. Really?"

Frank looked away, up and down the street. "As much love as one can have while I'm in New York, and she's here in La Habana."

"Frank, you're scaring me. You talk like a Cuban who's about to take a raft for Miami."

He shook his head and scratched the tip of his chin. "And Orlando?"

"He went to Marianao. He's working on his own relationship."

"¿Entonces?"

"Nada, chico. We'll take you to the airport. At what time is your flight?"

"No, qué va, I'll take the transport from the hotel. It's part of the tour."

"Let us take you. Besides, I'm sure Orlando would like to say goodbye."

"Gracias." Frank handed him an envelope with cash. "Here's something for all your help and for the gas. Half for you and half for Orlando, eh?"

"Coño, claro." Michi laughed and placed the money in his fanny pack. "Orlando and I, we're partners."

"I'll see you in the morning, then."

"Be careful," Michi said.

He walked away and when he turned the corner, he heard Michi shout, "Good luck with the mulatica!"

"Of course I love Cuban food, who doesn't?
But I have to watch myself around the membrillo and the flan.
Oh, the sweets."

—Singer Danita Rodríguez
Miami, 1996

The streets were sweltering. Neighbors gathered on street corners and on door stoops. On Calle Padre, four men sat at a table playing dominoes while an audience watched in silence. On another street, a large tanker truck blocked the road while people carrying buckets and cans formed a line along the sidewalk waiting their turn to collect drinking water.

Around the corner, a salsa orchestra rehearsed in a ground-floor apartment. The eight-member band—with a large drum set, congas, and a full brass section—could barely fit in the small room, but they jammed like they were playing the Palladium. People crowded around the window. The entire block had turned into party with people dancing all the way to Calle Lealtad.

When he arrived at Hilda's house, her neighbor pointed to the large door. "She's here. Go ahead and knock."

The house was cool and dark. "How's your friend with the hip?" Frank asked and followed her to the patio.

"Mildred? She's in some pain. You know, with things the way they are, it is so difficult to get the medication. She's going to begin her physical therapy in a few days, but the nurse confessed to me that she will likely need the aid of a cane for the rest of her life. Pobrecita."

The garden was blooming after the rain, filling the house with the fresh smell of jasmine.

"I assume," she said, taking his arm, "you would like me to continue telling you about your father?"

"If I'm not imposing. You left me in such suspense."

"Hijo, I thought you would have come sooner than today." She tore a dry leaf from a fern and walked to the kitchen. "Would you like a café?"

"If you're having one."

He watched her making the coffee, working the old espresso maker and carefully measuring sugar into a pair of small cups. Then she excused herself and went into another room. When she returned, she handed Frank an old black and white photograph of a group sitting at a large round table. The men wore dinner suits and the women long evening dresses. Scattered in the background, slightly out of focus where the light began to fall off, a group of bearded guerrillas in fatigues, holding machine guns, peered suspiciously into the lens.

"This young man here." Hilda pointed to a man at the center of the table. "Es tu papá. And this beautiful young lady is my sister Celia."

Frank inspected the photograph. The tones were beginning to fade and a pair of crease marks cut the emulsion in half. The man in the light suit was unmistakably his father, only thinner, younger. It was the same man who was in the photograph he had seen at the museum.

They sat in the patio. Frank leaned forward as Hilda pointed out the others in the photograph: "Éste, he went to Miami. This one also went to Miami. I later heard he was killed in Playa Girón. I do not know the women, but this man here became ambassador to...where was it? To Bulgaria, I think." She stared at the photograph for a while and her finger moved across the image, caressing the people she once knew. After a long silence she sighed. "It has been many years."

"Where was it taken?"

"They were celebrating the Triumph at the Habana Libre."

Frank sipped his coffee and looked at the photograph again. There was fear and joy in their eyes. It was eerie. "Where had my father been all this time?"

"Away, fighting. He joined Gutierrez Menoyo and other members of the Directorio in the Escambray."

"What's that?"

"The sierra, the mountains past Santa Clara."

"He was fighting for the Revolución?"

"Of course. But after the Triunfo, we did not see him as much. We were all very busy helping to bring changes to the country. Everybody was volunteering for something. People came from other parts of the world to teach, to cut cane, to help start a new country, one that would be proud and free of imperialism. It was a time of so much hope."

Hilda squinted. "When I saw your father after he came out of the Escambray, he had a different look in his eye. He had the kind of look one has after he has taken the life of another human being. I am a child of Eleggua, I can see these things."

Frank was silent. Images of his father as a rebel clashed with his own memories of a man obsessed with assimilation into American society. It didn't make any sense—the same man at opposite ends of two political ideologies.

He glanced at Hilda. "I just don't get it. Don't you think he would be proud of what he did? That he might tell his children about how he fought for something he believed in, even if in the end things changed? Exile is nothing to be ashamed of."

"I don't know, Frank. I am sure he had his reasons."

"But what were they?"

"No sé, chico. After the Triumph, the country was swept in a fever of change. I can still remember..." She paused to allow the memory to catch up with her. "Your father was still in the Escambray, but Celia and I went to see Fidel make his speech at the Campo Colombia. All of La Habana was there. There was a feeling in the air like the whole country was going to be born anew. At last things were going to change. We knew Fidel as a man of his word and a man of the people. When he spoke, it was like he was talking to me. Everyone felt that way. When he made promises, he kept them. He was like a prophet. And when he was delivering his speech and that dove landed on his shoulder, that was a sign from the Orishas. Everyone knew those were doves for Yemayá. Chico, one does not take such things lightly." She sat up straight and waved her finger. "Fidel was chosen!"

"But what happened?"

"What happened?" She sighed. "Let me tell you. I would rather be here today, in this house of mine that is in ruins, stand in line to receive my daily ration of bread, and mix my coffee with chícharos, but hold my head up high, proud to be what I am—a Cuban Yoruba woman who is truly free, and not some bitter, displaced coward in Miami. Chico, Miami must be like the old Cuba, all about money and power.

"We Cubans are a proud people, Frank, but the Cuba before the Revolución was a shameful place. It was a place of criminals and gangsters. The people who had money only cared for themselves. No, chico. I like how it is now. We all care for La Patria. There is no shame in suffering because suffering makes one proud and free. We are one people now. Soon our economy will change, and things will get better. You will see."

"I hope so, Hilda." But he didn't care about the revolution. He wanted to know more about his father. Why had he never talked about Cuba?

"It was not always like this, you know. There was a time when the bodegas had food. Besides, I am one who believes real happiness is in here." She tapped her chest with her hand. "And not in the pocketbook."

Frank leaned forward and took her hand. "Hilda, can you tell me what happened after my father came back from the sierra?"

"Yes, of course. I am sorry. I get carried away. Let me see." She looked at the brilliant flowers of the bougainvillea, then up at the sky. "When your father came back, he took Celia out. That was the same night the photograph was taken. But the next morning when I saw Celia, she was very upset. She did not talk to me or anyone else. She just packed her bags and went away to Santa Clara to work with a brigade. I had no idea what happened until many years later when she told me that while Filomeno was away, he had married Rosa. That night he told Celia he was going to leave Cuba forever. She was heartbroken."

"Why? What happened?"

Hilda shrugged. "I don't know. I wasn't there. After the Triumph, your father left for Santiago to settle his affairs. Then he showed up with Rosa and Pepe who was only a few months old. They stayed here, in your father's old room while they arranged for transportation out of the country.

"I helped your mother sew fifteen gold coins her father had given her into the fabric of her clothes so they could smuggle them out of the country. And while Rosita and I hid the little treasure, your father was busy getting the paperwork for your brother's passport. Pepe had been born in Santiago, but with all the chaos of the Revolución, they never got a birth certificate. Your father had to pay an acquaintance of his at the Civil Offices in Matanzas to issue him the documents so they could get him out of the country.

"Every morning your father would go to the airport while your mother and I waited here with Pepe and the suitcases all packed and ready to go. Finally, after almost three weeks, we got the call. Filomeno had the flight out. Rosita and Pepe got in a taxi. I never saw them again. Pobre Celia, she never even said goodbye to him."

"They left, just like that?"

"Just like that. Everyone who was leaving Cuba left just like that. There was no other way."

"It must have been very tough."

"It was very tough on Celia. She never had the opportunity to tell Filomeno that she was pregnant with Justo."

"Why—" Frank recoiled in his chair. "No. You mean by my father?"

"Claro, chico. Celia told me Justo was conceived that night at the Habana Libre."

"No!" Frank stood. He paced around the table and sat again. "I don't believe it."

"Justo didn't tell you?"

"Justo just showed up at the house one day. He said my father was his godfather. He never told us anything. He knew, but he never said anything? I don't believe it."

Hilda frowned and took Frank's hand. "And Filomeno never said anything about it?"

"No, never. I never even suspected. You know—" He lowered his voice, his eyes searching for compassion. "—because he's black. I just never imagined."

"Ay, Frank..."

"All these years," he whispered. "Why?"

"So much was going on."

But they were no longer talking of the same thing. He looked at Hilda and shook his head. "But for forty years?"

"These things are complicated. Celia said he wrote her many letters asking her to leave Cuba with Justo, but she did not want to go. She had so much faith in the Revolución. She wanted to stay here. Later, with Playa Girón and then the missile crisis y el bloqueo, it became impossible. After that, we never heard from your father again. Then, after Celia passed away, Justo left in a raft. About eight months later, we received a letter from him that he was staying with your father in Texas."

"But why did he hide it from us?"

"You know how it is. Politics still divide many families. This is our story. Here, every house has a hero, a combatiente or a gusano. It's heartbreaking."

His eyes darted nervously around the patio. "You want to know the worst part? I never gave it any thought. And Pepe too. We were never curious about Cuba. We didn't care. Maybe they never talked about it because we never asked. We weren't even curious about Justo. And he lived with us for three years."

"But that's natural. You and Pepe, you were preoccupied with your own lives."

He turned away. He and Pepe had been too selfish to consider anything or anyone else. He loved his father, but he had never respected him because he had wanted more from him. But it had been there all along. If only they had talked.

He leaned forward, his arms resting on his knees, eyes focused on Hilda. "Do you have any idea why he behaved like that? I mean if he loved Celia so much—"

"Hijo, that is a question you would need to ask him. I was simply a bystander. The only thing I know for certain is that Celia loved your father very much."

Frank stared at his shoes, at the tile and the cracks in the cement.

"Mira." Hilda stood and adjusted her dress. "I have some old letters from your father. Let me get them."

Frank felt dizzy. It had been too easy to blame Filomeno for everything. In the end it had been Frank who had invented his own sorrow. Like Hilda had said, happiness was something that existed within oneself.

He pressed the bridge of his nose with the tip of his fingers and swallowed hard, trying to block the tears he felt rising.

Hilda came back to the patio and handed him a pair of envelopes. "Maybe when you go home you can look for the ones Celia wrote your father. She wrote him a lot during those years."

The texture of the paper felt smooth and fragile between his fingers. They were postmarked from Pasadena, Texas. The return address was a post office box, also in Pasadena.

"You can have them if you like. What is an old woman like me going to do with someone else's memories?"

"What about you?" he said. "What did you do after the Revolución?"

She laughed. "Cortar caña, chico. Then I became educated. I attended the University. I taught thirty years at Ciudad Libertad, in Marianao."

It was strange how the simplest choices could alter the lives of so many people. "Do you think he's a good man?"

"Who, Filomeno?"

"Fidel."

"Of course. He's our father." She leaned back and waved. "Every father makes mistakes, especially stubborn fathers who want the best for their children. But he is our father and we love him."

The house was silent for a while. Hilda's eyes came and went with the memories. "All this nostalgia has made me very tired."

Frank stood. "Of course."

They walked arm in arm to the door. "When do you go back?"

"Tomorrow morning."

"Do you think you will come back some day?"

"Claro. I wish I'd come sooner. I feel as if my life has finally opened itself to me."

"It is not as bad as the Yanquis make it out to be, eh?"

He shrugged. "To each their own."

"I don't know if there is a food for broken hearts.
Maybe a cold gaspacho or a bistec empanizado.
I don't know, what do you suppose?"

—Singer songwriter Sindo Garay
La Habana, 1921

F rank found a taxi by the Capitolio and headed to the Malecón. He kept looking back, but there was no sign of the white Lada. He got off a couple of blocks from the Deauville Hotel and walked around the block to the faded blue building.

Eulina opened the door. She was wearing the same short dress she wore on the night Frank arrived in Havana. She had a small jar of red nail polish in her hand. "Ah, yes, El Yuma. She's not here."

"Where is she?"

She shrugged and rolled her eyes. "Forget about her."

"Come on, Eulina. Where is she?"

"She's gone."

He looked past her into the apartment and back down the stairwell. "I told your neighbor to tell her I was coming back."

"She told her. But she didn't care."

"When is she coming back?"

"She was very upset."

"But I have to see her, Eulina. I'm leaving—"

"She was in tears. All night."

Frank ran his hands over his hair and looked around him as if a solution hung in the dust of the crumbling walls. "But I can explain. I was almost arrested."

Eulina leaned her head against the door. She raised her hand and spread apart her fingers to study her red fingernails. "It's too late for apologies."

He glanced at the brown spots on the ceiling and took a long, deep breath. "When is she coming back?"

"¿Quién es, Eulina?" Yoselin called from inside the apartment.

"El Yuma de Marisol."

"Tell him he broke her heart."

"Sí," Eulina called back into the apartment, "I told him."

"You didn't say that."

"Well, you did. She waited for you." Eulina waved an angry finger at him. "She thought you were different, but you turned out to be just another hijoeputa. Big surprise."

"But listen—"

"You don't even know her. If you did, you would have been here. La pobre—"

"I'm sorry. I wanted to be here. I swear."

"But you weren't. Te jodiste. In Cuba there are no second chances."

"But I love her. I really do. Please help me, Eulina. I need to make this right."

"Se fue." She raised her hand to stop him. "She took the train back to Cienfuegos."

The shock knocked him off balance. Sounds and smells vanished. He shook his head. He leaned against the wall and looked up, trying to hold it in.

"Yes. She went home to her family." Eulina clapped her hands as if she were wiping dust off. "This life was not for her. She's too nice. Her heart's too soft. I always told her that."

Frank turned away and punched the wall.

"Yes, that's how it is." She dismissed him with a short gesture of her hand. "I had to sit and comfort her and listen to her laments all night. Then I had to help her pack and walk her to the station. She never stopped crying. Not once."

"Eulina," Frank pleaded, "I love her. And I know she loves me. You know it too. Why do we have to be like this?"

"Forget it."

"Please."

Yoselin came to the door, running a brush over her wet hair. "Maybe you're right. But you really hurt the poor girl."

"But I told you—"

"I understand." Yoselin grinned. "Marisol would find this amusing, me of all people, with a soft heart."

"What are you talking about?"

Yoselin nodded at Eulina.

"The train." Eulina looked at her watch. "There's a good chance it's late. It's a frequent problem."

Frank stared at her. "At what time?"

"Six o'clock to Cienfuegos."

He looked at his watch. It was five forty-five. "Thank you!"

Yoselin smiled. "Good luck."

Outside, the sun was nearing the horizon west of the city. The sky was shifting to a warmer hue. A group of tourists gathered at the corner, snapping photos of the Morro. The woman who sold cigarettes in front of the building was singing a soft romantic song.

Frank ran up to the Deauville and found a taxi. "I need to get to the train station. ¡Pronto!"

The driver looked at him through the rearview mirror and grinned. "Sounds like a line in a movie," he said. "¿España?"

"No. Just go. Vamos. Move it."

They started up Prado.

"Is it far?"

"No, just down here a ways, at the end of Monserrate, before the port."

Frank leaned back on the seat and closed his eyes. He told himself he would never complain about anything ever again. He would be thankful for whatever happened with the restaurant. He was sorry for anything that might have happened to Granudo. He swore it had never been his intention to hurt anyone. He promised he would take care of his mother. That he would never fight with Pepe or Justo and that he would live up to everything that had been expected of him. He would even go back to college and become an engineer or a businessman or an oceanographer. And suddenly he found himself apologizing to his father, for judging him and wanting to distance himself from him, and for not being Cuban. All he wanted, he said to himself—or to his father or to God—if there had been anything he ever wanted more than anything in the world, was to catch up with Marisol. He kept whispering to himsef, "Please, please, please."

"Here?" The driver slowed the car. The street was busy with people moving luggage. Old American cars were double parked with their trunks open while people loaded and unloaded bags and boxes. The entrance to the station was littered with bicycle taxis trying to get customers. Outside, vendors pulled carts and people sat, waiting on benches and concrete stoops, leaning along the iron fence, looking for relatives and friends.

Frank raced into the old terminal. It was dark, busy, disorganized. He ran to where a tall iron fence separated the terminal from the platforms. People were funneling slowly through one of the gates toward the trains, while another crowd made its way out. Frank walked quickly, moving between the people, bumping and rubbing against slow moving bodies.

There were only two passenger trains with big blue cars, relics of the Soviet Bloc. A man was checking documents at the end of one of the platforms.

"Señor," Frank interrupted. "The train to Cienfuegos?"

The man looked at Frank and shrugged. "You have to ask one of the terminal workers, the ones with the blue shirts. I only carry bags."

The woman who had been talking with the man pointed to one of the trains. "I just arrived from Santa Clara on that one. It must be the other one, no?"

Frank raced to the third platform, but it was deserted. All the activity was along the other platform, around the other train. He looked back. An official in a blue short sleeve shirt was walking away toward the terminal.

Frank ran and caught up to him. "Perdón, the train to Cienfuegos?"

The man turned and looked past Frank at the empty platform and to where the other train was standing idle. "It's a miracle." He glanced at his wristwatch. "I've been working here seven years, and that train has never left on time. Never."

"What?"

"Except today. It left at six."

Frank looked at his own watch. It was ten after six.

"There's another one leaving at eight in the morning."

All the sounds, the pandemonium of the station, were sucked out into a dead silence with Eulina's voice repeating, "She's gone. She's gone."

He left the station and walked up Monserrate. The sky behind the Capitolio was bright purple. He wandered, his shoulders slouched, hands in his pockets, his head bowed. He walked slowly down Prado, and inevitably found himself on the Malecón across the street from the blue apartment building. He took a deep breath. In Havana, the night reeked of rum and sex.

He walked across the street and knocked on the door again. "Marisol! Eulina! Yoselin!" His voice was weak and uncertain, as if he knew there was no use calling because there was no one home, but he still had to perform the ritual. He leaned his head against the door and whispered, "Marisol."

The neighbor poked her head out. "Compañero."

Frank stared at her in horror. "She's gone."

"I told her to wait. I told her what you told me to tell her, verdad que sí."

"And still she left."

"A shame, chico. You better try tomorrow because when those girls are out for the night, they're out for the whole night."

"I leave in the morning."

They both turned and looked down the hall where they heard the sound of a baby crying.

"Besides, she's gone. She went home."

"To Cienfuegos?"

Frank nodded.

The woman covered her mouth with her hand.

Frank looked around the dark stairwell, his eyes moist with tears. Then he glanced at the neighbor. "Do you have paper, something I can write with? I need to leave her a note."

"Sí claro, chico. Come."

Frank stayed in the hallway while the woman fetched him a piece of plain yellow paper and a pencil.

"Are you all right? Would you like some water?" she asked.

"No, gracias." Frank wiped his eyes with the back of his hand. Then he leaned over the handrail and wrote:

Mi querida Marisol:

I can only pray and hope this letter will find its way to your hands and into your heart. I have no other way to tell you how terribly sorry I am about what happened. There is no excuse for the way I treated you.

I need you to know this has been the most incredible week of my life, and it's all because of you. I didn't understand this at first. It happened so fast. I was afraid. I've been a fool. I swear it was never my intention to hurt you. My heart is in terrible pain for what I have done to you and to myself. I love you. I love you with everything I have. And when I think of the prospect of never seeing you again, I want to die.

If you get this letter, please write back. I promise I will do everything in my power so we can be together. I want to spend the rest of my life with you. You are all that matters in my life.

Marisol, if you only knew what you have done to me.

Te quiero, mi amor y vida,
Frank

He added his address and phone number at the bottom of the letter. He folded the paper and slid it under the door. Then he turned and looked at the neighbor who was staring at him with compassion. Frank forced a smile and gave her back the pencil.

"She's a good girl, that one." The neighbor smiled sadly. "I hope it works out for you two."

He walked slowly down the dark stairwell, feeling his way with his hands, his fingers running over the rough texture of the mortar, his steps weak and uncertain.

Outside the sky was black with a deep purple glow to the west. A rough texture seemed to cover the city. He crossed the street and leaned against the seawall. Cars raced past. In the ocean, he could make out the lights of a freighter in the distance.

His throat swelled. And then, almost unconsciously, he reached into his pocket and pulled out his father's letters. He slid his hand under the first envelope and pulled it open.

The letter was handwritten in blue ink. The paper was beginning to yellow at the corners and along the creases where it had been folded. At the bottom of the page a few smudges had caused the ink to blot. It was dated November 29th, 1959:

Querida Celia:

I am glad to hear the birth went without incident. I am proud of you, for your strength, and I am proud of our child. I agree with you that Justo is a good name. After all, fate has not been just with us, and I somehow feel that naming the child like this will be a symbol of our history together. I cannot help but wonder what misfortune befell us that we had to be born in Cuba, fall in love there, and become separated because of it.

If you only knew how much I miss you, my love. I long for your taste and your laughter. My God, how I miss your laughter. Every night I dream of the light in your eyes, assuring me of your love. I cannot help but wonder if it is still there, shining like a little star over those dark Caribbean eyes that captivated my heart. It has been almost a year since I last saw you, but I still remember every detail about you: the small beauty mark on the side of your breast, the softness of your shoulder, the gentle curve of your cheekbone and how that vein on the side of your neck swells when you sing Guantanamera.

Myself, I am doing as well as one might expect. You will be glad to know I have finally landed a real job at a refinery where I have been given minor responsibilities thanks to my engineering training. It is not the best job, but I prefer it to shoveling shit at the stables of the Country Club.

It is funny how the things one misses most are the simple ones, the ones we take for granted while we have them. You have no idea how I yearn for the streets of Centro Habana, a walk along the Malecón in the late afternoon, and a little café. It is almost impossible to find a good café in Houston. Some of the more expensive Italian restaurants offer something similar they call espresso.

I often wish I could turn the clock back to the day I met you. Knowing what I know now, I would change so many things and perhaps we could be together, drinking Bacardí and Coke in one of those little cafés in La Habana Vieja.

Celia, mi amor y vida. I miss you so much. Every day I wonder how I will live another day without you. Please come to Houston. I beg of you. I know you said in your letter that you wanted to stay in Cuba, but I have to ask you again, and I will ask you with every letter I write. I shall never give up. I love you that much. Celia, please come and be with the man who loves you and worships you.

Te quiero, Celia, mi amor y vida,
Filomeno

The second letter was written on a sheet of paper that had been torn from a notebook. The handwriting was different from the first one. The flow was erratic like it had been written in a hurry. It was dated March 23th, 1960:

Querida Celia:

I am very sorry to hear of the death of your father. I sit here and wonder if anyone will ever know the real cause of La Coubre's explosion. Will Cuba ever find peace? Around here, the latest rumor is that the exiles are getting ready to invade. I think they are playing into Fidel's hands.

Life has been completely sucked out of me. The United States is a machine, and I am only one of many who are the fuel that spur it on. Rosa insists we move to Miami, but I tell her if I am going to be that close to Cuba, why not just go back? I am afraid she has been brainwashed by the Yanquis.

Sometimes I think perhaps the United States is finally getting to me, infiltrating into my veins, repulsing me more and more. It is expensive, and it is extremely conscious of who we are, what color, what race, what accent. When I get offered some vacation time, I would like to go to the Caribbean. I long for the feeling of sand between my toes and the sun on my back.

Celia, my love, your most recent letter gave me hope when your answer was a simple no. Could you be changing your mind? Might you be considering leaving Cuba and coming here to Houston?

I want you by my side. Time is taking its toll against my memory. I am beginning to forget details of you. With your next letter, could you send me something of yours, something that carries your smell and your essence? A kerchief or a stocking, even an old rag would do.

There is the whistle. My lunch break is over. I will finish this letter now and drop it in the mail tonight.

Te quiero, Celia, mi amor y vida,
Filomeno

It was as if the letters had been written by a stranger. It made Frank jealous, even angry. It was as if his father was being unfaithful to Rosa. But there was something else: Filomeno cared. He cared for his country. He held strong political convictions. He had passion. Love, heartbreak. In death and memory, the image of his father began to grow.

He folded the letters and put them in his back pocket. Then he turned to face the buildings on the Malecón. His eyes got lost in the soft blue of Marisol's apartment building: the stone columns, the textured facade and the tall window of her bedroom. He looked up and down the Malecón. The city looked beautiful in the soft light of the night.

A young man walking on the sidewalk paused and displayed a cigarette. "Amigo, ¿tiene fuego?"

Frank stared at his eyes. Then he shook his head. The man offered a polite nod and walked away.

Friday night in Havana. Down the length of the Malecón, every other streetlight was out. Music came and went with a soft breeze like the breath of a solitary trumpet. The colors of the buildings: pastel pinks and blues and yellows, faded as the sky grew darker until only shapes and shadows remained. A man playing a guitar strolled with a woman at his side, singing the words to a Beny Moré song. They nodded at Frank as they passed, and the woman's voice faded with the tide, *La vida es un crucigrama que no sé cómo resolver.*

Frank could feel Cuba crawling on him like sweat. It was everywhere. The man standing on the seawall with a homemade fishing rod cursed. Frank glanced at him. The man shrugged. "Lo perdí."

He looked away at the road, thinking of everything he'd lost. Two teenage girls rode past on a bicycle. The one sitting on the back turned, made eye contact, and blew him a kiss.

Across the avenue, a man carrying a basket of homemade candied peanuts sang, *Maní, dulce de maní. ¡Tengo dulce de maní!*

Someone yelled something from a passing car. Then a large Camello drowned and killed everything with its noise, its size, its pollution. The faces of the people crammed inside, peering out like prisoners, cut through his gut and reminded him of where he was. Nothing in Cuba was perfect. It was raw and dirty. The country was scarred by history and communism and dictatorship.

He was not thinking of the recipe anymore. Maduros didn't matter. New York didn't exist. There was only Marisol.

Two teenagers climbed on the seawall next to him and sat facing the ocean. The boy put his arms around the girl's waist and kissed the back of her neck.

Frank closed his eyes and saw his father as a young man, the Filomeno of the black and white photographs, the Filomeno who wrote the letters. He was standing where he was standing now: the same time of evening, the same salty air, the same old American cars rumbling past. And the same music from the guitar in the hands of the man walking with the same woman and singing the same song. It was the same feeling of love, the same feeling of heartbreak. He saw Filomeno sitting on the seawall, his arms around Celia's waist, kissing the back of her neck and whispering in her ear, "Te quiero, Celia, mi amor y vida."

He turned to face the ocean and felt the ball in the back of his throat swell until he couldn't hold it in any longer. He dropped his head on his arms and cried.

"Compañero," the teenager sitting on the seawall said. "Are you all right?"

Frank glanced up, his cheeks glowing with tears.

The young man nodded. "It must have been a mulata."

Slowly, the Malecón came alive: lights, music, laughter, dancing. The heart of the Havana night transformed itself into a long, curving party from Habana Vieja to Miramar. But across the street, in the third floor window of the faded blue building, the light never came on.

Later that evening he went back to his hotel. He cut through the lobby to the bar and ordered a mojito. It had taken him a six-day trip to Cuba to fall in love. He was dizzy with anger, love, compassion, heartbreak.

The rum and the lime tasted bitter, but he drank regardless. He found an empty seat and watched the tourists and the jineteras. He kept stealing glances at the door, hoping Marisol might appear. He kept imagining her walking up the steps to the lobby in her short blue dress. He could see her smiling, waving at him. He could see the brightness in her eyes and smell her perfume. But it was never her walking up those steps. It was all the other Cuban girls and the German and Italian and Canadian men. Suddenly, the whole scene—the jineteras and the drinks and the trio of old men playing for tips—made him sick. He pushed his drink away and went up to his room.

*"Not even all the sugar in the world
could change how bitter I feel about what Castro
has done to my family and my country."*

—José Franjul
sugar baron, owner of Florida Sweet Sugar Corporation
The Palm Beach Post, 1988

E ntonces," Michi said when Frank joined him and Orlando at the
patio the following morning. "How did it go last night?"

Frank shrugged and looked away. But he still held hope. He
imagined Yoselin and Eulina coming home last night and finding the
note. They might mail Marisol the letter or call her. They would let
her know.

Michi leaned over the table. "Not so good, eh?"

Frank signaled the waiter for a coffee and scanned the lobby. The
tourists mingled at the entrance of the hotel, their luggage stacked by
the steps, waiting for the transport to the airport. Perhaps, he thought,
it was all a lie. Perhaps she hadn't left Havana.

He looked at Michi. "She's here. I'm going home to New York, and
that's the end of that. Besides—"

"Coño, Frank," Michi interrupted. "There's no need to be so
fatalistic."

He was angry with himself. It had all been his doing. He hadn't told
her the truth of his business in Cuba. What did he expect?

"It's not easy," Orlando said.

"But you know," Michi said. "I could see in Marisol's eyes that she
had feelings for you. It was different."

"It doesn't matter anymore," Frank said, trying to convince himself.

"You know what's worse about all this," Michi said, "Orlando and I, we can't even compete against a tourist, tú sabes. We don't have the money to take our date to the kind of places a tourist can afford. And a hotel? Coño, Frank, I live in a house where the rooms are divided with bed sheets hanging from the ceiling. Half the room is mine, the other half is the living room. There is a room for my parents, a room where my sister and her husband live, and another for my grandmother." He sipped his coffee and looked away. Then he turned back to Frank and changed his tone. "Besides, tonight you will be home in New Yor', far away from all the mulatas of Cuba. In a couple of days you won't even remember her."

The real Cuba—the one that existed between the cracks, the one that was full of poverty, suffering and hopelessness—was revolting. It angered him that people allowed it to exist. He drank what was left of his café. "Come on. I don't want to miss my plane."

They rode in silence. Frank stared out the side window, watching the city pass him by, thinking of Cuba and love and how difficult it was to have them both. They left the pretty neighborhoods behind and turned up Boyeros. The noise and smell of industry shook his sadness. He leaned out the window. He put his arm out like a wing and let the warm morning breeze run through his hair and caress his pores.

At the airport Michi insisted on carrying his bag. They wove their way through the crowded terminal and found their place at the end of a long line.

"Entonces, Frank," Michi said. "When do you think you'll be coming back?"

"Who knows? It took me thirty-three years to come for the first time. I only hope it won't take that long again."

"Coño, I hope not," Michi said. "We'll be old men by then. And just think, every day something changes in Cuba. Orlando and I, we could always use someone like you. ¿Tú sabes?"

Frank laughed. "Someone like me?"

"Coño." Michi winked. "You know what I'm talking about."

"No, I don't."

Michi's eyes narrowed. He punched Frank on the arm. "You know, Yames Bond."

Frank laughed. "But if things are changing, you won't need James Bond."

"Chico, there will always be a need for Yames Bond." They moved forward with the line. Michi leaned toward Frank and whispered, "I only hope one day you can come back and tell me what you did while you were here. Sabes, all that mystery with Eusebio and the business with Sordo."

Frank handed his ticket to the agent.

"And maybe we can open our own paladar. It could even be a franchise of your restaurant in New Yor'."

"Michi, what you need is a job."

"No, chico. I am not well suited for employment. It's not in my temperament. I perform better with a minimum of restrictions and plenty of freedom. Besides, Orlando and I, we're a team. Believe it or not, Frank, we do pretty well."

"I believe it." He wanted to say something about their time together and how much he and Orlando meant to him, but all that came out was, "I want to thank you again. You were a tremendous help."

"That's nothing." Michi gave him a pat on the back, and they moved away from the counter. "Just do me a favor, when you get back to New Yor', go to one of those steak houses you told us about and have the biggest, thickest, juiciest steak you can find. And remember us."

"And make sure it's nice and pink in the middle so the potatoes soak up all the juice," Orlando added.

"And when you come back to Cuba," Michi said, "bring me one."

"Frank," Orlando said quietly. "I wish you would have made up with the mulatica. It would be nice to know that at least one love story in Cuba has a happy ending."

Frank looked away. "Yeah, me too."

"Maybe in another visit—" Michi started, but stopped short.

Frank paid his departure tax and got in line for immigration. "I don't know, Michi, maybe if it was a different time, then everything would be different."

"No, there is no different time," Orlando pointed out. "All time is the same."

"Coño, listen to him," Frank said. "He doesn't say anything for a week, and when he finally opens his mouth, he's a philosopher."

"It's just that we can see you were taken with her," Michi said. "Listen to me, do not forget your friends in La Habana, because we won't forget you."

"No te preocupes, Michi. Even if I wanted to forget, I don't think I could."

"Yes," Michi said. "That is the curse of exile, no?"

Frank shook hands with Orlando and gave Michi a breif hug. Then he proceeded to the immigration booth.

The official flipped through the pages of the passport. He glanced at Frank, at the photo and back at Frank. "Delgado...Cubano?"

"My parents."

The man nodded. "They left after the Revolución?"

"Sí, señor."

"I have family in Miami...Coral Gables."

"Ah, qué bien."

The official shrugged. "First time in Cuba?"

Frank nodded.

"And, what do you think?"

Frank thought about it for a moment. He thought of Cuba like a song that had everything and had nothing, like a pleasurable pain. The naked Cuba is only naked because it cannot afford any clothes. "Well," he said at last, "it's full of contradictions."

The official pulled out the tourist card and handed Frank the passport. "Verdad que sí."

Frank looked back. Michi and Orlando were standing behind the yellow line, looking after him. He waved. Michi raised his fist in the air and called, "¡Aché!"

Later, when the flight was called, Frank joined the other passengers in a line that went to the runway where the airplane was parked. At the foot of the stairs to the airplane, two officers in olive uniforms made a final document check. The sun was glaring down on his face. A strong wind blew across the runway carrying with it the sharp smell of spent jet fuel.

Frank handed his documents to one of the officers. He hesitated. After consulting with the other officer, he asked Frank to step aside.

Frank glanced up at the door. It was only a few feet away. The airplane was crisp and clean against the blue of the morning sky. He watched the other passengers pass him and climb slowly up the stairs. The officer was still inspecting his passport, turning the pages, looking at it sideways, and up against the sunlight.

Frank told himself there was nothing to be afraid of. Then he put his hand in his pocket and handled the film canister with Aché.

"I apologize, señor Delgado." The officer frowned. "There seems to be a small problem. Will you come with me, please?"

"What do you mean?"

"Por favor." The officer took him by the arm and started him back toward the terminal.

"But I don't understand..." Frank protested. The officer tightened his grip and pulled him toward the terminal where Gaspar stood under the shade of the building.

Frank panicked. He glanced over his shoulder at the airplane. It was almost fifty yards away. His passport was in the hands of the officer. Ahead of them was the man from the Ministerio del Interior.

"Señor Delgado," Gaspar said cheerfully. "I see you are leaving us." He stepped forward and made a gesture toward the officer who handed him the documents, saluted and turned back for the airplane.

Frank watched him go. The line of passengers was getting shorter. He looked down and wiped the sweat from his forehead with the back of his hand.

Gaspar handed him the passport. "I wanted to apologize for our methods. I do not wish you to leave with an unfavorable impression of our country."

Frank looked back at the airplane and again at Gaspar.

"I also wanted to ask a small favor. You see, I have some family in Miami." He held out an envelope addressed to someone in Hialeah. "Perhaps you could drop this letter in the post for me when you get home. The mail from Cuba to the United States is very poor. It can take months, if it arrives at all."

Frank took the envelope and placed it in the side pouch of his carry-on. He was thinking of the night they beat him, of the rubber hose, the fear, the humiliation. He knew exactly what he was going to do with that letter the moment he got back to the States.

Gaspar smiled. "I appreciate it."

Frank nodded and started back for the airplane. All the passengers had boarded. Only the two officers remained at the foot of the stairs and a flight attendant by the door. On the other side of the runway, a soldier paced in front of a camouflaged security booth.

"Delgado!" Gaspar called.

Frank froze. He could see the flight attendant and the officers looking at him, waiting. He could sprint for the airplane, but it was a long a shot. They were in control. He took a deep breath and turned around.

Gaspar was marching toward him. "I could not help but notice you are walking with a slight limp. Perhaps this can be of some help." He held out the insole of his shoe.

Gaspar smiled. "Go ahead. Take it."

Frank took it and felt the soft texture of the rubber in his hand. He turned it over. The recipe was there under the Soleflex logo. He stared at it for a long while. A drop of sweat landed on the edge and he watched it run along the side and bleed into the fabric. Then he heard the flight attendant calling in the distance. When he looked up, Gaspar was gone.

"Fish. I eat a lot of fish.
With rice, grilled with onions, marinated in garlic sauce,
with sofrito. However my wife prepares it, I eat it."

—Photographer Raúl Corrales
Cojímar, 1994

New York still had a sharp spring chill in the air. Lights flashed, horns honked, neon blinked, people moved. The city was swarming with activity. Cuba quickly became a dream. Frank was exhausted. He leaned back on the seat of the cab and focused on the meter as it changed shapes—fragmented red lines forming numbers and adding up to fare.

When he walked into Maduros, it was as if he had entered a photograph in a glossy magazine. The dining room was immaculate—white and streamlined with a slight hint of blue from the lights beneath the bar. The place looked fragile. Cold.

He barged into the kitchen, set his bag to the side, raised his arms and called, "Hey Lucy, I'm home!"

Justo glanced up from behind the counter. "Coño, the spy who loved me is back."

Pepe waddled out of a storage closet and glanced at his wristwatch. "What the hell happened to you? We expected you hours ago."

Frank gave his brother a hug. Then he reached into the breast pocket of his coat and handed Pepe the insole of his shoe. "Here you go, hermano. Mission accomplished. And you." He pointed at Justo. "We need to have a little talk."

"Entonces." Justo winked. "Are the mulatas still as beautiful as I remember them?"

Pepe examined the insole, front and back. "What the hell is this?"

"That's it." Frank handed Justo the plastic film canister. "You're going to have to figure out what's in this Aché."

Justo opened the container and took a long whiff. Then he glanced at the ceiling and sighed. "Aché."

"¿Aché?" Pepe frowned. "What's that? What the fuck's Aché?"

"Listen, I need to have a quick word with Justo," Frank said and pointed to the back of the kitchen. "In the freezer."

"Sure," Justo complained, "in the freezer. Always in the freezer. Coño, It's a miracle I haven't turned into a popsicle."

Pepe waved. "What about me, am I not a part of this?"

"It has nothing to do with the restaurant."

They stepped into the freezer. Justo pulled out a cigarette but didn't light it.

Frank paced in a circle, condensation smoking out of his nostrils. "Coño, Justo, why didn't you say something?"

"About what?"

"About being my brother. All these years..."

"Coño." Justo plucked the cigarette out of his mouth and turned away. "I don't know."

"Justo—"

"When I arrived in Houston and met your father..." He took a deep breath and gestured back and forth with the cigarette. "Filomeno asked me not to say anything. Maybe he was going to tell you everything."

"But he never did."

Justo shrugged. "At first I thought he was ashamed of me." He ran his index finger up and down his forearm. "You know, because I was black. But one day he confessed that he had worked very hard to put Cuba behind him. It was very painful for him to remember my mother."

Frank turned away. "Unbelievable!"

Justo fished out his lighter, leaned into his cupped hands and lit his cigarette. "I can't say I knew him. But I think in his mind he thought he was doing the right thing."

Frank stared at Justo. Memories of Cuba seemed to come and go all at once.

"I was just glad he opened his house to me and that he treated me like family because when I came to this country, I didn't even know if he was going to recognize me as his own blood. Coño. He asked me not to say anything. What was I supposed to do?"

"Why didn't you say something after he died?"

"I guess I never found the right moment."

"Coño, Justo. That's lame. That's the lamest—"

"I was afraid," he said bluntly and backed away. "I mean if I said something, it would change everything, no?"

"No. Why would it? You should've just come out and said it."

Justo shook his head. "It's not that simple."

"¡Coño!" Frank stomped to the end of the freezer and punched a bag of frozen French fries. He was thinking of his father and all the truth he wished Filomeno would have told him when he was still alive. He saw him sitting in the living room of their house in Houston, watching one of his TV shows in silence, keeping his Cuban past locked away from the people who loved him.

Justo spread his arms and stepped closer. "Look, I'm sorry."

Frank stared at him. His throat burned and his eyes swelled with tears. "Coño, I don't even know if I'm upset or happy or what the fuck."

Justo touched his shoulder.

Frank nodded and lowered his head. Then he raised his eyes. "Does my mother know?"

Justo shook his head. "No."

"I wish I would've known sooner."

Justo exhaled a long cloud of smoke. "I'm sorry."

"You know, now you're going to have to tell Pepe."

"Me?"

Frank nodded, a sinister smile across his face.

Justo pointed at him with his cigarette. "But he's your brother."

"And yours too. Besides, it's your secret." In Justo's happy eyes, Frank could see Eusebio and Esperanza and Hilda. And even Filomeno. "You know," he said, "you have a really wonderful family down there. They were very kind to me."

"Coño, Frank. I envy you. I wish I could have gone."

"Maybe next time we can go together." He opened the door of the freezer and stepped out. "You tell Pepe the good news. I'm going home."

*"When it comes to Cuban food,
I don't think so much about the food itself. I think of
the social interaction that comes from sitting at the table
with my family and friends. It's a very communal thing.
I cannot imagine sitting down to a plate of
arroz con pollo or ropa vieja by myself."*

—Professor Rogelio Pedroso
Florida International University, Miami, 2001

F rank started south on 1st Avenue, pulling his small suitcase behind him toward the subway. He thought about Justo and Pepe and everything that had happened in Cuba. When he thought of Marisol, he felt more alone than he ever had. The city, the lights on the street, the wide sidewalks and the prospect of his dark, empty apartment depressed him. He turned around and walked north to 80th Street to the apartment Pepe shared with their mother Rosa.

The place was dark and quiet. Rosa was asleep. He set his bag in the hallway and folded his coat over the back of a chair. Rosa had left half a turkey sandwich on the kitchen counter for Pepe. Frank pulled a beer from the fridge and went into the living room.

Years ago, this had been Pepe's apartment. But when Filomeno died, they convinced Rosa to sell the house in Houston and move to New York. After that, the apartment became a replica of their house in Houston with a plain beige couch, a glass and tubular brass wall-unit, the old television, plastic flowers in a porcelain vase. And the mementos of a lifetime: photographs of the family at Six Flags in San Antonio, at Padre Island. Pepe and Frank's high school graduation portraits. It was impersonal and deliberate like his father.

The tabby cat was curled up in a ball in a corner of the couch. She twitched her ear, stretched and lay on her side. Frank scratched her belly. She turned over and Frank moved his hand to her neck so he could feel the vibration of her purring against his fingers. Then he closed his eyes. He expected to see his father's ghost, but all he saw was Cuba.

For the first time since Filomeno's death, he missed the old man. Cuba had opened a door—left it wide open, the wind blowing in, carying the dust of the past. Outside was a future he was only now begining to understand.

He heard a key turn the lock on the door. Pepe walked in and stood by the hallway that led into the living room. "What are you doing here?"

Frank smiled. "I didn't want to be alone."

Pepe sat down next to his brother.

"So?" Frank nudged him with his elbow. "Did he tell you?" Pepe took the beer from Frank and had long pull at the bottle. "Justo's aunt told me a lot about when Papi was young. Did you know he had a brother?"

Pepe didn't answer for a long time. Then he said, "I have this vague memory of him saying something about it." He rubbed his eyes with the tip of his fingers. "He died in a car crash or something, no?"

"He told you?"

"I was like ten years old. I had no idea what he was talking about. He was probably drunk."

Frank dropped his head back. "God, I wish I'd been there."

"Cuba haunted him."

"He should've told us about Justo."

Pepe waved. "He wasn't perfect."

"So?"

"He gave us a good life, no?"

"Yeah, but he should've told us."

"Shush!" Pepe turned and glanced at the hallway.

Frank lowered his voice. "You need to go to Cuba."

"I don't think so."

"You need to wake up the Cuban in you."

"I'm not going to Cuba. Not until Castro's dead and buried."

"Ay, coño, Pepe. What does that matter?"

"Because it does. And listen." He stood and looked down at Frank. "Let's not talk about this in front of Mami, okay?"

"Coño, you sound just like Papi.

"I was mistreated for twenty years, tortured even.
Well, when I finally got out, I went to a friend's house
in La Habana and his wife served me
a beautiful plate of picadillo with rice and beans.
I cried. I had been hungry for a very long time."

—Revolutionary Huber Matos
during an interview with *The Miami Herald*
after his release from La Isla de la Juventud prison. Miami, 1979

The following morning Frank woke to the salty smell of frying bacon and Rosa's animated voice gossiping with the cat. "I said no. I absolutely refused, but not her. She went to the baile. And unescorted, too. Pilar and María and I went to the movies instead. Then Mirta said..."

He walked into the kitchen and found his mother holding a piece of toast in one hand and a butter knife in the other as she talked with Caña. The cat sat on the counter licking its shoulder while Rosa went on about her friends and the church social where Mirta later claimed she'd lost her virginity to Raúl Montero.

"Buenos días, Mami."

Rosa startled. "I thought you were sleeping."

He kissed her on the cheek and sat on a stool at the counter.

"Why are you here?" she asked.

Frank rested his forearms on the counter and glanced at the cat. "I just wanted to see you."

Rosa pointed at him with the butter knife. "Pepe said you were in Miami."

"Ft. Lauderdale."

"Pepe said Miami." She glanced at the cat. "Didn't he?"

"Mami. Can I have a café?"

"Sí claro." She set down the toast and the knife and attended to the espresso maker on the stovetop. "Do you want it with milk?"

"No, gracias."

"Your father always had it with milk in the morning."

"But I'm not Papi. And please, Mami, don't put too much sugar in it."

But the coffee was too sweet. It always was. It reminded him of their house in Houston and Filomeno finishing his café con leche and kissing Rosa goodbye before leaving for work.

He watched her turn the bacon with a fork. She carefully picked a slice at a time and set them side by side on a folded brown paper bag. He had not had breakfast at his mother's house in at least a year. Nothing had changed. "Can I have another café?"

"Claro, mi amor." She took his cup, refilled it and put it in the microwave.

"Pepe sleeps late, huh?"

"And he comes home late. That is why I never see him. I go to bed after the telenovela. He does not come home until after Johnny Carson."

"It's Jay Leno, Mami."

The microwave beeped. Rosa took out the coffee, stirred in a few teaspoons of sugar and set it on the counter for Frank.

"Were you talking with Caña?"

"I was reminiscing. You know, the nostalgia of an old woman."

"Who's Mirta?"

"Just an old friend." Rosa cleaned the bacon grease off the skillet with a paper towel and pulled out a carton of eggs from the refrigerator.

"Can you tell me about Abel?" Frank said matter of fact.

Rosa paused. "Abel?"

Frank sipped his coffee, but kept his eyes on his mother's back as she went about preparing the eggs. "Papi mentioned him once."

"Really?" She cracked two eggs into the frying pan. "When did he do that?"

"I don't know, a long time ago."

"What did he say?"

"I don't remember. Something about Abel and the university."

Rosa sighed. Her fingers moved nervously around the handle of the spatula. "Abel was your father's brother. He died before we left Cuba."

"How come you and Papi never talked about him?"

"Ay, Frank, your father had his ways, ya tú sabes."

Yes, he knew his father's ways. He also knew Cuba, the Revolución and Filomeno's love letters to Celia. "So, how did he die?"

"Por Dios, Frank. Why are you so full of questions so early in the morning?"

"I don't know. I had a dream about Papi."

"Really?" Rosa set down the spatula. "I have dreams about him too. I tell Caña. She knows. I sometimes wonder if he's trying to tell me something."

"It was just a dream."

Rosa served herself a cup of coffee. She added a dab of milk and leaned close to Frank. "I will tell you about Abel, but you cannot tell your brother. He is too sensitive for these things, entiendes?"

Frank moved his cup aside and leaned forward.

Rosa gently pushed the cat off the counter and took a deep breath. "I don't know how to begin. Abel...Abel was born a few minutes after your father."

"They were twins?"

"But not identical. Abel was skinnier, and, I think, a little taller." Her words trailed off, and her eyes became moist.

"Mami, I'm sorry. You don't have to tell me."

"No, no. I want to tell you." She smiled uneasily. Then she glanced at the ceiling and continued. "Abel and your father had left Oriente to attend the Universidad de La Habana. One Christmas, Abel borrowed your father's car so he could go home and spend the holiday with your grandfather. On his way home, he had a terrible accident on the way to Santiago." She turned and took a tissue from a box and wiped her eyes. "I am sorry."

"Mami—" Frank came around the counter into the kitchen and put his arm around her shoulders, "—you don't have to tell me. I didn't mean to..."

"No, no," she said and dried her tears. She grabbed the spatula and scooped the eggs out of the pan and placed them on a plate. "No te preocupes, Frank. You need to know this. I am sorry that I never told you this before, but your father was always very sensitive about everything that happened to us in Cuba. He was the one who went to claim the body." Rosa sniffled and touched the corners of her eyes with a tissue. "When he came back to Santiago, he said the car had disappeared, and that Abel's face..."

"Mami," Frank said tenderly.

She raised her hand and took a deep breath. "Your father said Abel's face had been blown off by a gunshot to the back of the head."

She buried her face against his chest and sobbed quietly. After a moment she pushed herself away and looked at him. "We had to have a closed casket wake."

Frank could feel her sobbing, her body moving up and down against his chest. "Mami, I'm sorry. You don't have to tell me any more."

She moved away from him and pulled out another tissue. She picked up two slices of bacon and set them on the plate with the eggs. Then she glanced toward the hallway where they could hear Pepe moving about in his bedroom. "Your father...he accused the Servicio de Inteligencia Militar. He said they thought Abel was smuggling weapons to the rebels in the Sierra Maestra."

Rosa blew her nose and leaned against the counter. "But Abel was going to school to become a doctor. What business would he have with the Revolución? It had to be an accident."

The toilet flushed and Rosa and Frank looked down the hallway. A moment later Pepe walked into the kitchen.

"Buenos días," he said and gave his mother a kiss on the cheek. He sat at the counter and looked around. Then he focused back on Rosa. "Are you okay? What's going on?"

"Nada." Rosa waved and served him a cup of coffee with milk. "It's my sinuses."

Frank stepped out of the kitchen and hurried into the bathroom. He sat on the toilet. Everything that was Cuba—the tortured, the nostalgic, the real—was true. His mother, Abel, and then his father, Celia, Justo. Their exile was not as simple as it sounded.

"There is no real mystery to Cuban coffee.
It just has has to be very, very sweet and very, very strong."

—Marta Rodríguez
assistant for the *El Gordo y La Flaca* television show, Miami, 2002

Justo transformed the back of the kitchen into a cooking laboratory. He lined a dozen small bowls along the length of the prep counter, each with a different variation of the spice mix for the chicken. On another counter he had a miscellany of containers with spices, vinegar and sauces, and a notebook where he tracked his progress. It was trial and error. He worked through the process of elimination.

Frank moved back and forth along the counter, sniffing at the bowls. "How's it coming?"

"I'm not sure." He added a pinch of powdered cumin to a bowl and scribbled an entry in the notebook. "I'm trying to figure out what's in the Aché. But if I keep tasting it, I'm afraid I'll run out."

"It's all Eusebio could get."

Justo stepped away from the counter and wiped his hands with a rag. "Was it very difficult?"

"Getting the recipe? ¡Coño!"

"And no news of your uncle Nestor?"

"You mean our uncle."

Justo looked at him and smiled.

Frank shook his head and dismissed it with a wave of his hand. Then he dipped his pinkie in the Aché and tasted the spice.

"What do you make of it?"

Frank moved his tongue around his mouth trying to separate the flavors. "It's so confusing."

"It's really good."

Frank smiled. "Just wait until you taste the chicken."

"I hope I—"

"Ginger. I think it's ginger."

"Coño, ginger." Justo backed away and waved a finger at Frank. "Who would have thought? Ginger."

"But I'm not sure."

"No, no. I think you're right. Ginger." Justo searched among the spices for the powdered ginger. He added two teaspoons to his own Aché in one of the bowls and tasted it. He leaned over the counter and made a record of it in the notebook. Then he added more spice to another bowl and tasted the original Aché. He tasted his own mix, and looked up at the ceiling as he tried to decipher the labyrinth of flavors.

Frank sat on the counter. "Maybe I should try and find letters or something in Mami's apartment."

Justo leaned against the wall and crossed his arms. "When I was a little boy, I asked my mother why my skin was not as dark as my brother's. She told me I had a different father. Coño, I was so upset to find out I was not the son of my stepfather, a combatiente who had been with Che in Santa Clara. It took me a year to work up the nerve to ask her about my real father. But all she could tell me was his name and that he had gone into exile after the Revolución. If I ever asked her anything else, she would just say, 'la Revolución lo cambio todo'."

"You know, for most of my life I've felt as if something was missing. Like a piece in a puzzle."

"Maybe that's what it means to be Cuban."

"That's not it. I think I felt American, but what was missing was the Cuban part."

"And now you have it?" Justo said.

Frank shook his head. "I'm just as confused. Maybe more."

Justo pointed at him with a spoon. "You know what your problem is? You think too much."

Frank laughed and hopped off the counter. "I keep thinking about

Papi. He was so different when he was young."

"We all get older," Justo said. "I used to wonder what it would've been like if he'd stayed in Cuba."

"I'd give anything to talk with him."

"Óyeme, you could go see Ramón Juárez. He can check with the Orishas and make contact—"

Frank raised his hand to stop him. "If Papi refused to talk about his life when he was alive, why would he do it in death?"

"Maybe now he can see how tortured you are."

"I'm just curious. Don't tell me you're not?"

"Un poquitico." Justo shrugged. "But I suppose I've gotten used to it."

"I can't believe I was never curious about any of it until I went to Cuba."

"Do you regret going?"

"No qué va." Cuba had opened his heart in a way he could not explain. "It's my home."

Justo stared at him.

Then Frank slapped his hands together. "Well, enough of that."

Justo went back to his experiment, adding a pinch of garlic to the Aché. He took a taste and offered it to Frank.

"More clove, no?"

"And pepper?"

"I think just clove."

Justo divided the spice mix into four equal parts. He added more powdered clove to one of the bowls. Then he paused and looked at Frank. "But tell me something. Seriously, was there a mulatica?"

Frank looked away. Marisol walked toward him in her new bikini. He saw her floating in the pool, her arms extended, her figure cutting the water. He saw her smiling, telling him stories of what it was like growing up in Cienfuegos in the dim light of the Bodeguita.

"I knew it!" Justo clapped his hands.

"¡Coño!" Frank smiled and looked down at the line of bowls and the mess of spice.

"Come on, hermanito, tell me everything."

"No, I don't want to think about that." Frank walked to the front of the kitchen and looked into the dining room. The hostess had just arrived and was beginning to set the tables. "You know we're going to have to remodel the dining room."

"Thank God." Justo joined him by the door. "I never understood why we had to have such a pretentious-looking restaurant."

Frank laughed. "If we get this recipe right, we're going to have to make it more rustic. More Cuban. Like a place in La Habana Vieja with exposed rock and old wood and a wrought iron balcony."

"We can get some Cibaeños from Washington Heights to build us a palm thatch roof."

"We're going to need a lot of tables."

"Do you really think it's going to work?"

"It will if you can match the recipe."

They went back to the counter and the little spice bowls. Frank watched Justo do his work, looking more like a mad scientist than a chef. He thought of the difficult time he'd had accepting Justo when he first arrived in Houston. He hadn't been fair.

"Listen," he said quietly. "I know we've had our differences in the past, and—Coño, I've been a real comemierda at times—but Justo, I'm proud that you're my brother."

"Sure." Justo waved him off.

"Coño," Frank said, "I'm trying to apologize."

"Yes." Justo looked up. "I heard you. Apology accepted. Now go figure out how we're going to remodel the restaurant. Anda—"

"But I mean it, Justo—"

"Go on." Justo picked up a knife and waved it in the air. "Enough with the sentimentality. Get the fuck out of my kitchen!"

H ello?"

"Frank?"

"Justo? What is it? What's wrong?"

"Nada, chico. Call Pepe and get your lazy culos down here. I got it."

Frank hung up the telephone and sat up on the futon and stared into the darkness. It was two in the morning. He shook off the sleep. Then he called his brother and told him to meet him at the restaurant.

When they arrived, Justo was sitting on top of the counter smoking a cigarette. "It's in the oven," he said and glanced at his wristwatch. "Diez minutos."

"How do you know this is it?"

"Because I know, Pepe. I have been killing myself for the last two weeks tasting every possibility. And you know what it was? Naranja agria in powder form and a pinch of clove. I didn't think about it because it's already an ingredient in the marinade, but it's also part of the Aché. The effect it creates is unbelievable."

"Really?"

"Bitter orange. Amazing. The most Cuban of Cuban ingredients. But it's such a complicated recipe. I have never seen or even imagined these spices working together. It's crazy. Whoever came up with it is a genius." Justo pushed himself off the counter. He took a long drag of his cigarette and extinguished it in an ashtray by the counter. He checked the thermostat and looked at his watch. When he finally opened the oven, the smell of Cuba after a long spring rain flooded the kitchen.

"¡Coño!" Frank cried. "That's it!"

Justo took in the smell. "It makes you smile, no?"

Frank rubbed the palms of his hands together and laughed.

"Come on," Pepe said, "let's try it."

"Hold on. We need to let it sit a moment. You'll burn your mouth."

Frank fetched beers from the bar. They sat in a circle on the dusty dining room floor. All the tables and chairs had been sold to a restaurant supply reseller in Queens. Piles of wood and dried palm fronds and construction material were scattered on the ground. The crew of Cibaeños had finished texturing the walls and were half way done with the palm thatch ceiling.

They looked at each other, their eyes blazing with anticipation. Frank picked up a leg and looked at his brothers. Justo and Pepe grabbed pieces of their own.

Frank sunk his teeth into the hot, crisp texture of the chicken. The complex and familiar taste of nostalgia exploded in his mouth. Marisol was lying naked beside him, the moonlight falling on her flesh as it filtered through the shutters of her bedroom window. She reached across the bed and caressed his arm. Her touch engulfed him with a sensation so real he opened his eyes and glanced at his arm.

Justo chewed with his mouth open, his eyes half closed. All the tiny muscles of his face flexed and bulged with each bite. Pepe laughed. He was chewing so fast and smiling like when they were little boys and their father brought home barbecue from City Market in Luling.

Frank dove back into his own piece. Once again he was in that other world, the naked Cuba. He could hear Marisol's voice talking of love, saying things she had never said when he was in Havana. His heart raged against his chest, his body covered in goose bumps.

"Dios mío!" Justo was euphoric. "I saw my mother. She was standing by the window of our house in Havana and the neighbor from the corner was calling that they had meat at the bodega."

"I saw Papi," Pepe said, "and he was smiling. He looked happy."

"This is it!" Frank howled. He dropped the bone of the leg and took another piece. Marisol never left him, even between bites and sips of beer. She was always there, in person, talking, touching, leaning against him. He could even smell her.

"Cuba is all about food.
And food is nothing more than a metaphor for nostalgia."

—Poet Guillermo Cabrera Infante
after the publication of his book *Tres Tristes Tigeres*, 1967

T he new sign outside the restaurant now read: **SOFRITO**. The construction work was finished, and the picnic tables had been delivered. Behind the bar, an impressionistic mural of Viñales with its imposing cliffs and vast tobacco fields dotted with small bohíos covered the wall.

Justo had rearranged the kitchen so there was a single long counter dividing it in half. One side was for the preparation and cooking of the chicken, the other was for the side dishes.

Frank stood on a ladder checking the inventory in the storage closet. Then he noticed Justo pacing behind the line cooks, guiding them through the recipe, one ingredient at a time, as they mixed a batch of the marinade. He jumped down and pulled Justo into the freezer. "Coño, what the hell are you doing?"

"What?"

"The recipe."

"Coño, Frank, don't worry about that. I set it up so no one will know all the ingredients. Besides, I will be the only one to mix the Aché."

He stared at Justo. Suddenly he realized the consequences of owning the recipe. It was as if he were riding a merry-go-round and he would never be able to step off.

"Frank?"

He blinked and saw Justo's eyes and his hand reaching for his shoulder.

"You okay?"

"I'm just cold," he said. "Let's get out of here."

In the afternoon, Rosa walked into the restaurant loaded with Macy's shopping bags. "Pero, look at this place," she said, looking around the dining room. "It is very nostalgic. Pero qué bonito. And Viñales. If only your father was here to see this. It would make him so proud."

"Maybe he's watching from up there." Frank went behind the bar and mixed a batch of mojitos. But these were not blueberry or mango mojitos. These were the real deal. He only used fresh yerba buena and squeezed key limes by hand instead of using lime from a pre-squeezed bottle. And he put a little less rum than he used to and added cane sugar to balance out the flavor.

Rosa placed her hand on Pepe's arm. "I hope the new menu is real Cuban food and not more of those dishes with exotic fruits and funny mushrooms."

"They're shiitakes, Mami."

"I don't care what they are, they are not Cuban."

Frank brought the drinks and sat across from his mother. "Don't worry about that, Mami. What matters is that we're all together, no?" Frank lifted his glass and they had a toast to the new restaurant.

Then Justo came out of the kitchen with a large tray piled high with chicken. He placed it at the center of the table. Rosa glanced at the ceiling the way she did when she was in church. "Pero, Dios mío. It smells like Cuba."

Justo smiled and rubbed the palms of his hands together. "Serve yourselves. Go ahead, put a little bit of Cuba in your life."

Rosa reached for the chicken. Frank and Pepe and Justo waited. She picked out a piece and inspected its color. She inhaled deep and long, then took a small, delicate bite.

Her expression changed. She stared at Frank and frowned. "I think," she said, "I should tell you the rest of the story."

"Claro." Frank smiled. "But only if you want to."

"You deserve to know. You all do. We should have told you this long ago."

Pepe looked at Frank.

"Filomeno blamed himself for Abel's death," she said. "You see, it was his car. I was too young, too naïve to understand. I was devastated by his passing. So when Filomeno took me aside at the cemetery and asked me to marry him, I thought it was terribly romantic."

She took a deep, long breath. "But Abel was not the saint Filomeno made him out to be. He was as flawed as any man. Abel and I had been dating for months. And we were both young and weak. It happened after he proposed to me when I came to La Habana, when I visited him at his little apartment in Vedado."

"What happened?" Pepe asked.

Rosa looked at him. "You happened, mi amor."

"What?"

"Filomeno wanted to replace Abel because he knew I was pregnant with you." Rosa stared ahead, past Pepe and past the restaurant, her eyes glazed with nostalgia and the illusion of the past. "But you cannot force love. It was all a farce. A woman knows. We have intuition about these things. I had been suspecting it for years, but I suppose I made excuses for him. I wanted to avoid the truth. Then I figured it out the day we learned that Che had been killed in Bolivia. We had just moved into the new house, and we heard the news on the radio. I looked at Filomeno, and I saw it. He had the same look in his eyes when he came back from Las Tunas with Abel's body. That was when I knew he did not love me. He could never love a woman the way he loved that stupid Revolución."

"Enough," Pepe said. "You don't have to talk about this."

Rosa smiled at him. "But I do. You need to know. We did not leave Cuba because Filomeno was running away from Fidel or communism. We left because he was trying to give me the life he thought Abel would have given me."

Frank lowered his head, glanced at his hands. He knew the truth. It was Celia. Filomeno had to get as far away from her as he could in order to remain failthful to Rosa—and to his brother.

Rosa leaned forward and locked eyes with Frank. "And that's why he insisted on naming you Frank. It was to honor his good friend, Frank País."

Pepe glanced at Frank. "Who's Frank País?"

Tears found a way out of the corners of her eyes and traveled slowly down the sides of her cheeks. She dropped the chicken on her plate and pulled at the lapel of her black dress. "I don't wear black every day to mourn Filomeno. I wear it for Abel. I wear it for Cuba."

Pepe reached across the table. "Mami..."

"How did you do it?" she whispered.

Everyone was silent.

She smacked the table with the palm of her hand. "How?"

"Justo did it," Frank said quickly. "He's a genius."

"No. It's impossible. This is Uncle Nestor's recipe. This is the chicken from El Ajillo."

"It was Eusebio." Justo glanced at Frank. "My brother. He sent us the recipe."

Rosa wiped her tears with her napkin. "I would like to go home now."

"In Baracoa, they cook with coconut oil and lechita,
the milk from the coconut. In the evenings,
if you walk the streets of the town, you can smell it.
The air acquires a soft musky smell that is very pleasant.
It lifts you up and makes you feel like
everything is all right with the world.

—Santería priestess Fatima Marú
Baracoa 1992

The next evening they arranged the tables in diagonal rows from one end of the restaurant to the other, cafeteria style. Justo, Amarylis, the line cooks, and the waiters carved names and slogans on the tables. Someone put a Sonora Matancera CD on the stereo and the voice of Carlos Argentino wrapped around the room like a humid afternoon in La Habana Vieja.

Frank arrived with a case of beer and passed them around. He paused where Justo was leaning over a tabletop carving letters with a small kitchen knife. "What are you writing?"

"The names of all my family in Cuba."

"And Pepe?"

"He went home after the painters left," Amarylis said. "He's still trying to make sense of it."

"I think he's still in shock," Justo said. "Coño, how would you feel if you found out your father was not your father and the one who was really your father was killed before you were even born?"

"He should be proud." Frank sat on one of the tables and set his beer down. "I mean, in the end it doesn't really change anything."

"Trust me. It changes everything."

"Give him time," Amarylis said. "Only time heals all wounds."

Frank forced a laugh. "It didn't for my father." Then he nodded toward Justo. "It's odd how it turns out you and I are connected by my father—our father—and at the same time Pepe became disconnected."

"True. But we're connected just the same. Maybe that's what Filomeno wanted with the restaurant, to create a thread that would tie us together because we're brothers, but we're not brothers."

Frank smiled. "I was thinking the same thing."

He leaned over the table and carved his name. He thought about it for a moment, and then wrote, 'Marisol.' He took his time sipping beer, listening to the music and contemplating the carved wood, his fingers tracing the grooves where the letters of her name curved at the top of the R, around the S and all over the O.

He drank another beer and when he looked up, only Justo and Amarylis and two waiters remained in the restaurant.

"You ready for tomorrow?" he asked.

"Claro, Frank. It's not such a big deal. You think it will get full?"

Frank was surprised by the question. "Amarylis, did you like the chicken?"

"Don't laugh. But when I was eating, I saw a child. A little boy." She looked at Justo. "It was ours, mi amor."

Frank glanced at Justo. "What else do you want?"

"The same thing you want."

Frank smiled and continued carving. After a while he paused and looked down at the table and was surprised to find he had carved all their names: Michi and Orlando, Nestor Quesada, and even Gaspar and Verónica.

He focused on the names and they blended together, taking the consistency of something that was uniquely Cuban, like a good sofrito. It took him back into the heart of Havana. The sun was setting low to the west covering the city with its golden light. The waves crashed against the seawall where fishermen stood with their lines cast out to sea. And from the streets of Centro Habana he heard the lyrics of a bolero between the cry of gulls and the broken exhaust of an old Chevy that rumbled past. He saw Michi and Orlando sitting on the hood of the blue Moskvitch, leaning back with teen bravado, smoking Marlboros and drinking Cristal. A group of Pioneros skipped past them, past the men playing dominoes in the shade, and past the old lady peddling Popular cigarettes from the stoop of the faded blue apartment building where on the third floor he could see Marisol through the open window.

Then she was gone.

The window was empty. A knot tightened at the pit of his throat. He suddenly realized that hole—that dark window—would grow and weigh on him the same way it had done with his father. Filomeno had made the choices he had to make. Life was not easy. There was no right or wrong in what he had done. But because of it he had suffered until he exhaled his final breath.

"No," he said out loud, surprised at the sharp tone of his own voice. He came out of the dream knowing he could not live the rest of his life like his father, broken, bitter.

"Frank?" Justo was staring at him.

"I have to go." He stood and dusted off his pants. "I have to go back."

Justo smiled. "Smart idea," he said. "Get a good night's rest because tomorrow is going to be the first day of the rest of our lives."

"Exactly." Frank waved a finger at him. He smiled nervously, proud and a little confused at his decision. But he knew he was doing the right thing. His father had made all the wrong choices and suffered all his life for it. He was not going to make the same mistake. He backed away and felt the heavy weight of his father's ghost lifting off his shoulders. "I have to go back to Cuba," he said and rushed out of the restaurant.

They had the recipe. Pepe and Justo and Rosa would be fine. But not Frank. He was not going to let it end this way. He was not going to let her disappear from his life. He would fly out first thing in the morning and go back to Cuba. To Cienfuegos. To Marisol.

He walked quickly down the wide sidewalk, his hands buried in his pockets, his head forward, face turned sideways against the cold wind, a small confident smile on his face because at long last it was love.

And he was not going to let it get away.

Acknowledgments

One would think writing a novel would be a lonely, solitary journey, but in the case of *Sofrito* nothing could be further from the truth. There are a number of people I must thank, starting with all my friends in Havana and Miami who contributed to the story in multiple ways. Early on Julie Barer and Nancy San Martin gave me valuable feedback on the manuscript. I would also like to thank my peers at the University of South Florida, especially Jaquira Diaz, Kimberly Karalius and Christine Lasek. Rita Ciresi, John Fleming, Ira Sukrungruang, Katie Riegel, Danita Berg and Helen Wallace have all gone above and beyond for me. A shout out to Stephany Evans for her guidance and support, and a heartfelt abrazo to my friend Tony Diaz. Thank you.

I have no words to describe the welcome I received from the family at Cinco Puntos Press: Lee, Bobby and John Byrd, you all are the best. Gracias!

And finally to my lovely and patient wife Lorraine. A man is only as good as the woman he loves. Thank you for putting up with me, for your love and support, and for reminding me of the important things in life. I love you.